Wolf of the Crown
And Peril of the Crown

Also by J.E. Moncrieff

Part of the Black Axe series…
Shadow of the Crown

Other titles…
The Tower Grave
Pride of Blood

Wolf of the Crown

And Peril of the Crown

J. E. MONCRIEFF

Estuary View Publishing

First Edition

Published by Estuary View Publishing 2025

The moral right of the author has been asserted

This novel is a work of fiction. The names and characters, other than those clearly in the public domain, are the product of the author's imagination and any resemblance to actual persons, living or dead, is entirely coincidental.

This book is sold subject to the condition that it shall not, by way of trade or otherwise, be lent, resold, hired out, or otherwise circulated without the publisher's prior consent in any form of binding or cover other than that in which it is published and without a similar condition, including this condition, being imposed on the subsequent purchaser.

A CIP catalogue record for this book
is available from the British Library

ISBN: 9798303038349

Copyright © 2016 James Moncrieff
All rights reserved.

For Iris, my mum. I will miss you forever.

PROLOGUE

Prologue

Summer 1572

The oldest man in the room sat silently watching as the six around him mumbled to each other softly, waiting for the meeting to commence. Only three of the seven men present knew the true role of everyone there and as he caught the eye of the grey-haired but younger man opposite him, the man they all knew as their boss, the head of their organisation, the Black Axe, he inclined his head silently and the other man cleared his throat.

"Gentlemen, thank you for coming," he said. "You are here as the heads of each strand of our brotherhood and I am grateful for your attendance. We have much to discuss, not least with the fact that I hear Edward Rothwell is still alive?"

"Yes," said a dark, bearded man sitting under the window. "I was told he fought viciously and was lucky when his whore was killed."

"He did indeed," said the leader. "I *was* present, after all. But am I correct in saying he remains alive even now?"

"He is alive and well," said the oldest man. "He cannot be removed yet."

"Please elaborate, Silver," said the leader, using the code name the older, white-haired man had been given.

"For a start, since he found us the queen has kept him tightly in her corset. Why, we don't know. We cannot know what she knows, but he is surrounded by soldiers and officials permanently. We cannot risk showing out or losing any more men. And secondly, we need to know what he knows about us and therefore who he has told."

"What could he possibly know?" asked a younger man known as White due to the shining scar that ran the vertical length of his right temple and cheek.

"He knew to seek us. We believe it was him who sought us in Spain last summer. It coincided with his visit to gather intelligence from King Phillip, after all. When we killed his whore he heard our proceedings. I doubt he was there simply to save her. And when he entered the vaults of the Abbey last year, he asked questions he should not have been able to. Gentlemen, I was there when we burned his family home a decade ago. His family took their own lives to save him. They knew to sacrifice themselves for his secret. Even the daughter knew who he was. We absolutely need to know what he knows as well."

"Has that not always been the case?" asked White with his Irish accent.

"Of course, which is why we did not blindly kill every Edward Rothwell we found," continued Silver. "But now he hunts us as we hunt him. He will die, sure. It is our life's objective. But not until we secure the objective of the lives of generations within our brotherhood." He stopped, looking at the men around him before nodding subtly to the one they all knew as the Black Axe.

"Then we must get close to him," said the leader.

"Who knows him the best?"

"Blue and I both know him well," said Silver, nodding at the bearded man.

"And he trusts us," replied Blue. "He does not like me, but he trusts us both. He has no suspicion of either of us and neither of us were at the conference with his whore when he arrived."

"That is true," said Silver. "But I do not believe he would open up to us about this. He would have done so already."

"We need someone extremely close to him then, but without knowing who he has told, who do we interrogate?"

"We will need to put someone in," said the man they knew as the Axe. "It will mean slower progression but we can monitor him and tap him slowly. We will get an idea of how loose his lips are and whoever goes in can play whichever role is needed to get him to open up, whether it requires a close relationship or not."

"I will do it," said White, sipping his ale and holding his chest as though to restrain a belch. "If I have a way in, I can get close to him."

"I would have suggested you, White, knowing your skills in artifice," said Silver. "I can get you in. I will see if I can recommend you to get you some work on the periphery of his business and as you gain the trust of the Queen's closest, you will be next to him in no time."

"Thank you, Silver," said the leader.

Silver nodded.

"Let us get this done then," he said. "We can finally put an end to this chapter and bleed the bastard."

PART ONE

Chapter One

August 4th 1572

Edward and his best friend Marcus chuckled as their colleague Rutherford recounted a story of his late friend being caught as a young man by the father of a girl as he climbed from her window. That very friend, Edward had killed in self-defence two years before and he remembered the hatred he had felt from Rutherford for doing so as he first joined the ranks of Queen Elizabeth's 'Shadows'. The work of the secret investigators under the Lord Burghley William Cecil had been hard through Rutherford's scrutiny and distrust; and despite Edward's rapid promotion and success in preventing what they called the Ridolfi Plot to kill Queen Elizabeth, it wasn't until Edward's girlfriend had been murdered and his secret exposed to his closest colleagues that Rutherford finally gave him a chance.

Edward smiled ruefully as Rutherford spoke animatedly atop his horse before them, and he looked around as they scouted the path ahead of the queen's entourage. The two men had risen to join Edward in Francis Walsingham and William Cecil's team of international spies known as the 'Wolves', and although they had spent months as the coordinators of the queen's personal protection contingent, their lives had been pushed on several occasions following up intelligence. In turn, they had become inseparable as friends and colleagues.

Marcus laughed out loud as Rutherford's story reached its punchline conclusion and spotted Edward lost in thought.

"You ok, Ed?" he asked.

"Of course," replied Edward. "I'm just thinking."

"About?"

"The last two years, how we are now, how we were, if we will ever get back to our jobs instead of living our lives as glorified bodyguards."

"It is an important role, my friend."

"I know, and I am honoured. But we do have a job to do."

"You know full well that while there are threats at your head from whoever those bastards may be, she will not ever let you out of her sight. She loves you; you know that."

"Don't start with this again."

"She cannot say it or act upon it, she is the queen as you are the peasant. But she is a single, red-blooded female and she is permitted to be smitten occasionally."

"And I suppose you find it hilarious?"

"Who wouldn't?" Marcus laughed. "You know everyone calls you the royal toy-boy behind your back!"

Edward punched him in the arm.

"You are such a bastard," he said, making both men laugh.

"Here we go," Rutherford interrupted, seriously, as a soldier on horseback approached them from behind.

"Everything in order?" Edward called as the horse

covered the ground of the woodland path in seconds.

"Yes, sir. Her Majesty requests your presence in her carriage."

Edward closed his eyes at the timing of the request and glanced over his shoulder to see the grins of his two friends before shaking his head and riding back towards the queen.

He stepped from the summer heat into the cool and comfortable carriage to find his queen relaxed with quill and parchment on a tray before her.

"Your Majesty," he said, bowing.

"Hello, Edward," she replied with a smile. "We are a day behind, as you know. I was planning to ignore it and arrive as we are, but as we have the Habsburg Ambassador coming for the event tomorrow, I would like you to send ahead a rider to Greenwich and let them know we will be arriving this evening. We *will* be there this evening, yes?"

"Of course," Edward replied. "Ma'am, if you don't mind me asking, you seem nervous about this meeting?"

"Edward, Maximillian is the first Holy Roman Emperor to truly make efforts to unify Christianity in his realm. We cannot agree on faith as he is Catholic, of course, but he too has seen turmoil in Austria and Germany and to have strength in the east on the side of peace, we could put to rest all but the pope and the Spanish. We in England sit here as one religion while the south enjoys the same on the other side. But the countries in the middle, Edward; France, Austria, Germany and the Netherlands, they are split down the middle in unsolvable conflict, and it needs to stop. I want it to go well."

"It will."

Elizabeth smiled at Edward, then dropped her expression as she was startled by a roar outside the windowless carriage. Edward checked his basilard, a two-foot double-edged dagger secured at his hip, and bolted through the door without a word.

He swore as he saw the soldiers outside the carriage fighting viciously against double their number in scruffy, blade-wielding men that poured from behind the treeline. He took sight of the entire scene for a moment, then ran to the front of the carriage where the soldiers faced the most aggressive attack, leaping over the shoulders of a guard and plunging his blade deep into the chest of a middle-aged man, while another soldier took a wound to his navel and dropped to the floor next to him. He spotted Marcus in the fray as he fought off a much younger man holding a blacksmith's hammer, then shouted over the din of metal-scrapings and yells of anger to grasp his attention.

"What happened?" he bellowed as he edged closer to his friend.

"From the trees," Marcus managed to shout back before being forced to turn away and face an attacker. "They came from the trees."

Edward killed the man before him by driving the point of his weapon into the young throat, and then turned in an uncontested moment to see five or more new men run for the rear of the carriage and the door to the queen.

Edward counted the men in defence. The dozen soldiers that had been present with the three wolves had dwindled to just over half of their original number, though he counted at least fifteen attackers lying sprawled around them. He ran to join the two soldiers holding the door and ducked inside the jab of an old rusty spear before lunging forward and catching the man in the groin with the top inch of his blade. The spear swung again as the man ignored the wound but tailed off gently as Edward dropped to the floor and the spearman's eyes glazed over at the loss of blood. Edward watched from the ground as the body dropped into a heap behind the stamping mess of feet, then jumped at a small explosion to his right as the body of another falling soldier landed next to him.

Another of his men filled the gap fighting as Edward surveyed the scene and looked for the source of the sound. He hadn't expected the unfamiliar blast and as the attackers fell and were replaced by more, his eyes fell on a young man of no more than fifteen years standing in the tree line attempting to reload what Edward assumed was a pistol. The boy filed something into the long barrel then poured a sprinkle of powder into the same place. Turning the weapon, he filled another part of its body with the powder before picking up a wooden match that had been burning on the floor next to his feet and lowered it towards the gun.

Edward stood and fought frantically through the countless peasant-like men in front of him and slammed his head into the face of an older man, receiving a heavy object in the side of his own face in return. The scene around him went dark momentarily, then returned to life as each clash and grunt echoed loudly through his head. He watched through hazy eyes, swinging his dagger wildly, as the young man at the trees raised the barrel towards Edward then lowered the match down into the top of the pistol with the other hand. The flash and bang made the entire crowd duck in response and a scream erupted immediately behind Edward as the melee around him changed into one of panic.

As his mind cleared, he slammed his long dagger into the mouth of the man facing him, then pulled it free and put it straight into the upper-back of another. The last remaining peasants fought and dropped as Edward turned back to the boy in the tree line and set into a clumsy run as he began to sprinkle his powder into the final section of the weapon once more. Edward caught the boy's eye as he closed him down and finally managed to gather his legs and sprint away from the crowd that held him. The shooter hurriedly threw down his powder, bent for the match with shaky hands, and raised the barrel perfectly for Edward to hit him square in the chest with a diving tackle. Without the match, the weapon cluttered uselessly to the floor and the boy slammed hard into the tree behind him, letting out a whimper as Edward's moving body doubled the impact.

Edward pulled him roughly to his feet and held his dagger up to strike, stopping as he saw the fear in the young blue eyes opposite him. He had blonde hair, similar to Edward's own, and his tiny, malnourished frame quivered in fear just as Edward's had in France over a decade before.

"Who ordered this and why are you attacking the Queen of England?" he demanded instead as the scene behind him finally fell quiet besides a cacophony of nervous laughter and grunts of agony.

"The queen?" the boy replied in terror. "It cannot be. They said it was a noble carriage, not royalty. Please, I did not know it was the queen and would never be here if I did."

"You didn't know? Look at the uniform of the soldiers and the crest on the carriage. How could you not know?"

The boy shrugged with a blank look.

"I have never seen the queen," he said.

Edward sighed.

"Then why did you attack this noble carriage?"

"Because we are starving. We have had no harvest, nothing to trade. We need coin to eat through the coming winter. We are desperate."

"Then where did you afford a matchlock?" said Marcus suddenly, standing behind Edward.

"A what?"

"The pistol. It's a matchlock."

"It has been in my family for years," the boy replied. "My grandfather received it in Portugal when he was young."

"And it is now yours?" asked Marcus.

"My father's, but you killed him," he said, defiantly, looking at Edward and holding back tears. "He is dead on the floor behind you."

"Who organised this?" Edward replied.

"It came from higher up, my father said."

"Did he say who or where?"

"I shouldn't say."

"What do you mean, 'you shouldn't say'?" Edward mocked. "Listen, lad, I can help you. Right now, you are hung, drawn and quartered for treason but with help it could get better."

The young man looked at him with a twinkle of hope

before his expression changed and he looked over the shoulders of his interrogators in terror.

Edward frowned in response and turned only to be startled by the flash of a sword swinging over him to embed its point into the chest of the young attacker. He watched in shock as the boy's eyes glazed over with a gurgle and he slid from the blade to land in a heap on the ground.

"What the hell was that?" Edward bellowed, turning on the soldier who stood panting behind him and clutching a blood-soaked eye.

"The little sod shot me in the face, sir," the soldier replied. "I can't bloody see and I will never work again because of him."

Putting his suspicions on hold momentarily, Edward reached up and moved the soldier's dripping hand from his face.

"No, you won't," said Edward, taking in the horrific sight. "It must have hit you from the other side. It has taken your eye and the side of your face with it. You seem calm, does it not hurt?"

"It does, but not as it will later."

"You are lucky it wasn't straight on, it would have gone straight out of the back of your head."

"Lucky?" the soldier said, quietly. "I would rather die than be kicked out of the guard and left to live on the streets in poverty and humiliation while my family starves to death, *Sir*."

Edward watched him for a moment.

"Nevertheless, your reckless vengeance has cost us valuable information. Get this man attention from a surgeon immediately!" he shouted to the rest of the soldiers. "We will cover the costs but we will still have to question you about this, you understand? You killed a man mid-interrogation as he was about to tell us who ordered an attack on the queen. After you're fixed up you will be returned to the Tower under guard until I can speak to you." The soldier nodded in realization and grit his teeth to hold back the moisture in his remaining eye. "But if everything is above board," Edward continued, lowering his voice, "I will see to it that you are looked after in your retirement or employed elsewhere if preferable. You were injured protecting your queen, regardless of what happened afterwards, and I promise it will not be overlooked. Now go. And remember, you seriously fucked this up today."

The soldier nodded a third time and let out a breath as a tear spilled onto his cheek. He turned and walked to another soldier who stood waiting with a horse.

"Everyone else, let's move these bodies to the side of the road and collect the fallen soldiers," he said, before turning to Marcus.

"So what is a match-lock?" he asked, quietly.

"It is, in essence, a small hand cannon," Marcus replied, picking up the weapon. "A lead ball and gunpowder go in the barrel; gunpowder goes in the flash pan; then you lower down the...where is it? Ah..." he picked up the now extinguished match. "And using the match, you light the flash, which sends a flame into the barrel, lights the charge and projects the missile forwards. I am surprised you haven't seen one."

"I have heard of the hand cannons but no, never seen

one."

"And I have never seen a match-lock pistol, only a long-barrelled version."

"Why are there not more of these? Why don't we have them?"

"Cost, bias, practicality; you wouldn't want one of these. Unless you light the match it cannot be fired, and if it is lit it'll give away your position in the dark, go out in the rain or burn your clothes if concealed. It must be fired one-handed so that you can light it, and you, my friend, would be much more deadly with your blade. Especially that long thing you carry around."

"It's for guards then?"

"They toyed with the idea, but it is said that to keep the match-lock lit all night for one sentry on night-duty for a whole year, it would require a mile of match."

"A mile?" Edward coughed.

"A mile. It would cost a fortune. And, well, some at the top feel it is a gimmick when compared to the sword, the axe, the bow or bolt. No, these won't be around any time soon. They have more on the continent."

"Edward," said the queen, unscathed and unshaken from her doorway.

"All clear, Your Majesty," Edward replied.

"I will need an update while we travel on. And I can see you have fought hard for me," she added, loudly, so that all could hear. "Your country thanks you for protecting your queen; and I thank you for saving my life. You will all be honoured, as will those soldiers who fell today. Let us move on to Greenwich safely. Sergeant? When we reach London,

I ask that you re-bolster our contingent with replacement numbers from the Tower Garrison."

The soldier who stood panting at her feet nodded dutifully, then turned to rally the remaining men.

"And Edward…" she added.

Edward nodded as his queen stepped back into her carriage.

"I am not chuckling this time, my friend," said Marcus. "We will get to the bottom of this. See you in a few hours or so, we will be up front."

Chapter Two

Edward climbed the stairs of the royal quarters in Greenwich Palace to see the queen as summoned. Since arriving that day, nine hours after the attack, he had washed and re-dressed in his own luxurious chamber and prepared himself for court as he had been forced to learn to do in his role. As the lead on Queen Elizabeth's protection contingent, Edward had been afforded the perks of life usually reserved for only the nobility and courtiers of the queen herself and he shook his head at the cards he had been dealt in life. With no one to support except an elderly friend, Albert, he had no reason not to enjoy the finer benefits of his work; though he admitted he should make an effort to visit the old man more frequently.

"Your Majesty, Edward Rothwell," announced a young court-servant through the queen's open double-doors as Edward approached.

"Thank you, Jacque," Edward whispered as he met the man he had begun to know well, then he turned into the doorway and bowed deeply.

"Hurry up and come in," said Elizabeth as she stood from where she sat on the foot of her bed. "I told you to stop bowing like that in private meetings. Close the door, Jacque."

Edward stood as he heard the doors close behind him and smiled at his happy-looking queen and the ever-cheerful Lord Burghley William Cecil standing beside her.

"Hello, Edward," said Cecil, beaming.

"Hello, Lord Cecil," Edward replied. "I wasn't expecting to see you here, though it is a pleasant surprise."

"I asked him to come," said Elizabeth. "We have much to discuss with you."

"We have," agreed Cecil. "Edward, we want to thank you for stopping the ambush. The numbers we lost are shocking and I understand it was quite a fight?"

"They had a pistol, which certainly didn't help."

"A firearm? Which kind?"

"A match-lock, so Marcus said."

"You did not know yourself?"

"No, I know nothing of firearms. At least, I didn't."

"We will have you trained. I am sorry, that was an oversight by me. Their regularity is growing and it concerns me, quite frankly. How have you been? And how many attempts on your life have you counted since you revealed yourself? We have been listening out."

"We? Who else knows about me?"

"No one else. Just the three of us here right now, Francis Walsingham, and your two colleagues."

"Excellent. Well then, there have been no attacks, nothing at all."

"Apart from the ambush today?"

"That was not for me."

"There is no intelligence suggesting they were actually targeting the queen."

"That is because they weren't. They had no idea she was in there. The lad with the pistol told me it was intended as a robbery."

"So said this boy?"

"Yes," replied Edward more firmly. "He was scared, he told the truth."

"He also looked like a peasant but could afford a match-lock pistol. And he fired it towards you specifically twice?"

"After the countless interrogations I have carried out for you, my intuition on truth is yet to be trusted?"

"Of course it is, but the evidence suggests on this occasion that it may be incorrect."

"What are you saying?"

Cecil sighed.

"I am simply saying, Edward, that we cannot confirm that this was not an attack on you. We simply cannot rule it out."

"William..."

"I am sorry, Edward," Cecil said, cutting him off. "But if this *was* an attack on you by this, Axe, then we must also consider how close it came to killing our queen; and, therefore, whether it is safe for you to be that close to her operationally at this time."

"That is madness. I would never let anything happen to you, Your Majesty," Edward protested.

"I know, Edward," replied Elizabeth. "And believe it or not, my own safety is not *my* worry. I am more concerned with you. But hear what William has to say. Please."

"We are looking into this with you," continued Cecil

as Edward nodded. "But we need some distance while we do it. Tracking you has given us nothing and we can look harder with the risk removed. We believe your disappearance may prompt them to be more overt in their actions."

Edward frowned.

"I am listening," he said.

"We are also of the opinion that they will not target the queen, but your proximity simply puts her at risk."

"Fine, so what are you saying? Please be clear now, William."

"I am sending you to France," said Elizabeth.

"But they operate in France, we know that. How can it help?"

"It will help because Francis and I need you in Paris on official business. It is only short-term while we sort this here and you manage some business there, but I would have deployed you in any case."

"The only difference now is that you will go in secret," said Cecil. "Deployed officially but only the three of us here know you are leaving the country and Walsingham will meet you in Paris."

"And what is the business?"

"Francis is our ambassador in the French capital. He is there, on the face of it, as a token of good will to maintain our relations with France. But in reality, we still face the threat from catholic action against us and France teeters on a knife-edge of tension between the catholic population, including the monarchy, and the protestant Huguenots, thousands and thousands strong. Their three religious wars have torn the country to shreds. The Huguenots actually control La Rochelle in the west as well as La Charite-Sur-Loire and Montauban. They are large, heavily populated towns, Edward. And, we heard that in May a Huguenot army under Louis of Nassau crossed into the Hainault Province in the Netherlands and captured Mons and Valenciennes. Both were once important catholic strongholds. Louis is the brother of a man they call William the Silent who leads the Dutch revolt against the occupying Spanish. Louis governs Orange in the South in his absence.

"Seems like quite a place at the moment."

"The country is at war," Cecil continued. "We need to keep an eye on all that happens. Paris is intensely catholic and full to bursting with action and plot. We must make sure our Huguenot brothers at least retain *some* clout and safety. And we need to know if and when the catholic strength grows. Without the protestant resistance in France and the Netherlands, the Pope along with the French and the Spanish will run riot and come straight for us."

"Also, Edward, there is a wedding planned in Paris this month," said Elizabeth. "The king's mother, Catherine de Medici, makes out that she is trying to secure peace in France and has facilitated a wedding between her daughter Margaret and King Henry of Navarre on the Eighteenth of August. Henry is protestant, and Paris passionately catholic, as discussed. They are not happy and tensions are high."

"You will work for Francis as his runner, his eye and his protection," said Cecil. "He needs a wolf at his disposal and we need you away. It is a win-win, as they say."

"A win-win for whom?" asked Edward.

"Do it for me?" asked Elizabeth. "Please. I would

have needed to send you anyway."

"And I would have gone at your word. Very well, when do I leave?"

"Now," said Cecil. "It is imperative that no one knows you have left and we will run it like a covert evacuation. You will go straight from here to Dover, there will be a ship waiting for you to get you to Calais, and then there will be a line of horses for use to Paris. I will provide you with a list of roads and inns to use as we have allies in place from top to bottom through western France, with family lines left over from the days of Plantagenet rule. They will know your coin but not your name or the nature of your travel. What you call yourself, I will leave up to you. Francis will not address you by name until you introduce yourself."

"Right, I guess it's all sorted then. I will gather my items from my room and head off."

"There will be an aide waiting for you at the palace stables. Take him with you and keep him as your servant until you return. I imagine from your upbringing that your French is still fluent?"

Elizabeth closed her eyes as she remembered what Edward had once told her.

"It never was," Edward replied. "I was kept away on an isolated farm with English parents. I scraped by on the streets after they died but language is one of the reasons I came to England."

"I had forgotten," said Elizabeth. "French is as much my first language as this one and I was confused by Edward's lack of it when he arrived. I apologise, Wiliam."

"Not to worry, your aide will speak French," said

Cecil.

"Thank you, Edward," said Elizabeth suddenly. "Good luck and please return to me in one piece."

Edward bowed deeply at his dismissal and caught a twinkle of emotion in his queen's eye as he backed to the door and turned away. He walked through the corridor as excitement and nerves fought for attention in his mind.

"What a strange hand of cards I have been dealt," he whispered to himself.

Chapter Three

August 13th 1572

Edward chuckled for what seemed like the fiftieth time that day, as Jacque urged his horse to catch up and shook his head in feigned embarrassment.

"She wasn't interested?" Edward asked as they rode away from the pretty village-girl Jacque had attempted to talk to.

"Oh she was, her eyes said it all," he replied. "It was her mother in the window with the blade that wasn't sure!"

Edward laughed again and glanced over his shoulder to see a wide-spread, middle-aged woman tearing into her beautiful, twenty-something, French daughter outside their home. He glanced back to Jacque and shook his head. The man was a verbal beast and had a way with women Edward had never seen. The moment he had been dismissed by the queen, Edward had asked for Jacque as his aide. The protestant Frenchman had played it cool on the two-day road to Dover, but had released his inner-stud the moment they landed in France.

"What *do* you say to them?" Edward asked.

"As I always say, Ed. I just tell them they are beautiful," he replied with a grin.

"And as I always reply, I don't believe you."

"It is true, my friend."

"Then why did your girl in Allonne kneel to me when I walked into the room?"

Jacque laughed out loud.

"She did ask where you kept your crown."

"I knew it!" Edward shouted.

"Listen, it has served you well. In almost every coach house you have had a local girl beg to stay with you. That is almost five-days straight. It would have been five, in fact, if not for that Mayor's daughter."

"She could have said," Edward replied. "I nearly lost my balls."

"She would have been worth it, she was a beauty. It was difficult to choose between her and her friend."

"What? You choose?"

"Of course, the tactics are different depending on who I select for each of us and which one I use to get us close."

"That is unbelievable."

"One for me and one for the English prince," Jacque added, smiling.

Edward laughed.

"You will get us beheaded," he said. "Still, I am impressed. Your success rate is near perfect and it was all worth it to see you riding bareback with no trousers when we ran from the Mayor's guards."

"I am not sure I remember it so fondly. I still have the bruises," Jacque winced.

The young men chuckled together as they wound their way along the final miles of road towards the city of

Paris looming in front of them.

"It has been one of my more enjoyable road-trips," said Edward.

"It has for me too," said Jacque. "What are we to expect in Paris?"

"I am really not sure yet, though I believe Walsingham will let us know soon enough. Word has it, religious tensions are through the roof."

"They were when I left. Montauban, where I grew up in the south, has been a Huguenot town as long as I can remember. The Catholics surrounding the area hated it and there was always violence."

"Have you been to Paris?"

"Never, but I hear they are different to the rest of us. 'Arrogant and unforgiving, the Parisians,' my mother always used to say."

"That they are."

"You have been before?"

"As a boy, yes. I lived on the streets there alone."

"An English boy alone on the streets of Paris? I am surprised you made it out at all."

"Strangely, those on the streets with me were not prejudice. The merchants and nobility though? I used to pretend I could not speak rather than reveal my English tongue."

"Are you concerned now?"

"Not this time," Edward smiled. "In any case, I fear your beliefs will bring us more trouble than my accent."

"I will keep them to myself while we are on official business. What about your beliefs?"

"Ha! Any God who sanctions the atrocities that I have seen deserves no worship of mine. No, all I need put faith in is the air in my chest, my instincts, my friends and my sword. I will worry about what happens after death when I get there."

Jacque looked at Edward with his eyebrows raised and nodded.

"Maybe the whole world would calm down if we all thought like that. It is refreshing; though I am quite happy with beautiful women and fine wine in the clouds when I am done, thank you."

Edward laughed.

"The gates are close," Jacque said. "Shall I speak?"

"Translate for me instead, if you would?"

"Of course."

Edward looked around as they drew up under the northern entry point of the city and the relaxed guard stepped in front of the open gate known as the Porte Saint-Martin.

"Puis-je vous aider, messieurs?" the guard said as they stopped. "Toutes les affaires étrangeres á etre annoncé."

Edward opened his mouth to answer the apparent question but Jacque had already leapt into a stream of French language that had him baffled. Initially the guard listened with a twisted smile before roaring with laughter and stepping out of the way. He said something brief as he waved them through then nodded with a blush as Jacque spoke over his shoulder and winked.

Edward waited until they were well out of ear shot before turning to Jacque with a grin.

"What did you say?" he asked.

"It is best you do not know," Jacque replied before looking at Edward's expression and breaking into laughter. "I simply said nice things about the both of you. You and he," he added.

"What nice things? Jacque, he blushed."

"Of course."

"What do you mean, 'of course'? Why would he blush? I understand if an attractive woman had paid him a compliment or invitation, but you?"

"I think he would have chosen either one of us over any woman, if you understand my meaning. Did you not get that impression of him?"

"What impression?"

"You English men are so blind and uncultured. Listen, if you see him in a tavern, just do not offer him a drink. Or show him your backside for that matter; that is all I am saying."

Edward paused for a moment.

"You mean he is..." his eyes opened wide and he gaped with a broad smile. "...And you said that I...? Jacque, I am going to cut your ears off!"

"It allowed us to enter the city without question or revelation, did it not?" Jacque laughed.

Edward chuckled and shook his head.

"I guess so," he said. "You are a strange beast, my friend."

"Handy though?"

"Very handy."

Edward headed towards the river then south along

the upper-eastern bank as directed until he came to the only white house on the strip of the western end of what he assumed were the enormous gardens of Tuileries Palace. The garden, and indeed most of the palace, had not been there when he last had; but he recalled the royal residence at the Louvre Palace and took his bearings from there.

"This is it," he said suddenly.

"This white house? How do you know?"

"Because it was described to me and is the only one here."

"I am impressed. You said nothing, you read nothing. Your ability to recall detail is staggering."

"And so will yours need to be, I am afraid. You are no longer a door-minder or servant. You are operational. In any case, Paris isn't as complicated as it looks. If you know the areas, you can find what you need. Here on the east side of the river is the Louvre Palace, the Tuileries Palace and the gardens. As well as the covered market, Les Halles, but I have less than pleasing memories of that place. On the west side is the Latin Quarter. It houses the main body of the university and the catholic students learn in the language, of course. It is there that they lodge. In the centre of the river here is the Ile de la Cité with the old palace and the Cathedral of Notre Dame. There is a small version of the cathedral on the left bank also, do not get them confused. I lived in the centre here, as well as inside the gates of Saint-Antoine in the east and Saint Denis in the north. If we need the other end I am afraid we will both be learning from scratch."

Jacque nodded.

"Got it," he said. "In my downtime I will explore and

map the city as I see it to help us should we need it."

"Good idea," Edward replied, raising his eyebrows. "Come on, let's meet Walsingham once more."

The two men tied their horses and knocked on the large front door of the white house. A pale and silent staff-member opened the bolted, oak door and looked at them with a squint before recognition appeared in his eyes and he stepped back allowing them to enter without a word.

Walsingham stepped down into the hallway from a wooden staircase moments later and smiled as he looked at Edward.

"Mister Walsingham," Edward announced. "I am James Williams. I have been deployed by Queen Elizabeth of England to act as your runner, your eye, and your protection. This is my aide, Jacque; a servant from the Royal Court of our Queen."

Walsingham nodded in appreciation of the introduction.

"Good afternoon, Mister *Williams*," he said. "You are welcome within my staff and will be put to work as soon as you are settled." He nodded at Jacque in greeting. "You worked for Her Majesty, Jacque?" he asked.

"For three years, sir," Jacque answered. "I worked directly to the queen herself."

"You are French?"

"Yes, sir, from Montauban, north of Toulouse."

"Excellent," Walsingham smiled. "James, I understand you must have instruction papers with you?"

Edward nodded and handed over a folded letter with Cecil's seal still intact. Walsingham opened it sharply and smiled as he read.

"Understood," he said, finally, folding the note and nodding subtly to each man. "Jacque, please go with my doorman here and unpack your items for long-term lodgings. James, I need you to go somewhere for me. I will hand you a new note to pass to a friend of mine in the faculty of the college. It is best you do not reveal any religious preferences, or indeed your accent, while you are there." He waited while the doorman and Jacque left the room then turned back with a whisper. "You are going to love this," he said.

Chapter Four

Edward followed the directions he had been given past the impressive structures of the Ile de la Cité and the shop-lined bridges that serviced it, then on into the Latin Quarter and the very heart of the catholic University of Paris. He ambled his way through the busy, tree-lined, afternoon streets and down into the basement vaults of a large, square building with a bell tower three turnings south of the Petit Pont. At the bottom floor, he walked the torch-lit corridor until he came to a door marked 'Prof. Giraud' and knocked once as instructed. A groan and a shuffle sounded behind the wood as heavy items were audibly slid aside and a slightly-overweight man in his fifties opened the door with a smile.

Edward flashed his coin and pulled the note from inside his shirt once they were inside and alone.

"Interesting letter from Francis, Monsieur Williams," he said in a strong French accent. "So you are his new man and you are here to learn about firearms?"

"Is that what it says?" asked Edward.

"Yes, is it wrong?"

"No, I guess not," Edward grinned. "Just unexpected, is all."

Professor Giraud smiled.

"Arrivals from Francis often act that way. Fear not,

you will get to know me quite well in time. The cover for experimentation here is second to none. I am Pierre Giraud, a researcher at the college. And you are?"

"James Williams, as it says in the note."

"Ah, of course," grinned Giraud. "Come with me, Mister Williams."

Edward followed the hobbling, stumpy body through a series of dark doorways and corridors until he came to what looked like an indoor archery range, only smaller, with long-barrelled firearms on the wall rather than bows.

"My king pays me directly to study the power of the Asian gunpowder and the European designs to use it," Giraud said, gazing at the wall. "They would like me to come up with something better but, at present, having me in post for *my* country is only directly helping yours.

"You have heard of a matchlock firing mechanism?"

"Yes," Edward replied. "I have seen one fired accurately."

"Surprising, as they can only be shot single-handed. They are heavy."

"It was a pistol."

"Really? Well the shorter the barrel, the more inaccurate the aim, despite the reduction in weight. Even so, they have their uses but are expensive and impractical. Following the matchlock, a clever man designed this, the wheel-lock," Giraud said, holding up a short gun. "Again, impractical, taking a full minute to load, prepare and fire. But useful for explaining how they work. Take hold of the gun…" Edward did as he was told. "The wheel-lock," Giraud continued, "Creates the spark by spinning this steel wheel against a small piece of pyrite, known as *fool's gold* for obvious reasons not limited to it's colour."

"Like flint?" asked Edward.

"Quite. Except flint is far too hard and would wear away the grooves of the wheel. The grooves here, rub on the pyrite, causing a spark that lights the powder in the flash pan. That flame, in turn, shoots through the touchhole into the barrel where the main charge and missile are waiting. The result is as expected, when it works."

"Simple but clever, I like it."

"I can tell by your eyes you want to have a go. In case you come across one, I will show you how to prepare it but we will practice on the snaphaunce, which is what you will carry from now on."

"Carry? I'm not sure," said Edward.

"You will be once you fire one. The wheel-lock, however, must have this side-lever, *the dog*, put into the safe position, which opens the pan. Powder charge and ball into the muzzle, though I won't do that now, then use the spanner attached to turn the square part of this wheel shaft on the side until a click is heard. Just over halfway. It is now locked."

Edward looked at the complicated mechanism in disbelief. It had seemed so simple.

"Powder in the pan," Giraud continued, sprinkling a small amount of black powder from a sachet into the small open disc, "Then shut the lid. Dog back to slip the jaws of the wheel onto the pyrite…" He lifted the gun and pointed it towards the wall. "And…fire," he said as he pulled the trigger and both a large flash and the sound of an explosion filled the room.

Edward jumped back and shouted as noise filled his senses. Giraud laughed.

"Fear not, James," he chuckled. "It was simply a flash in the pan. Wait until you hear it with a full charge in the barrel. Strangely enough, the bang is not so loud when you shoot the things yourself. Know it is coming, I imagine. Anyway, the snaphaunce..." He put down the wheel-lock and picked up two much shorter pistols, though they were still the length of Edward's forearm. "Seen one of these?" he asked.

"No. It is lighter though," Edward answered, taking one of the weapons.

"Yes. It shouldn't be, but it is. Now this will have less range and accuracy due to the shorter barrel, but I do not expect you to pick people off of horses from a rooftop. This will sit nicely hidden within your cloak, loaded and safe until you need to pull it in close quarters for a quick kill. If you need it and the noise isn't a problem, this will certainly save you a dangerous fight."

"How does it work?"

"The snaphaunce? Simple. This lever at the back is the cock. Click it back and it locks out of the way. Here, where it will land when released, is a small area we call the *steel*, and the tip of the cock has a flint held firmly in place. The old snaplock required you to open the pan-cover yourself but this one is automatic and has a safety feature in that you can simply bring the cock forward, close the pan and stop it tapping. If the flint cannot strike the steel, the weapon cannot fire. Main charge and ball through the muzzle, flash pan full, cock back and locked, aim, pull the trigger to release the cock and bang. She fires. Tap, spark, flash, charge, fire. All in one instant."

Edward smiled, making Giraud laugh.

"More like it, eh?" the Frenchman chuckled. "Load it then, my boy. There's a target on the wall. Stand at the line and see what happens."

Edward grinned, surprised at his nerves, and followed Giraud's lead, packing powder and a lead ball into the barrel, then filling the pan with powder from a sachet. Giraud cocked his snaphaunce pistol and stepped up to the line, aiming and firing once with his arm outstretched. The noise again made Edward jump and he smiled, his heart beating as Giraud whooped and looked at the hole on the outside of the target twenty paces away.

Edward took a breath and stepped forward. He raised his right arm, cocked the pistol with his thumb and pulled the trigger. The explosion made his arm rattle with shock and he looked forward expectedly, feeling his heart drop from his throat to his stomach as he saw no new holes since Giraud's.

"Do not worry," said the professor. "My wall is soft and the missile will not bounce. It will now be buried in the stone. Young man, reload and try again. This time, raise it to eye level, look down the barrel so the top length is almost lost from sight and the end itself is married up with the centre of that target. Let your firing shoulder stretch forward and keep that arm straight."

Edward nodded and reloaded slowly under the watchful eye of his new tutor. He did as he was told, raised the weapon and tried to slow his breathing. He could see instantly how his aim became clearer, as though he was looking down the bolt of an arbalest crossbow. He extended his arm and shoulder, let out his breath and pulled the trigger, staying firm and absorbing the shock as he did so.

The small puff of smoke cleared and he could see, to his delight, a new hole just inside the last one made by his instructor. It was a way from the centre but on the target. He needed another go.

"Go on then," said Giraud, spotting Edward's expression. "Good shot. Go again."

Edward reloaded and fired again. Another hit, just inside the other. Giraud cheered out loud as the second shot to hit the target revealed its position behind the smoke and he stepped over to Edward with his hands wide.

"One shot can be lucky but two in a row? You seem to have talent, James. Keep going."

The two men took turns to shoot and reload the weapons a number of times and a small wager for a portion of the cost of the pistol saw them compete in a three-shot match. *Twelve* shots each later and Edward took ownership of the pistol for free, grinning at his four best shots, all only a finger's width from the centre of the target.

"You are a gambling man," he said, chuckling at Giraud's continued 'double-or-quits' offers. He'd halved the price repeatedly until he ran out of numbers.

"You should only gamble on yourself, I always say. But I have learnt not to gamble when shooting with you. Are you that natural with a sword?"

"With sword, without a sword, I am not bad,"

Edward replied. "But I am useless with a bow. Not a hope in hell for me there."

"Well it is the fifteen-seventies, my friend. Who needs bows?" Giraud winked and Edward smiled, stowing his new, deadly toy in his waist band along with its ammunition and gunpowder, then tying his light jacket around his waist to cover it.

"Thank you, Giraud. You have been most welcoming and extremely helpful."

"Not a problem, James. For you and for your *protestant* queen."

Edward nodded in understanding and turned to leave the room.

"I will see you again," he said, glancing over his shoulder and catching the professor's wave. He walked back through the corridors and out into the street. He couldn't help but smile. Protection duty was over; he was an agent again. He was armed, and he was dangerous.

Chapter Five

Edward wandered back through the Latin Quarter watching the bustle of people living and working around him. It meant nothing to him, the divide of people across Europe, yet to the passionate locals, he was behind enemy lines. Rounding a corner, he had finally spotted the river ahead when he heard a shriek from an alleyway across the road. Running through, he took a moment to process the vision of a young woman hanging from the upstairs window of a two-storey building, clinging on with one hand and the crease of one elbow while her legs wriggled silently beneath her. Edward jogged over, stepping over the scattered wooden pallets that had clearly slipped from beneath her and tried to work out how to address her without making her jump.

"Bois stupide. Super, et maintenant?" she whispered to herself.

"Stay still, I'll help," he said, smiling in surprise as she chuckled in response.

"Thank you, Englishman!" she whispered again.

"Why are you whispering?" Edward asked as he began to stack the pallets.

"Please, when I get down…" she said, quietly.

He finished the small, wooden tower and stood back,

his hands held out wide, cautiously. Her feet squirmed and stretched a foot or two over the platform.

"Where is it?" she called.

"It's done. Why is it so short? That is all the pallets."

"What about the box? The wooden box underneath?"

Edward looked around, spotting the flattened sides or what appeared to have been a flimsy, wooden box, laying crumpled beneath the stack.

"It's flattened underneath," he said. "It must have lost its shape and fallen away underneath you."

"How far away are my feet? Can I drop?"

"No, it'll break," Edward said, looking for ways to support the structure. "I'll come up instead."

He climbed up in silence, feeling his poorly built tower tip and shudder beneath him as he clung on to the rough render of the wall with his fingertips. He slowly extended his legs and stood next to her, smelling her flowery scent before seeing up close for the first time, her soft, well made dress and slim torso inside it.

"I'm here," he said, quietly, looking at the soft, lazy ringlets of copper hair falling over her shoulders. The smell of her perfume hit him again and he wondered what her face would be like. How her eyes would look at him.

"What do you want to do? Can you take my waist and lower me? Will that work?"

"It should do. Do you mind?"

"Mind you holding my waist? As opposed to falling into a pile of rough wood and iron nails? No, I don't mind."

He took a breath and put his hands either side of her,

feeling her rib cage and steadying his feet.

"Ready?" he said. "On three, lower yourself down and I'll support you to the pallet.

"One, two…"

She did as instructed on the third count and he easily held her, slowly lowering her until she touched down and turned to face him. The tower wobbled as she turned and his first look at her face caught the surprise of her light blue eyes along with the mischievous "O" shape of her mouth atop the unsteady platform. He said nothing.

"It's going to fall," she said, bringing him back to reality.

He intimated for her to jump down and took her weight by her hand as she stepped down lightly to the floor. He opened his mouth to speak as she let go of him and his weight shifted on the wooden stack.

"Get down," she whispered hurriedly as he tried to regain his balance. He clawed for the wall, scraping his knuckles as the solidity of the tower buckled and tipped his way, sliding him off noisily and throwing him to the floor before clattering back into place as though it had never been touched.

He managed to land on his feet awkwardly but grazed his thigh and side on the way down and grimaced at the raw burning of skin.

"Are you ok?" she asked, stepping over to him.

"Fine," he lied, trying to ignore the searing pain. He cursed himself. He'd been stabbed, beaten and tortured in his years since leaving France as a teenage boy, yet in that moment, nothing seemed to compare to the distracting pain of the skin ripped from his torso by rough wooden pallets.

"Let me see," she continued, lifting his shirt and wincing at the graze. "Thank you for helping me."

His world evaporated again as the freckles on her nose came into view and he felt himself stare for what seemed like long moments until the roar of male voices around the corner snapped him back into place.

"No problem. You'd clearly slipped in your attempts to…" He paused and looked at the window. "What *were* you doing?"

She looked down embarrassed as her expression struggled back and forth between a blush and grin.

"This is my father's Paris-house," she said. "Sorry, that sounded arrogant. Rather, as a family we live in La Rochelle but when he has business here, the merchant that he is, he rents this house and I come with him. It is good to study at the college.

"He insists on me being escorted everywhere I go so sometimes I slip out of the window to avoid his minders. They don't mind so they say nothing but if I walk past them they are not permitted to turn a blind eye. My little steps here have remained true for months. This time, I guess I chose my footing poorly."

"Steps? Is that what they were?"

She laughed. "Once, yes. Thank you, Englishman."

"James," he said. "My name is James."

"And mine is Amelie." She extended her hand and he shook it gently. Smiling back at her.

"You speak English very well," he said.

"I hope so. And your French?" she asked.

He shook his head and smiled ruefully.

"Anyway, I should go," he said. "I have work to do."

"Ah, you work here. Well, I will be here for weeks yet."

"Right here?"

Her nose crinkled. "Nearby."

"Well, then I hope to see you again," he said as he backed off, holding her gaze.

As he reached the corner of the alleyway where he had found her, he saw a rabble of men talking between him and the river in what he assumed was angry French. One then raised his voice firmly and spoke to the group who listened intently before dispersing.

He watched from the corner before he felt Amelie brush up next to him.

"Who are they?" he asked, covering his acute awareness of her elbow against his.

"Locals," she whispered. "Don't let them hear that you're English."

He stayed quiet as the leader and his entourage passed them and looked closely at Edward with narrowed eyes.

"Why does it matter that I am English?" he asked quietly, watching the group move out of earshot.

"Because they are Catholics. Wait, *Parisian* Catholics. They hate the English and can be violent when they want to be."

"But you don't hate me," he teased.

"I am not Parisian! Nor am I Catholic," she added, grinning. "But don't let anyone know that. My father says it is good for business if we follow Rome and speak Latin in the market. And quite frankly, in Paris, it *is* good for business. Anyway, you are sworn to secrecy or you'll get me killed as well. Now get out of my quarter."

He smiled and backed away, watching her grin and bite her lip for a moment before turning and crossing the bridge with a smile as wide as the river.

Chapter Six

Monday August 14th 1572

Edward let his gaze follow the swirl of the mead in his hand rather than watch the piercing eyes of Sir Francis, deep in thought six feet in front of him. He looked out to the palace gardens from their bay-window armchairs inside the white house and smiled to himself at the sight of the upper class boy chasing his dog in what seemed like zig zags thanks to the skew of the waves of the small, square panes of glass that encircled them.

"It seemed innocent enough," he offered. "They were angry but it could've been anything, even some kind of trade or employment union."

"They do like to moan and disrupt here in Paris,". Walsingham replied. "Of course, life is far from balanced and equal but at least the English take it on the chin. Here, a riled crowd can turn to riot for a lot less than a protestant queen. That's what worries me."

"It concerns you?"

"I wonder if they were talking about what's happening in the palace. Edward, I need you to do something."

Jacque coughed gently and rose to his elbow from his relaxed position on a rug by the cold fireplace.

"Shall I leave?" he asked.

Edward shook his head but looked to Walsingham for confirmation.

"Definitely not," the ambassador continued. "There is something dangerous afoot here, I can feel it. It is going to take all three of us to survive it, let alone prevent it." He paused again, squeezing his nose with his fingers. "Tensions are extremely high at the top. We have the most powerful protestant man walking the city on official invite to the royal wedding and he is not alone. The Catholic factions are furious."

"Will they rebel?" Jacque asked.

"I don't think they dare. At least, not through anger as they need the favour of the king and his mother. But anger isn't the problem here; the protestant Huguenot army is camped outside the city and its leaders sit unchecked in the palace. They won't rebel through rage, but who knows if they will rebel through fear. If not with a pre-emptive strike, then with a retaliation to the slightest provocation."

"Have you heard them say as much?" Edward asked, leaning forward.

"No. I'm an outsider. Who trusts an English ambassador in Paris? I am struggling to work out who would drive the response and therefore who to cultivate. But even then, they may not be the problem. Admiral Coligny has such sway across the country and the king admires him for his courage and record in battle; much to the fury of his mother and those around him. The awe and fear he commands is what concerns the Catholics. The power of confidence can turn the tides among thousands."

"But they aren't planning to attack," said Edward.

"Who knows? The Catholics are in fear of such an event and they know the opportunity is present. Why bring an army? I cannot say they won't. It could be catastrophic.

"This is why I need you to speak to Coligny and need Jacque on the ground," Walsingham continued. "Coligny is even less popular among the Catholic masses and Paris is angry. Harvests have been poor and food prices are through the roof, the city has put taxes up yet they spend a fortune on a royal wedding to protestant Henry of Navarre of all people. A mob here tore down the entire house of Phillips de Gastines a few years ago and erected a large cross on the land. He was a prominent protestant figure and even execution wasn't enough for them. The city only managed to take the cross down last year due to a fear of reprisals.

"No, the nobles may not fight but the commoners could. One wrong move to put Coligny down could spark a riot from either side, whether he lives or dies. And if he dies, god help the Huguenots across the continent, and God help us when that tide turns."

Edward smiled, feeling his excitement grow in time with the ante of his deployment.

"So, I'll get to Coligny," he said. "Jacque will keep his eyes and ears in the Latin quarter to monitor the mood. And you, I assume, will keep close to the king?"

"Exactly that, though Coligny won't be easy. I need you to find out what the Huguenots are planning and feeling and we need him to watch his back so there is no cause for retaliation. He is a tough man and he is arrogant. He will be open and question why he should talk to the English. Explain your concerns. Explain *my* concerns, and those of the queen. We are all on the same side after all. Be upfront and he will accept it. He will lie to you, but he will accept it and we can gauge him, even if we don't get answers. He will recognise your coin so will know your message comes from the top. I will do the same with the king, he is young and understanding so can be steered. His mother, not so much."

Edward nodded.

"And *James*, once this is done, I must ask more of you," Francis continued, lowering his voice despite knowing beyond doubt that they were not overheard. "I have had word from Rome, from one of my men there. There is something large occurring, something that cannot be ignored. Yet the route from Paris to Rome is corrupt so he cannot risk putting the news in writing. I need you to go to Rome and collect the information."

"Rome?" Edward repeated. "Is this another one of Cecil's diversions to keep me away from the Queen for longer? As though I still put her at risk?"

"Of course not, and please never think I would use such a tactic. I would tell Cecil to be straight in his direction or nothing at all. And he was direct when you last saw him, was he not?"

"He was."

"Well then, it will be so. The fact of the matter is, I have contacts all over this continent, but only a handful that I can trust without doubt. You are one of those and you are here. I would need to get word out in writing with the details of my Roman contact or else wait for someone to come into the unrest of Paris to receive the message if I go elsewhere.

You are here, you have the skills, I need you."

"Very well," Edward agreed. "It will be done. Now let's get to Coligny and stop this volcano losing its head."

Jacque laughed out loud and elbowed Edward where they stood facing south in the afternoon sun against the balustrade of the Pont Au Meuniers between the Il de la Cité and the left bank. Edward turned to see the source of Jacques' humour on the river when his eye caught a familiar sight that took his breath away.

"It's her," he said.

"Who?"

"Amelie. She's there."

Jacque frowned at his friend's expression, as unfamiliar as the name he spoke.

"Wow," he said as he saw the red, wavy hair and beaming smile aimed at Edward. "She's like autumn in motion."

Edward grinned.

"Autumn with summer in her eyes," he said.

Amelie approached them and stood smiling with both amusement and confusion at Edward's dumbfounded expression.

"Nice to see you," she said.

"And you, Amelie," he replied. "I didn't expect to see you again so soon."

"Is that a problem?" she smirked. "I would expect you to wash whether you were planning to see me or not, Englishman."

Jacque burst into laughter and Amelie chuckled as her sarcasm defeated her new friend.

"I am Jacque," he offered, holding out his hand.

"Amelie. You are French?"

"Of course, though I maintain this young man's dialect so he does not get lost."

"Ah," she said. "It seems we all must. Nice to meet you."

"You too. I will have a stroll around and leave you two to it, I think." He looked to Edward and grinned as his friend caught up and nodded back silently.

"So," Edward said as Jacque slipped away across the bridge. "I *was* hoping to see you again."

"You were? Why is that?" Amelie offered back with a smile.

"Because I have never been lost for words before, and with you, it seems to be a regular occurrence."

Her nose crinkled again ever so slightly, warming his heart.

"Carry on."

"I simply don't know what to say around you. Twice we have met and twice I haven't been able to think beyond your freckles."

"Well, my favourite Englishman, you are going to have to try if we are going to get to know each other."

Edward grinned and nodded his acceptance. They stood together talking, watching the jostling of boats in the crowded Seine below and the time passed easily as he gazed back and forth between the water and the fascinating movement of her mouth. Once in a while he caught her mischievous sideways glance as though she knew he watched her and he marvelled at how both confidence and shyness was clear in her expression.

"Looks like you two are having a good time," Jacque said suddenly, grabbing both of their shoulders and making them jump out of a trance. "Are you meant to be working, James?"

"I am working," Edward offered back, slyly.

"Well, he is trying," Amelie added, making Jacque laugh again.

"I found this, my friend," Jacque added, holding up a flyer. "There is a meeting here in two days. A rally at midday. It doesn't say what, but says, *'Join us to have a voice. Take back our city. Take back our God.'* So I am guessing it is something related to the unrest."

"Excellent, Jacque. Let's be there. Amelie, I must go now, but will you be there? At the meeting?"

"It is not really my kind of meeting, but I can meet you here on the bridge when it finishes?" she offered, gently.

Edward smiled.

"The date and time is on the flyer. I will see you then?"

She nodded, smiling, as Edward backed away with a grin then nodded to his friend who winked mischievously, and turned to walk back into the northern part of the city.

Chapter Seven

Edward took a long breath to slow his heart as he walked the quiet streets just north of the Louvre and the Tuileries Garden. The ever-expanding fortress turned palace and its brand new neighbour beside the gardens dominated the northern bank of the river. The roads narrowed and darkened in the shadows of the low, evening sun and Edward stopped, counting back the turnings and referencing the stored instructions in his mind to make sure he was in the right place.

He stood at the tight T-junction, looking into the mouth of the alleyway and watched the humble front door chosen by one of the most powerful men in France. He spotted no movement but a gentle light flickered from the upstairs window and confirmed a human presence inside.

He waited a moment longer and was about to move when quiet voices sounded around the curve of the road to his left and the accompanying footsteps moved into view. Edward put his head down, wishing for a cloak in the summer heat, and attempted to look busy while cursing himself for his lack of cover. He waited while the two men neared and risked a glance as they slowly passed him. He felt the familiarity in one of the faces, who in turn caught his eye and squinted as recognition dawned. The man had led the initial rally in the Latin quarter and had eyed Edward with suspicion the day he met Amelie. Neither could escape the fact they had both spotted and *been* spotted in the heart of the royal territory within fifteen paces of Coligny's front door, and neither of them said a word.

Edward waited with frustration for the figures to pass beyond the corner to his right and when the steps had faded, moved forward to the Admiral's door. He knocked quietly and waited for it to open, flashing his coin to the bearded Frenchman who stood as a silhouette against the low light behind him. The man eyed the coin for a moment before looking up and down the alley from his door and then stepping back to hold it open without saying a word.

"Why would a strange Englishman be knocking on my door at dusk?" he said in English as he eyed Edward.

"Admiral?" Edward asked.

"Clearly. You?"

"James. Thank you for allowing me to speak with you, I speak on behalf of Queen Elizabeth of England and Francis Walsingham."

Coligny barked a laugh.

"I knew Francis wasn't here for the celebrations. What do you want, Englishman?"

"Are we alone?"

Coligny nodded.

"My presence here in France is not known to any other but the two names spoken, my aide and yourself. We are concerned, Admiral, that the unrest in Paris is at boiling point and will spill at any moment. We are concerned that the Catholic masses will target you and the resulting vengeance will tear the country and our chance at protestant expansion apart."

"I have no fear of attack. The king will not allow it and my army would not retaliate regardless. We have our objective and no squabble will allow us to deviate. None of us are bigger than our goal."

Edward couldn't help respecting the sheer force of the man before him. A gravitas that overwhelmed him. He said little but what he did say was iterated with absolute conviction and belief.

"And that, I believe without doubt," he said. "But it is the mob itself that worries us. The living, breathing beast that forms among thousands in fear. Panic and bloodlust resulting in a frenzy of violence. It is the mob that we fear may attack you, and it is the mob that may then attack if *they* fear your retaliation to their own pre-emptive strike. What are your intentions here in Paris? I am sure you are not here just for celebrations either."

Coligny allowed a smile to take control of his mouth.

"I don't have to answer to anyone, especially an Englishman."

"No, but we do share a common interest," Edward replied. "We can protect our interests, and in turn yours, if we at least understand your objectives."

"It is simple, James. The Peace of Saint-Germain-en-Laye is a treaty I myself signed with the king two years ago. It was supposed to put a stop to our fighting and give us, the Huguenots, the respect we deserve. We were awarded four towns for security and were allowed to worship in any town we controlled at that time along with a couple of suburbs within every province except Paris and the Royal Court. But it is not equality, young man. The Catholics, they never accepted it. Last year in Rouen, forty Huguenot worshippers refused to kneel for Catholic communion and were butchered for it. Forty. For nothing. When they were free to choose.

"I am here for the minority and I am here to talk to the king of the injustice within our treaty. We will speak after the wedding and I will not leave until we have a resolution that includes the rights to worship God our way right here in Paris. We will not fight but we are here with permission and the city will know we mean what we say."

"The Catholics aren't happy."

"Of course they are not happy. But the only family that concern me are the Guises and they will not step over the king while he and I speak in trust."

"Then I guess there is not more to say," Edward added. "I respect your courage and your objective. Please remember, you can trust Francis Walsingham and we will be here to help you should you need it."

"Very well, Anglais. Maintenant laisse moi en paix."

Edward frowned but took the hint as the grizzled admiral held open the door with a smile. He nodded respectfully and stepped outside, hearing the door click gently behind him. He took in the darkness that had settled over the alleyway, lit only by the weak candlelight in the overlooking windows. He retraced his steps back to the T-junction and left towards the palace.

"Pourquoi voudriez-vous rendre visite à l'amiral, je me le demande? Qui es-tu?" said a voice in the shadow beside him. "Qui es-tu?"

Edward was baffled by the man's language but said nothing in order to hide his own. He watched as the face he had passed earlier stepped out of the shadows and two others joined him from each direction at the junction.

Edward shrugged.

One of the men stepped forward and spoke harshly only inches from his face, washing him with sour breath. Edward pushed him back and turned to a neutral position between the three of them. Another shouted, only to growl at Edward's lack of response and jumped in with a swinging arm in the darkness. Edward took a dull thump to his face without seeing it and grabbed a handful of cloth before him, hammering his forehead through twice to connect each time with a crumpling face. The figure dropped from his hands and he turned to overpower the next, holding him around his neck and armpit and tripping him with his feet to slam himself down on top of him, forcing a single grunt from the man as the two bodies collided with stone.

He jumped up again and turned in blind rage only to find the final man from the Latin Quarter on his back, wriggling silently as Jacque sat behind him, constricting his neck with his arm.

Edward nodded to Jacque, loosening his aide's grip and looking at the man from across the river. The constructed face grimaced in pain in the darkness and gurgled as it gasped at the small amount of air it was permitted, uttering a few broken French words. Jacque shook his head at Edward, then whispered into the ear beside him before dropping the man back to the floor and standing up to wait for instruction.

Edward intimated for them to leave and they did so, as quickly as they could, disappearing into the shadows of the Parisian streets.

"He called us shadow men," Jacque whispered as they got further away. "I said we were here to help."

Chapter Eight

<u>Wednesday August 16th 1572</u>

Edward took a breath as nerves threatened to overwhelm him. On the two occasions he had seen Amelie, he had encountered her by accident and had never had the anticipation of meeting her. It had been only eight months since the death of his former love, Maggie, and it was not lost on him that Amelie was only the second woman ever to truly enter his heart. He despised the idea of yet again putting someone he cared for at such risk but he had learned to confront the fact that Maggie had been turned by the Black Axe; and had she not succumbed, she would be alive today.

He left Jacque behind to assess the mood south of the river and stepped onto the bridge early, laughing in surprise to see Amelie already there waiting for him.

He saw her hair first, the only red ringlets on the bridge, and then he saw her smile as she bit her lip and stepped over to him. Her hair was gathered to the side of her neck and fell across her chest in waves that only she could muster. The rest of her took away the breath he had worked so hard to control.

"You look beautiful," he said, taking in her long, emerald green dress and open neck. Her collarbones stood out ever so slightly above her tanned but gentle bust and her shoulders were more delicate than he had realised as the cloth hung to their edge like fingertips on a cliff.

She thanked him with a curtsy and took his elbow with her fingers to allow his lead across the bridge.

"I have been quite nervous," she said with the full strength of her accent.

"As have I."

She smiled at him and they walked for a while in silence, across the bridge and right along the north eastern bank of the river. The warmth in Edward put Paris in a different light and he felt, for a moment, as though he was a noble at peace, admiring the beauty of one of Europe's most powerful cities and courting the high-born daughter of a lord or baron.

To her, he thought, they must simply be enjoying each other's company where words cannot do justice to the mood. To him, however, he had tried more times than he could count to speak and had swallowed the words like water.

"Tell me about yourself, James," she said suddenly, stopping in front of a public garden on the bank and holding both of his hands. "Where are you from? Why do you have scars? Why are your eyes both hard and kind all at once?"

Edward smiled. He hadn't considered talking of his past but somehow she made him want to open his heart.

"Well, believe it or not, I was raised in France."

"In France? But you don't speak French!"

"That's true. And I'm not sure why. There are many answers about my life that still elude me. My parents were English and we lived in isolation, generally. When I was fifteen, my family died. Both of my parents and my little sister. So I came to Paris for a while then ended up in London. The scars are from my time on the streets as I wasn't bad in a scrap."

"If you were a handy fighter, why did you get so hurt?"

"It was a way to make a living," Edward added, with a wince. "Sorry, I don't do that anymore."

"And that bruise on your cheek?"

Edward shrugged and she grinned.

"Don't say sorry to me. You are an interesting man, James. Though I think there is more to you." She reached forward and felt his shirt. "You don't feel like you live on the streets."

"Thankfully, I don't. I was given an opportunity and now use my *skills* to do good things." He looked at his shirt and held the hand she held against him. "And, I now have access to fine resources."

She smiled and laid the tips of her fingers against his stomach, looking down for a moment then back to his eyes.

"What about you?" he asked. "I know you are not Catholic, I know your father is a merchant, what of your mother, what of your life?"

"I have lived my life in La Rochelle, on my family estate outside the city. My mother died from sickness when I was small and my father has been somewhat overprotective ever since. He is a merchant, yes, and he deals in arms: hardware, weapons, armoured accessories. He has contracts with various garrisons and weapon resellers around the country and he takes me with him wherever he goes. In more recent years, as a grown woman, I have refused to go, and so he started to gather clients in various businesses and households outside of the military. He did so in Paris intentionally so that he could talk me into studying at the college. The sessions are in Latin, of course, but language has never been a problem for us. I've had tutors pestering me all my life. Now he spends most of his time in Les Halles, making deals or making men drunk so that he can make deals. He is good at what he does, but it does not leave such a life for me."

"Maybe it is time you walked a fresh path?"

"And what would that be?" she grinned. "You want to whisk me away to London, English knight?"

"If you would let me, then yes."

"Maybe I would," she whispered, looking up at him, then inside her own thoughts for a moment. "Still, you would have to get through the old bull first."

"I do like a challenge," Edward replied with a chuckle.

"What happened at the gathering today? Did you go?" she asked, suddenly. "I was thinking about you. They do not take kindly to the English that side of the river."

"Not much. Three men spoke from a platform, making the crowd excited and filling them with rage. I doubt they were pulling the strings though," he added, thinking of the men from near Coligny's house whom he had seen bruised, watching the demonstration from the side. "They made a lot of noise about protestants being here in Paris and outside the gates, protestants in their stronghold towns, protestants in the Netherlands and shouting that the English church was heresy."

"It frightens me."

"It frightens me for you. They made no actual plans to cause harm, yet. But the people were scared. They think the Huguenots are here for a fight. The men on the platform told the crowd that the Catholics had support from the nobility and that as soon as the wedding was over the Huguenots were meant to leave but would not. He told them to arm themselves in case of attack and to make the city as hostile as possible.

"I do not think it is safe, Amelie. Maybe you and your father should leave."

"And what about you?"

"I must stay for now."

She closed her eyes and shook her head.

"It is crazy, I know, I have met you three times, but...I wouldn't want to leave without you."

"Nor I without you."

They looked at each other for a long moment in silence before Edward finally spoke.

"I am falling for you, Amelie," he said. "It has only been days but I have never met anyone like you."

The sound of church bells seemed to steal the words from her mouth as her lips parted and she turned to look across the river to the Latin Quarter in the distance. She bit her lip then turned back to Edward, taking hold of his collar with her hands then pulling him close and kissing him firmly on the lips.

Edward watched, stunned, as Amelie spun back to him and lifted herself onto her toes to kiss him. Her lips landed on his softly, then pushed deeper, parting ever so carefully so that he felt the slightest touch of moisture against his own. He was lost for a moment, then she released him, bouncing back down onto the soles of her feet and smiling up at him. He grinned back.

"It is four in the afternoon. I have a session at the college starting now."

"I will walk with you."

"No, it is fine, I can cross the river at the next bridge along the bank and get to the college quickly. But thank you."

"Very well," Edward replied, suddenly sad.

"Can I see you soon?" she asked.

"Tomorrow?"

She smiled again and her nose crinkled once more.

"Tomorrow. Same time, same place" she said. Then she turned and ran, and she was gone.

Chapter Nine

Thursday August 17th 1572

"What is it?" Edward asked as he walked into the front room of the white house and found his leader rubbing his temples in frustration.

"Something isn't right and the palace is the problem," said Francis.

"Coligny seems to think the king wouldn't dare," replied Edward.

"The *king* wouldn't. He appears happy and isn't even considering trouble from what I can see. But his mother? Catherine is strong and angry and determined. What about the streets? What is happening out there?"

"Not much. They're angry but they're not planning anything. They want to arm themselves just in case but in reality, they just want the Huguenots out as soon as the wedding is over."

Francis nodded then looked up as the front door of the house was heard to slam and hard soles were rapped against the hard oak floor of the hallway.

"James," said Jacque as he pushed open the door. "Amelie is outside. Something is wrong."

"She's here?" asked Edward, concerned. "At the safehouse?"

"Of course not. I left her halfway across the gardens near the river bank and made sure she couldn't see my route. She was standing there alone then saw me, ran over in panic and asked for you."

Edward shook his head, confused, gathering his blade and his gun under his light jacket.

"Is anyone going to tell me who Amelie is?" interrupted Francis, looking unsettled.

"A woman," said Edward. "A woman I met. We have become close."

"Close?"

"She knows my pseudonym only, and nothing about me, apart from the feelings underneath."

Francis smirked.

"This isn't advisable, you know that. I should forbid it."

"I know."

"And she only knows your current persona. It is...immoral."

"No, it isn't like that. She knows my…"

"…Feelings underneath. Yes, you said. Well, you're my best. I trust you enough to know that you know what you're doing. You've surprised us all over the last few years with your less than standard techniques. But, James, if it gets in the way, it ends. The job first."

"Of course."

Edward moved gently from foot to foot, waiting for Francis to issue a dismissal, given the circumstances. The older man nodded slightly and Edward bolted for the door and out into the gardens, taking a long route around knots of trees spread throughout the northern side before moving down to the river.

He saw her sitting on a bench facing the Seine and felt his heart leap at the sight of her as he jogged over.

"Amelie," he said, making her turn. "Are you ok?"

"Of course, but *I* am not why I am here," she said. "I do not know why you are here in Paris, or even in France, but I do believe you are here to keep us safe. Something tells me that."

"Are you not safe? What is it?"

"I am. My father…"

"Is he ok?"

"Yes, James. Please, I must finish. My father has heard many rumours and had word of violence. In the markets, in the college, in taverns. From all of his circles. Something is happening. I don't know what," she added, seeing the questions on Edward's face. "There have been meetings of leaders in the Catholic community. They meet in the college and the alleyways around it. They have discussed a plan. The royal wedding is tomorrow and I wanted to let you know in case it was important to you. I am a little scared."

"Thank you, Amelie, it means so much. Who is in charge of the group? Who leads them and calls them together?"

"I don't know, and neither does my father, though he thinks it is Catherine de Medici, the king's mother. Please, I feel like we are in danger. I feel like you should leave the city. My father will not. He said it won't affect us as it'll only touch the nobles and the poor. A few examples made here and there. But I am not so sure and I want you to be safe, so that one day I can see you again."

"I am not sure it will come to such violence but it could. The city is bubbling and it is ready to spill over. Stay safe, stay away, stay home as much as possible. If it becomes dangerous, I will come for you."

Amelie nodded, her eyes filled with tears. Edward watched her and his biggest fear grew before him: that he would not see her again if they parted. He touched her cheek with his thumb and kissed her briefly, feeling the breath from her nose on his face as he did.

He said his goodbyes and jogged back via the trees to the white house, wishing the whole way that he had told her he loved her.

As he entered the white house, Jacque was waiting for him in the hall and Francis walked out at the sound of the door.

"Any news?" he asked as he came into view.

"The city is bubbling over," Edward replied. "Amelie's father is a successful merchant with his fingers in pies right across France. He has heard in the nobility, the military, the upper circles and on the streets that things are being planned and tensions are about to spill. He thinks the king's mother is coordinating it all."

"Why would he tell you?" said Francis.

"He didn't, he told her and she came to me as she is concerned for my safety."

"You're sure? She's not trying to flush out your true

purpose?"

Francis eyed Edward deeper than he found comfortable and he knew the spymaster was hinting at the betrayal by his former lover.

"I am sure," he said. "She isn't working for anyone or against us."

Walsingham nodded.

"Then we must act. The wedding is tomorrow. We must be ready."

"You shouldn't go. It could be dangerous," added Edward.

"I must or it will raise suspicion. We will all be there in one capacity or another. We need to be able to either react effectively, or recognise when all is lost and get the hell out of this city before it gets us as well."

Chapter Ten

Friday August 18th 1572

"Pain chaud doux et choix de viande rôtie!" called a voice above the din of a thousand conversations.

Edward looked around at the heaving crowds and smiled to himself. The weather was ideal and the mood light; where he was at least. If not for the threat of so many innocent deaths in the back of his mind, it would have been a perfect royal wedding. He had never witnessed such an occasion before and shook his head at the pointless, holy quarrel that tarnished the event. People held their children aloft on the bridges that led to the island in the Seine and the Notre Dame that stood upon it, pointing and laughing at the street entertainers and the food sellers who argued their way to an advantageous spot. His nerves prickled as he stood in the crowds not far from the looming western entrance to the cathedral and he spotted Jacque among the mob in the distance, keeping watch professionally for the slightest hint of trouble. The two caught each other's eye and nodded subtly before turning their attention back to the masses. The jubilance made Edward suspicious, though he enjoyed the feeling of tension, he admitted to himself, and was grateful to be back in the field.

Edward turned his attention to the steps under the

cathedral doors as the soldiers who guarded them moved into a forceful march a few paces forwards. They held a line one-man deep but made their weapons known as they pushed the crowd back to make more room around the three arched doorways and the carved saints that lined them. Edward looked at one of the supposed rose windows that sat above the doors on the west side of the building. It didn't look red to him, he thought, though he guessed it must have the name for a reason.

The crowd entering the cathedral behind the guards thickened and Edward smiled to himself as he saw Francis walking alone up the steps in fine robes. The older man took one nervous glance around him then stepped into the darkness inside with his head bowed.

'*Henry of Navarre would be waiting inside*,' Francis had told him. Along with his men and the Cardinal de Bourbon, who would carry out the ceremony. Edward watched the crowds of lucky guests as they chatted and laughed on their way through the grand arches until they were gone and emptiness embraced the steps once more.

He felt the mob shift as the stairs to the cathedral fell silent and the guards struggled to hold the surge. Shouts called from the line of armed men and the crowd around Edward grew in vigour. Edward struggled to make sense of the angry exclamations and searched for Jacque in the crowds. Pushing back against a scramble behind him, he heard a baby cry close by and turned to see a fearful mother clutching her child and whispering words into its ear. Edward chose to save at least the one he could and threw an elbow at a sweating man who yelled and pushed beside him. He began to move more forcefully around the woman, knocking aside those who complained and creating space so that he could move her to the wooden stall of a souvenir seller at the side of the street.

He assumed she was thanking him as she called out and began to cry, so he offered a tight smile in response and threw a leg up onto the stall to scramble onto its roof, ignoring the blasphemy of its owner beneath. From the top of the stall he was able to see Jacque, safely tucked out of the crowd and surveying them for an indication of their intent.

A fanfare sounded around the Notre Dame and the crowd roared collectively. The surge continued and a call among the soldiers that echoed off of the doorways of the cathedral led to the line of men stepping back to draw their swords and then stepping back into the crowd in an attacking stance. A handful of those at the front were cut and dropped to the paved surface of the island as the fanfare increased in intensity and the crowd fell silent in a ripple from front to back.

Edward caught Jacques' eye and shrugged, unsure of how to gauge the crowd. Jacque blew through his cheeks, raising his eyebrows once before turning to the church in response to a sudden cheer in the masses.

Edward looked up to see shining soldiers and flags march into view followed by the royal entourage in their carriages. The crowd continued to roar in excitement as the spectacle moved fully into view and came to an abrupt halt before the saintly arches.

Edward whistled at the impressive sight and watched with a childish grin as the royals stepped out of their carriages, waved at the crowd and entered the premier place of worship in France. Finally, when all had entered and royal aides had lined the steps with bowed heads, the final carriage opened and Princess Margaret alighted, adorned in the finest fabrics so white that they reflected the light of the sun as they hugged and flowed from her body. The image was beautiful and Edward thanked his luck that he was able to witness such a day.

The princess entered and the doors were closed behind her, leaving the crowd silent for a moment before they turned internally and began to laugh and dance among themselves. Edward looked up at the steps to see the bodies removed and the soldiers at ease, then glanced to Jacque to see the Frenchman laughing back at him with obvious bewilderment.

Edward had allowed himself to relax and enjoy the time while the wedding took place. The stall owner had said no more and Edward had kept his position above the crowds, allowing him to watch the people and their day of departure from monotonous city life with both interest and mirth. Language meant nothing, he realised, as he followed the stories that unfolded below him and whether it be a romantic moment, a chance reunion, a troublesome quarrel or an inquisitive child, he knew exactly what was occurring and kept up with ease. It was an interesting aspect of communication, he mused, the expression and body language of others. One he would study and exploit.

Yet another fanfare shook him from his thoughts as

the doors to the cathedral were opened and both soldiers and royal aides filed out to line the steps. The men that held the front line moved closer together in a defensive stance but the crowd held back and shouted with glee, holding children aloft and pumping their fists in the air.

The newlywed royal couple stepped out into view, to the roar of the crowd, and moved slowly down the steps before boarding a carriage that awaited them. The entourage built slowly until all those permitted were in place and were pulled into movement by the call of the royal guards, the first steps of a march and the creaking of reins against the sweating backs of the mounts.

Francis moved out of the doors among the crowd and spotted Edward immediately. He nodded subtly, just visible at the distance between them, and moved into the crowd towards him. Edward spotted Jacque awaiting instructions and signalled for him to join them.

They met together as Edward climbed down and his new colleagues arrived at once. A scramble nearby made them jump and two men began to fight as another few arrived, pulling aside their cloaks to reveal soldier's uniforms and bared blades. The fighting men subdued and all involved melted into the crowds once more.

"They have some interesting security," said Edward.

"They're paranoid," Francis replied, looking around with his head dipped.

A man nearby glanced over with a raised eyebrow and Jacque launched into storytelling mode in deep, expressive French, speaking directly to Edward and Francis and laughing as he did so, moving animatedly. The inquisitive man shrugged and turned away leaving them to share a glance and exhale collectively.

"We better keep our voices down, they won't take kindly to our tongue. Let's go," said Jacque.

The three of them moved into a slow walk through the crowd as Francis made sure he wasn't overheard.

"Well it seems to have passed but it's not over," he said. "The wedding was smooth inside, though there was no shortage of glances between factions, both angry and perturbed. I take it nothing occurred out here?"

"Nothing more than a boisterous mob," Edward replied. "Any information on the motives and causes when it went awry, Jacque?"

"No sign of a motive as such," Jacque said. "And certainly nothing religious. Just a large crowd, some crushing and some excitement."

"Ok, then we have passed today unscathed, I think," continued Francis. "Coligny is determined; the Huguenots said they intend to stay in Paris and talk to the king about the treaty. It seems it may end without bloodshed."

"I am not so sure," interrupted Edward. "There have been plans discussed. Something is intended and I do believe it will happen."

"But is your *source* reliable?"

"She has proven to be so far, and I know she didn't hear it first hand but it is certainly corroborated by everything else that is occurring. I don't think we can overlook it."

"And I agree. Why would Amelie think it comes from Medici?"

"I don't know. Though Medici arranged the wedding

for reasons we cannot fathom and you have said yourself that only the king admires Coligny. Not his mother. What a cover to pretend to make peace while drawing Huguenot leaders to Paris and then blaming the mob for their action?"

"But the mob cannot take on the Huguenot army."

"I don't think they need to, the army are outside the walls. They can't fight without their head and their head isn't safe without them."

"An assassination?"

Edward nodded.

"Then we should warn them," said Francis.

"Warn who? There are too many targets. Navarre?"

"No, it would be bad for her daughter."

"She has sons," offered Edward.

"No, it is too close. Were there not Catholic men from the Latin Quarter wandering around near to where Coligny is staying?"

"Coligny," Edward nodded. "Take him out, blame the mob, bar the walls and the job will be done."

"Have you been watching the house since then?"

"Yes, between the two of us. He has barely returned all week."

"Ok, then we must assume it is him but be open to others. You two should be ready to monitor him and see if he is being followed, and I will get news to you if it looks like he intends to leave the palace. I'll keep an ear to the ground in the heat of the talks and let you know if there is anyone else we need to watch or warn. Discussions will finish in three days, I believe. He will be safe while he is at the palace and may stay there throughout the talks but that may make them impatient and force them to act rashly to finish him before he leaves the city and rejoins his troops."

"They will strike him as he leaves the palace."

"I think so."

Edward shared a glance with the others before shaking their hands subtly and moving away into the crowd. He would meet Jacque later to set up a plan, he thought. The excitement of being back in the field had turned to nerves once more as the stakes rose sharply. Once again, the life of an important figure and the prevention of the inevitable unrest that would follow sat upon him. This time in a foreign world where *he* was the enemy, and he had no idea what *his* enemy said around him.

Chapter Eleven

Tuesday August 22nd 1572

Edward blew into his shirt to cool his chest as the high summer sun wore down on him as though it was only six inches away. He watched the doors of the Louvre Palace as he waited for the most powerful men in France to emerge. Francis had sent him word of the talks drawing to a close and brought him closer to keep an eye on Admiral Coligny. The Huguenot leader and battle veteran was apparently irate at the inconclusive discussion and his departure could be either one of his last actions alive or the moment he spurred on the religious war to its crescendo. Edward glanced around himself feeling nothing but silence in the peaceful, upper class atmosphere of the royal quarter. The silence made him uneasy and he missed the reassurance of his new partner, though he knew Jacque was better placed in the Latin Quarter, listening and charming people into talking to him as he did.

In an almost startling fashion, the doors to the palace flew open and the sound of aggressive confrontation emanated from the shadowy portal. Francis stepped out into the light first, taking in the sight of Edward without expression and looking down to move out of the way while a small group of Frenchmen emerged with Coligny at their head. The older man turned to those that followed and grunted something at them angrily. They each nodded in turn and split off in different directions to leave the area with nothing more than a disappointed mumbling of farewell.

Edward kept his head down as Coligny marched past him with another in tow, reeling off orders and statements while the second man nodded under the pressure of too many mental notes. He looked up to Francis for assent to continue then fell in behind them, sweating under the hat that helped cover his face.

He kept a suitable distance as Coligny's unknown companion showed an unsettling level of awareness, looking around constantly for anyone who may be following. To Edward's surprise, he appeared to say nothing to the Admiral, who himself had not glanced away from the pavement several feet in front of him. He briefly said his goodbyes and then peeled off into a side street away from the vacant wave of a powerful man under pressure.

Edward's spine tingled at the sudden change and he glanced around to see if another followed. Whether Coligny's colleague had spotted him or was part of a set up himself, Edward didn't know, but something wasn't as it should be and he felt exposed to be so openly on the tail of the man. The area had become familiar through the weeks and he chose to take a side street himself to skirt around Coligny's path and either throw off or flush out anyone that may be behind him.

He took a sharp turn into a sweeping alleyway that he knew would curve wide but allow him intermittent views of Coligny and bring him out closer, ready resume his surveillance. He knew if he moved quickly he would both be able to keep up with the Admiral's pace on the shorter, direct path, and see anyone emerging from the tight corners within the alley as they looked to see which direction he took. He broke into a gentle jog and worked his way through the twists and turns, hurdling a number of Parisian street sleepers as they called out to him from the floor and turning into the first long, narrow opening ready to spot Coligny move past. He was sure he had timed the run accurately but despite more than a moment's wait, the grizzled veteran never moved into view at the end of the path. Edward guessed he must've missed him and moved on more quickly to the next opening. He noticed no one tailing either of them but let his mind forget that possibility as he focused on the greater threat of losing his target. He sprinted to the next outlet that led to Coligny's path and darted down it.

He passed a number of doorways as he ran blindly towards the opening onto the wider road where Coligny walked and skidded into the daylight of the open road without stopping to ensure he wasn't seen. He cursed himself for his stupidity as he looked ahead to see how far Coligny had walked and then spun at the feeling of a presence behind him.

His eyes locked onto the Admiral's as he turned to find them only metres apart and in the short moment between Coligny's recognition and the time it took for Edward to speak, a loud explosion rang out behind them and the old man's left arm shook violently with a spray of blood.

Coligny fixed Edward with an expression of anger and disbelief as he felt the betrayal of the Englishman, then looked to his ravaged arm and dropped to his buttocks with a thud.

Edward looked around at the streets but saw nothing. No one stood in the open, no sound of footsteps could be heard. He spotted movement in the curtain of an upstairs window but knew not if it was the shooter or a frightened witness. He ran to the wounded man and crouched beside him.

"Admiral," he whispered. "Admiral, how badly are you hurt?"

"How dare you approach me," Coligny growled in reply as he grimaced in pain. "I would not have thought this of Elizabeth's men. You must be one of the Pope's."

"No, Coligny. I am here to protect you only."

"Liar!" the old man roared once more. "You follow me here and I am shot twice!"

Edward noticed for the first time that both the Admiral's left elbow and his right hand were shattered and bleeding, though he only heard one shot. He looked around once more at the sound of many well-timed footsteps approaching and knew he would soon face soldiers.

"Admiral, it wasn't me, I swear it. But I must go."

"Coward!" the old man yelled back weakly with his eyes closed as he dropped his head back to the stone of the road.

Edward opened his mouth to protest but knew he had to find Francis. He shuffled around for his dagger and felt the outline of his pistol in his cloak. He would seem even more guilty, he thought, as he closed his hand around the barrel. He had to leave.

He stood up to run as men came into view at the end of the street and one shouted to him. He turned on his heels and ran, glancing over his shoulder only once to see a handful of men chasing him while one peeled off to tend to Coligny.

He ran with everything he had, sprinting past a number of openings to create space between him and the armoured men, and then ducked into an alleyway to weave through the twists and turns of the Parisian Royal Quarter. Though he moved at his best pace and the majority of footsteps behind him faded, two heavy feet remained close behind him as though only ever one corner away. He felt himself tire beyond endurance and realised he would have to fight to shake away his pursuer.

He had covered half the distance of a narrow path when he found a suitable corner on his right and ducked into the shadows. He took a breath, listening to the steps approaching and readied himself to ambush the fast moving body. But though he waited, the relentless soldier seemed to sense his trap and slowed his pace at what sounded like twenty paces away. Edward heard him call out with heavy breath, what could only have been his location to the other soldiers and then the footsteps restarted as a slow creep along the path.

Edward waited a moment longer before facing the inevitable. If he waited for the soldier to reach his hiding place, the others would catch up and he would face them all. He had no choice but to run on or face the man. He cursed at the sound of a blade being drawn as he had no desire to hurt an innocent soldier. He had simply tried to protect the old man and would now have to fight to the death to avoid being treated as his assassin.

He took one deep breath, trying to gauge exactly where the soldier was then leapt from his position to sprint directly at the man who chased him. He took several hard steps as his mind adapted to the new view and found himself within moments hurtling into the unsuspecting face of a tall soldier barely old enough to wear a uniform. He dipped his shoulder as they connected and drove it at the lower rib cage of the man, knocking him into the air to land flat on his back. He dived on the man before he had a chance to adjust and raise the blade he still held, and drove his head down hard into his face. His forehead connected with the soldier's nose, flattening it with a crunch. The head lulled with confusion to one side as Edward slammed his head down once more into the exposed temple, knocking out the man in a moment. Edward winced at the sound of the cracking cheekbone as their heads connected and jumped up, looking down at the unconscious body before spotting a woman watching him from an overlooking window. He shook off his inevitable feeling of regret, held up his hands and turned on his heels to continue sprinting through the alleyway, around the corner and on towards the river.

Chapter Twelve

<u>Wednesday August 23rd 1572</u>

"Come on, Jacque, where are you?" Edward whispered to himself as he wandered the streets and alleyways of the Latin quarter. He had set out to find his partner mid-morning after waking to find that he had not returned and was yet to hear of the shooting. He did his best to avoid being seen by someone who might recognise him while making himself visible in case Jacque spotted him first. He listened in to the hurried conversations as he walked but had no idea what was said despite the animated expressions worn by those who spoke.

Edward had briefed Francis when he arrived home and they had discussed both of their concerns and their strategy. The intended assassination had missed its target and Coligny was alive with only the vision of Edward jumping out from an alleyway as the shot was fired. He knew not that he worked for Francis Walsingham but knew he carried the coin of Elizabeth, which put all Englishmen in Paris in danger. To Coligny, with Elizabeth an ally of the Huguenots, an assassination attempt by her man could only mean a changing of sides and an immoral stab in the back.

Francis had felt the white house remained safe as an unrecorded residence and as only Coligny and the soldiers had seen Edward at the scene, they reassured themselves that it would be safe to redeploy him to the Latin quarter.

Edward continued to walk, side-stepping children and ducking through animated conversations until he came across Amelie walking towards him in the opposite direction. He caught her eye, making her smile, and indicated with his head towards a narrow alleyway opening halfway between them.

She reached the narrow path first as he ducked in behind her and she turned to face him, grinning. He pulled his hood up and his cloak around them both, then pulled her tightly towards him, kissing her deeply and feeling her mouth open to admit his tongue to meet hers. He felt himself harden as they kissed and he pressed himself against her in instinct, causing her to gasp mischievously and smile as her tongue reached out to his.

"I do love French girls," he said as they finally broke apart.

"All of us?" she replied slyly.

"No, just you. I have fallen in love with you," he said.

"I love you too."

"Are you ok?" he asked.

"Yes, of course. Though there is a lot of talk around here. They are saying that Admiral Coligny was shot."

"He was. In the arm, I think. I was there. What are they saying? Are they angry? Excited? Are they planning to fight?"

"Most are scared," said Amelie. "There is an army outside the walls. Most are innocent, James. They are not fighters."

Edward nodded. He knew she was right. Plots against the innocent public, for any reason, were vicious and unjust. He didn't know what to do. How could he and Francis protect a city alone? Francis was barely welcome in the royal court and Edward's presence could never be more than a whisper.

Edward opened his mouth to speak but Amelie held her finger to his lips. A multitude of deep voices grew louder around the corner in the alleyway and were within inches of coming into view.

"They're talking about Coligny," she whispered in warning. "About planning, and arming."

As she whispered, a dozen or so men moved into view slowly, with some walking backwards to face the others while they held a slow-moving meeting. One of the men turned and saw them, then hushed the others as he pulled them closer. Another, who emerged afterwards, looked beyond his shoulder and recognised Edward instantly. He growled in French as he pushed his friends out of the way and converged on him.

Edward moved his hand to his blade as he recognised him as one of the men from the alleyway outside Coligny's house and readied himself to fight. Amelie stepped between them both and spoke loudly in French.

The man stopped in his tracks and watched Edward through squinted eyes as he listened to Amelie's words. She raised her voice again as she spoke, pulling the attention of all the men with her beauty and gravitas. One asked a question with both anger and interest showing on his face. Amelie turned to look at Edward with concern, and then turned back to answer. They listened intently as their suspicions waned and after she clearly changed her tone for a moment, they conceded with a nod and continued their meeting in Edward's presence.

Amelie gave Edward a strained look that convinced him to play along silently and he watched the men, pretending to listen to their gibberish while studying their body movement for an indication of both their intentions and their ability to fight.

As the meeting finished, they glanced between each other with acceptance and gestures of farewell, before departing and leaving only the man from Coligny's alleyway to face Edward. He stepped closer and put his right hand on Edward's shoulder, fixing him with a gaze that tried to pull the truth from within him. He spoke quietly but forcefully to Edward then waited, watching him for a reply. Edward saw Amelie nod her head slightly behind the man and Edward followed suit. He nodded gravely and took the man's shoulder with his own right hand. The man nodded again, squeezed Edward's shoulder once, then moved away to disappear into another, even narrower side-alley.

Amelie looked at Edward, her eyes wide, and indicated for them to walk on. They did so in silence until they had put enough distance between them and the rabble of Catholics.

"What did they say? What did *you* say?" Edward whispered, finally.

"At first, they were talking about the Admiral being shot and that you had been seen there at the time."

"How do they know that? One of them must have

been the shooter."

"I don't know. But they said the shooting came from the top, from the Guises, and that you are a spy for the other side, working against them. I asked them, 'Whose man do they think you are? Of course you were there. That the Guises only knew where Coligny would be because of you.' When they asked why you don't speak, I said that to reveal your tongue would be to reveal political allegiances that cannot be discussed." She paused. "I said that is why I am here with you."

Edward shook his head as his heart dropped into his stomach.

"You put yourself at too much risk," he said. "Anything that happens with me now, they will associate with you."

"It was necessary. So I said to them, 'Of course it came from the top. Leading Catholics support his deployment, so they must also'."

"And they were content with that?"

"It seems so."

"Thank you," Edward said. "Thank you for everything. You may have saved a city."

Amelie nodded.

"So, what was their plan?" Edward asked.

"Well, Coligny survived and apparently the king has been to see him already?"

"He has?"

"Apparently. They said that Coligny wants revenge and he has four thousand men outside the city walls. The first place they will come is the Latin Quarter. They agreed to arm themselves and take care of warning a sector of the quarter each. If the soldiers do attack, they plan to chain off the streets and kill the protestants."

"Which protestants?"

"All of them," she said, solemnly. "All of them in the city. They say have word from the very top. If anything changes, they will know."

Edward nodded as the news sank in. He wished he'd killed them when he had the chance.

"Thank you," he said. "I must go, right away. If it goes wrong, I will come for you. Keep an eye out for Jacque and tell him to head back to us as soon as he can, if you see him."

He leaned in and kissed her for a long time, then looked her in the eyes.

"Keep safe, keep away. I love you." And at that he turned and sprinted back to the bridge and north towards Francis.

Chapter Thirteen

Jacque chuckled as he tucked his loose shirt back into his trousers and fastened his belt. He looked down at the palace maid who watched him, still entirely undressed and displaying herself while her hands stroked unashamedly in the dim light of the breaking dawn.

"Won't you stay?" she asked in her strong, Parisian French.

"I cannot," Jacque replied, truthfully. His enquiries had led him back over the bridge as he heard word of conspiracy in the palace, and almost without effort he found himself to be a trusted ear to one of Catherine Medici's chambermaids. He'd made all efforts to extract information from her covertly but she had only one thing on her mind and even her subsequent pillow talk was less than useful in their race to stop catastrophe in the city. Nevertheless, she had the body of one of the ancient Greek goddesses and knew how to use it, he reasoned. She was one to remember.

"Which way shall I go to leave the palace unnoticed?" he asked.

"You are directly opposite the royal chambers. You will need to pretend you belong here as you will certainly be seen. Look presentable and be ready to face anybody, but they should all still be sleeping and we get time off, so that is the best reason why you are not in uniform."

"Ok."

"But go left and stay left, whatever you do. If you enter the chambers without invitation you will be in serious trouble."

Jacque nodded as the maid giggled back at him. He felt a stirring in his trousers again and shook away the urge to climb back on top of her, despite the renewed glisten of her obvious readiness in the dim light. Instead, he straightened his clothes, winked once, and then ducked out of the door.

'Go left and stay left,' he said to himself as he padded silently along the shadowy corridor, lit only by candles despite the light of the new sun only a wall away. As he neared a doorway on his right, he slowed to check that he wouldn't be seen before hearing voices and slipping past to see the shapes of what looked like the king and his mother inside the room

His heart beat wildly at the potential of torture and execution if he was caught listening but their heated conversation could not be missed. He slowed down on the other side of the doorway and moved as close as he could, doing his best to assume a position that could keep moving as though in motion if seen.

"You are my son but you are the king!" said an authoritative female voice, giving them both away. "I cannot let you get bullied by either side."

"But they tried to kill him," the king replied. "We brought him here under truce. He trusted me, he trusted *us*, and as soon as he was out of sight, they went for him. I cannot let it go. I *must* not let it go. I couldn't protect him."

"It was beyond you. You cannot control every citizen in this city regardless of how close they are."

"But it is my law. My word should stand."

"In the midst of a religious war? There are many who think only God can give them orders. There are many who do not think you are above them."

Jacque listened hard as a sudden silence stretched.

"Was it you?" the king asked, quietly.

"Coligny?" she paused. "No, of course not. The Guises are angry about the wedding and are the most likely culprits. But they could lay blame on us, on the royal house. To exonerate themselves."

"They wouldn't."

"Or else risk your wrath as well as Coligny's? They would. And they could. They could say they don't have the power to issue such orders over the king's word. And that only the king could have ordered the shooting. The talks didn't go as planned, Charles. The Guises could say they were relieved. *They* were relieved but *you* were not.

"Their word would force a war," she added.

Silence stretched again as Jacque saw the old lady's tactics as though they were written down in front of him.

"They would come for us, the Huguenots. And their numbers, they are strong," the king said.

"Us? They would come for you, my son. They have already burst into this palace and demanded revenge in the last day alone. The Admiral's own brother in law has four thousand men outside this city."

"So what to do? Ideas?"

"Take them out."

"Coligny or the Guises?"

"The Huguenot leaders. All of them. You must not leave one who could rally for revenge. There is no other way."

The king barked a single, nervous laugh.

"No other way?" he cried, incredulously, but then paused. "You are right. And wrong."

"Wrong?"

"It is worse than that, mother. This is a religious war, as you said. And in the eyes of God, people do not need leaders. Leaders stand from the shadows, from the ashes. Men and women gather around those of courage. They do not follow the noble ancestry of Gaspard de Coligny, they follow his courage and the scars of his battles. No, this is bigger than the leaders. We must crush the masses. All of them. And finish this war for good. We must send our men into the streets to take out the leaders, then force word into the commoners to kill every protestant they know."

"You want to bring down the city?" she said with mock fear, though Jacque heard the excitement in her voice.

"No, just the heretic half of it. I cannot believe I am agreeing to this."

"It was your idea, Your Majesty. A wise and courageous idea."

Jacque's heart beat almost out of his chest. He knew he had to get to Edward and Francis immediately and work together to find a way to prevent such a massacre. He went to slip away as Catherine's voice sounded much closer only inches away on the other side of the door frame and he stopped still holding his breath.

"Send the orders," she said as she emerged from the doorway and stood with her back to him, looking back at the king.

Jacque almost laughed at the ridiculous position he found himself in under a foot away from the king's mother. The shadows were nowhere near dark enough to hide him and he knew that if she turned, he was dead. If it came to it, he would have no choice but to kill her, he knew. And suffer the punishment of a martyr assassin.

Catherine Medici stood still and watched her son for a long moment before nodding and walking away from Jacque into the darkness of the corridor.

"Follow her as always," the king said after a moment. "If she speaks to anyone at all, I need to know."

"Your Majesty," said a quiet, more elderly voice as the king's footsteps were heard to disappear into the distance followed by the closing of a heavy door.

Jacque waited a moment longer before finding himself face to face with an older man wearing the uniform of the king's service. Jacque said nothing, looking cannot back into his eyes. The man looked him up and down and then around once to make sure they were alone before speaking in a hushed whisper.

"Do you work in the palace?" the servant asked.

Jacque nodded.

"Do you agree with what you just heard?"

Jacque took a breath then shook his head. The man nodded gravely.

"Then warn as many as you can," he said before

walking away and disappearing in quiet pursuit of Catherine.

Jacque felt a huge amount of air escape from his body, then turned to hurry through the corridor, being sure to stay left.

Chapter Fourteen

<u>Thursday August 24th 1572</u>

Edward pulled at the neck of his loose shirt in an attempt to ignore the sweat that trickled at various points of his torso as he and Francis jogged through the Royal Quarter towards the small infirmary where Coligny was being treated. Dawn had broken only a handful of hours before and yet the sun had risen high enough to pierce every corner they ran through. He looked across at his employer, appearing considerably less athletic than he, and yet the older man seemed to plod gently without an ounce of discomfort while Edward's body had begun to complain some time ago.

Jacque had woken them in a hurry not long after dawn with news of the king's intentions and only the gravity of what they faced had prevented Edward from laughing when he heard how Jacque's unmatched escapades with the female form had led him to within inches of Catherine Medici in one of her most private moments. Francis had congratulated Jacque on his skill before making the order to dress immediately so that they could warn Coligny themselves.

Noise in the city had grown in the minutes since they'd left the white house and they slowed to listen to the frantic conversations that the residents of Paris had begun to shout between them.

"What are they saying?" Edward asked as Francis lost colour in his face. "Is it Coligny?"

"It is worse," Francis replied. "It has already begun. They are saying there has been a murder on the steps of the church at Saint-Germain L'Auxerrois."

"Where is that?"

"It is a church near to the Louvre," he replied, absently, while listening further. "The Swiss Guards, they kicked the visiting nobles from the Louvre and slaughtered them in the street."

"My God."

"*Someone's* God, at least." Francis replied, glancing at Edward and quickening his pace. "Every one of them was a protestant."

"Jacque was right. And the catholic commoners thought it would be the protestant commoners that would cause trouble. Will they follow suit, is the question."

"I think so, through fear."

"Or bloodlust."

The two men ran through the streets as the small crowds grew in number. It wasn't far before they turned the corner into the square in front of the two storey infirmary housing Coligny and skidded to a stop, their mouths open.

The noise was deafening as a crowd of men used tools to strike the building and pull down its decoration. The unmistakable sound of lethal fighting could be heard from inside the building as more of the mob lost their control and stormed inside.

"That's Coligny," Francis whispered as a loud voice

roared above the others only to be cut off and replaced with a moan. The ferocity then grew further as an upstairs window was smashed above the square and the men below stepped back with a cheer, only to fall silent as the form of Coligny was forced, screaming, from the small, empty frame to land in a dull, crumpled heap on the floor. The men around him stood still in shock for a moment before the Admiral lifted his head in dazed pain ever so slightly and inadvertently sent a signal to those around him to return in frenzy.

One man released an animal-like scream and pounced on the old man, swinging and hacking with a large knife. The others then followed suit until one raised Coligny's head above them all and they roared with crazed intensity.

Francis spun around as the door opened and an arrogant man of money stepped out into the square, looking upon what he had clearly led.

"That is Henry, the Duke of Guise," said Francis. "He will know me. I mustn't be seen."

Edward nodded silently, watching the men as they calmed ever so slightly. The man in charge looked between them then up at Edward with a squint. Edward saw him call out to his accomplices while indicating towards Francis and he, and then saw the man from the Latin Quarter look over and respond loudly.

"Who are they looking at?" Francis asked urgently.

"Me. What did they say?" Edward replied.

"One asked who you were and another said he is your man. The first disagreed and said he doesn't recognise you."

"You need to go, they are coming."

"What about you?"

"I'll distract them, you can't be seen. Go. Go!"

Francis nodded without reply then immediately set into a run in the opposite direction as Edward pulled out his pistol and pointed it at the crowd, his face stern. They slowed slightly but continued to advance and by the time Francis had a good lead, Edward had only a moment to make his escape. He launched into a sprint in the opposite direction to his leader and grinned when he saw the entire contingent follow him instead of the ambassador. Nevertheless, they were behind by only the length of several men and he knew it would take all of his stamina to keep ahead at full speed.

He sprinted back through the main streets, winding between the groups of people that blocked the route and whispering thanks in relief as the group of men behind him were slowed by the bottlenecks that were caused.

He continued running then turned south towards the river. His lungs burned beyond endurance as he neared the water and with both the bridges and banks beginning to fill with people, he allowed himself an unlikely idea as his options wore thin.

The water was deep and fast moving at high tide as he pushed his way through the crowds to the midpoint of the bridge between the north bank and the island in the Seine. Looking back once only to see the men come into view between the nearest crowds, he fired his pistol into the midst of them once, dropping a man and drawing a scream from the crowd, then jumped over the palisade to the water below, hitting it like an almighty slap to the back of his thigh and being pulled under in rush of mud and bubbles.

Edward held his breath and tried not to swallow the brown water that swarmed around him as he was pulled along the riverbed across rocks and debris. When the rush finally pushed him back to the top, he took a deep breath and looked around, wiping his eyes to see how far he had been swept. He knew not how many bridges had passed but the one behind him was not the one he had jumped from and he saw no one chasing him along the bank. Looking around as a small ripple slapped him in the face, he saw the bridge nearest to the Tuileries Palace and the white house approaching then pulled himself towards it, kicking his legs and feeling the energy drain from him with every stroke.

He clambered out of the water onto the narrow, stoney bank at the base of the wall that led to the river walkway. Grateful for the heat of the sun, he stowed the wet pistol in his waistband and pulled himself up the wall, ignoring the looks of the bystanders as he rolled onto the walkway and stood to jog as quickly as possible through a winding route back to the white house.

Francis looked up with relief as Edward slipped through the front door and closed it quickly behind him.

"No one saw me come here," he said, panting.

"Excellent," Francis replied. "I can see you took an unusual route."

"Yes. I had no choice but it paid off. That river is fast though. I do not recommend it."

"The Seine? Fast and dirty. Bathe and rinse your mouth with fresh water as soon as you can. I am glad you are safe. What you did for me back there, it was vital for the country but it was appreciated far more by me personally. Thank you."

Edward nodded.

Jacque hurtled down the stairs of the white house at the sound of Edward's voice.

"My friend, you are safe. Welcome back," he said as he embraced Edward's soaking clothes without a flinch. He stepped back and looked into Edward's eyes with the focus of hidden meaning. "What is your plan?" he asked.

Francis looked up at the same time but waited for Edward to speak first.

"I will stay to protect Francis and enable him to continue his business."

"You have already done that, young man," Francis added. "You should leave the city. You deserve to be safe now."

"Leave the city? Now? But we have to prevent this catastrophe."

"Alas, we cannot stop a mob and no one listens to us as Englishmen. It is only a select few now but the frenzy will grow and this city will be rioting within hours. I am safe in this house and no one in Paris knows where I stay."

"Then it should make no difference for me to stay either."

"But I will need to leave the house as the violence subsides to show England are not involved. It is my duty as ambassador. But you, you are now known. Not only to the Catholics bent on violence but to the soldiers who saw you stand over the body of Admiral Coligny. Your cover is over and if I am seen with you it will endanger our country. You must disappear and Jacque must disappear with you."

"Very well, but I must warn Amelie. If I cannot protect her then…"

"No," Francis interrupted. "It is impossible. You must leave the girl."

"Leave her? I cannot."

"You must and I won't hear more of it."

"I must not," Edward replied. "She could have blended into the background as a good, catholic girl in the Latin Quarter, but instead she stepped up, put herself at risk and saved both my life and our operation. She got us the information we needed. They have seen me since and they will go for her if they see her. She doesn't even know it is coming."

Francis looked at him for a long while.

"I need to get to her in the Latin Quarter," Edward continued. "After what happened to Maggie for saving my skin, it cannot happen again. It must not happen again. Our operations are not worth the lives of the innocent."

Francis nodded finally.

"Very well, but it is vital you live. I have an assignment for you."

"An assignment? Why didn't you say?"

"It was on my agenda for this conversation. You may visit your Amelie and advise her to leave the city, but you do it under the cover of darkness tonight and then you leave at that moment. Until then you bathe, you rest, you plan, you wait."

"Agreed."

"Then I need you to go to Rome from here. Both of you. Before this happened, I received news from a contact down there that there is a plan occurring involving the Vatican and England but it cannot be put in writing. No one can be trusted. The news cannot get across France due to the unrest and it is too sensitive to trust with messengers."

"Be honest with me, Francis," Edward said. "Is this because Cecil wants me out of England longer?"

"It is not, I give you my word. I am here, I have only you here to send, and quite frankly, you are the only man I know with the skills to get there and get home. The first coach house loyal to our cause is ten miles north-east of this city. Get there, mount up, get to Rome for me before word of this mess heads south, then get the message back to Cecil from there by water."

Edward looked up at the last sentence.

"You *are* going home," Francis said, smiling. "You are just taking a long route."

Edward nodded.

"Very well. Rome it is. Jacque?"

"Certo amico mio. Sono con te fino alla fine," Jacque replied, making Edward smile. "Let's do it."

Chapter Fifteen

Edward looked up and down the street from the door of the white house, then across the gardens of Tuileries Palace to make sure they could not be seen. The sound of savage mania had slowly risen outside the house throughout the day with screams emitted and cut off as people were killed on the spot. A house nearby had been raided only hours before and excited voices outside had announced to each other that the gates of the city had been closed to trap the protestants inside and keep the Huguenot army out. Francis informed Edward that Professor Giraud had told him of the Paris sewer system and its uses. Built two hundred years before, a three hundred metre sewer ran under the Rue Montmartre, north of the Louvre and Les Halles, the market not far from the white house. The straight sewer was well known to the public, unlike the smaller offshoots that were built in secret independently and ran with multiple entry points between the main sewer and the outside of the Fortress of Saint Antoine, a gatehouse known as the Bastille in the city wall two miles east of the Louvre.

Having already said their goodbyes, Edward looked back to let Jacque through and nod at Francis once in silence, before slipping from the doorway and closing it gently behind him. He met Jacque's eye as every step into the summer warmth brought the sound of more voices and violence in the distance. The darkness was heavy but offset by the glow of large, distant fires throughout the city. The two men, adorned in black clothes and darkened faces, padded forward silently towards the river and the bridge into the Latin Quarter. The gardens were quiet yet the violence always seemed only moments away.

As they approached the river, Edward watched a group of men on the bridge with clubs and knives, running towards them and laughing as they headed into the royal quarter with savage intent.

"How do they even know who they are killing?" he whispered. "It is not as though the two sides look any different."

"I guess, if you're a sensible catholic, you are either killing or you are on the other side of the river," Jacque replied.

"You're right. Only confidence can keep us safe now."

The men passed and the night fell quiet once more, the silence only interrupted by distant screams and the violent sound of destruction.

The bridge was deserted apart from a couple who lay against the balustrade, stabbed and bludgeoned to death and then left arm in arm as though they watched the scenery, presumably in some attempt at cruel humour.

Edward shook his head further and they darted across the bridge into the busier Latin Quarter, alive with the activity of its residents, running excitedly and armed down to the last child.

Edward raised his fist in joy at two men running past him, who howled and cheered in reply, and then nudged Jacque, bringing them both into their own run through the frantic affray.

"Are we too late?" asked Jacque, panting, as he spotted the two large men standing outside the open front door of Amelie's large, Parisian house.

"What did you do?" Edward roared, breaking into a sprint. "Where is she?"

The men looked up at the sound and turned to face him, one in a ready stance, the other with barely an eyebrow raised. Edward launched himself at full speed only to crash into the large frames that grew with every step and moved together to form an impenetrable barrier of muscle and beard.

Edward felt his heart and lungs batter the inside of his ribs as he hit the wall and halted with a jar of his neck. He bounced back to his feet and attempted to rebound only to be hit with a hoof-sized fist and knocked to the floor.

"Where is she?" he shouted again as he leapt to his feet and was joined by Jacque. "Amelie!" he called as he frantically raised his own fists and jumped back in between the men in a clumsy attack that was held back with ease.

"James!" he heard from behind them, making him pause. "James! Laisse moi passer!" The men relaxed and parted, allowing the tiny frame of Amelie to step between them. "James," she said as she hugged him. "You are here."

She looked to Jacque, smiling and mouthing the word 'hello', and then pulled them both into the house between the men, who stepped in and locked the door behind them.

"These are my father's men," she said. "I am safe with them."

Edward looked up at them watching him coolly and nodded his head.

"Pardon," he said, causing them to shrug silently and turn away.

"They're good," he said.

"They are, and we have many more. James, what are you going to do? How will I see you?"

"I am returning to England and won't be able to return to France. Where are you going?"

"We are heading to our estate in La Rochelle," she said, handing him a piece of leather with an address inscribed. "I will be okay."

"How will you escape? I will wait here until you are safe."

"You would remain in this storm for me?"

"Amelie, I would stand in the rain for hours for one moment with you."

They shared a grin and she pushed him lightly.

"James, you need to go. We will make it. Come to me at La Rochelle if you can."

"I will, I will get to you. And if you get trouble, I can help you in England." He took a breath. "James is not my real name."

"I know," she said, shrugging and smiling. "I guessed as much."

"My name is Edward. Edward Rothwell. I work for the Privy Council of England. If you get to London and request me at the gate of the Tower, they will find me and I will get to you."

Amelie nodded.

"I love you, Amelie," he said.

"I love you too."

Amelie smiled as Jacque focused on a corner of the ceiling with unbroken interest. They watched each other for a moment, then she pulled Edward in and kissed him hard on the lips.

"The gates this end are barred," she said. "How are you getting out?"

"We know of a way out through the drains. As long as we can get to an entry point, we can make it."

She nodded again.

"Then go, and get word to my estate to let me know you're safe."

"I will."

They kissed again as Jacque patted one of the guards on the shoulder and they opened the door. They said their goodbyes and ducked out into the roaring night once more.

"Ready?" Edward asked, knowing Jacque understood their plan.

Jacque nodded and they broke into a run, showing their excitement and joining a rabble as they ran towards the river, their weapons held aloft and their laughter growing with every excited step.

Edward's stomach lurched at the sight of bodies floating by in the Seine like logs and as they hit the northeast bank, they peeled off without being noticed, pushing quickly through the dark gardens that remained quieter despite the growing violence around them. Pockets of violence broke out nearby as they ran between sporadic trees and they ducked behind a thick hedge as a lone man sprinted for his life only feet away and was chased down by a group of armed teenagers like rabid dogs on a scent. Another group of teenagers stood laughing while one of their number continually kicked a woman in the head long after her life was extinguished and the dark gardens were littered with random, disfigured bodies as they ran; some alone, some cowering as a couple or family. There was no sense in dying to stop such acts that could not be prevented elsewhere, Edward reasoned, and they jogged as a pair, hidden by the shadows, until they reached the streets on the north eastern side of the gardens.

The heavy, acrid scent of smoke stung their eyes and lungs as they crept into the narrow streets that lay in tatters, the silence broken by the crackling of wood ablaze and the screams of protestant victims. Edward looked up and down as they came to a stop.

"The streets really are chained up," Jacque said, peering around a corner into a main thoroughfare. "There is a blockade at each end of this street. We can get past on foot if they are not manned but the people have no chance of escape. Not without leaving their lives behind."

"Francis said we must head east from here towards the Bastille. The drain entry should be only a number of junctions away."

"Can we be sure we are on the correct street?"

"I am sure. You will see the fortress. There are forty towers on the eastern stretch of the city walls. The gatehouse in the centre will be dead ahead of here."

Jacque nodded, checking their path and nodding to confirm it was clear.

The two men crept out and padded along, staying out of sight as much as possible. Edward felt his heart leap as the first blockade appeared abandoned and then jumped from his skin as he began to climb over and was faced with three young men in their early twenties, their faces marked with soot and streaks of dried blood.

They shouted at Edward and Jacque to which Jacque spoke back quickly and loudly. Edward heard the word 'catholique' as Jacque held up his hands and caught the gist of his cover story.

They looked to Edward and spoke again, spitting words at him that he could not understand. Jacque went to speak but was silenced by the first man who held up his hand. He fixed Edward a stare once more and spoke quietly, weighing a long, heavy kitchen blade in his hand as he scrambled slowly over the blockade, followed by his accomplices.

Edward glanced around himself to see they were alone then watched them climb in assessment, smiling inside at their lack of balance and allowing himself to return from the sharp minded spy he had become to the fast acting violent delinquent that had once fought in the pits of Southwark. The lead man held his blade clumsily while the two behind him shone with incompetence, one overweight and bare-faced, the other clearly malnourished despite his bravado and bloodthirsty grin. Edward smiled at them and cocked his head, making the lead man pause for a moment.

"You leave me no choice," he said, unashamedly in English, bringing first confusion then realisation and rage to the lead man's face.

The man opened his mouth to roar as Edward pulled his own blade and slammed it into the gaping hole, smashing through the roof of his mouth and severing his spine in a moment. He ripped it free again as the body dropped and kicked the skinny man's knee, sweeping him from his feet then stabbing him in the throat as he hit the ground.

The fat man scrambled for the blockade as Jacque leapt onto him and pulled back his head by his hair, slicing his throat before he could cry out and leaving him to crumple onto the upturned carts in a heap of eviscerated bodyfat and bubbling blood.

"They may be many but these townsfolk are made even worse by their frenzy," Edward whispered. "We will make this if we can avoid being vastly outnumbered."

Jacque nodded and gripped his shoulder as they crept over the blockade then continued along the street. Voices sounded behind them as Edward glanced over his shoulder and saw a group running towards them beyond the blockade.

"Maybe they didn't see us," he said, as he ducked low and looked back through a gap in the pile of rubble, now yards away.

"No, they saw us," Jacque said, listening to the words. "They're coming for us."

"We need to get off this street," Edward shouted as they broke into a sprint once more and darted into a dark, side alley. "We can lose them in these corners," he panted.

Edward did his best to gauge their direction and spun

the route back towards the main street and the drain, turning corner after corner, through the mix of the homeless, infirm and deceased underfoot.

They emerged back at the main route to the drain with only silence behind them. Edward poked his head around the corner to see if the group still roamed on the street. There were men in various packs marauding in the distance but the stretch to where the drain would be was clear besides two men sitting by the next barricade. Edward looked to Jacque who had spotted the same pair and nodded in silence.

With large and dangerous groups only a shout away, only stealth would see them safely to their exit point. They crept quietly side by side into the centre of the street so that they were sheltered from the two men by the highest point of the barricade, then with a hand-gestured count of three, slipped up at speed, reached around the stack of wood and cut the throats of the two men.

They slipped over the barrier in silence, checking the road once more then darted across the building line in a crouched scramble.

Edward turned and nudged Jacque as he spotted the entry point to the drain in the side of a building as described. Bars covered the man-sized hole though they had been assured that they could be removed. Jacque nodded once again in reply and they began to make their final sprint as noise erupted behind them. Edward stopped and crouched in order to confirm they could still enter the drain unseen. He could see a large group of men had passed the barricade and were forcing entry to houses one by one along the other side of the street and setting them ablaze.

"They haven't seen us," Jacque said. "If we move in the shadows we can get across."

Edward watched in horror as one old man opened his door from the inside and held up his hands in protest only to be knocked to the floor as a bottle was smashed on his head and then stabbed in the face by its broken remains. He looked up and down the houses, wondering how many innocent people would be slaughtered so needlessly, then saw the eyes watching him from a second floor window opposite him.

His initial reaction was to slip back into the shadows to avoid being seen but his eyes took in the tears on the young woman's face and the baby in her arms.

"Don't do it, Edward. We can't help these people," said Jacque, watching Edward look at the girl then back down the street at the men in an obvious assessment of their available time.

"We can't leave her. They'll kill her."

"They'll kill them all."

"But the others haven't looked at me in plea and terror, Jacque. How can we turn away?"

Jacque sighed, looking down the street.

"We have moments only. If you want to go, it must be now."

Edward grunted and moved forward as more men burst out of a house further down from the inside.

"They must have backdoors," Jacque called, stopping him.

Edward glanced to his right as the group spilled onto

the street then back up at the window as the woman's face turned to terror and a pair of hands wrapped around her from the shadows. They pulled her head back, then forced her body through the window, child clutched to her chest, to fall screaming until she landed in a heap on the stone floor below.

Edward looked on helplessly as she lifted her crumpled face lazily from the floor then looked down at her baby, broken beneath her, with a cry of despair.

"Come on, Edward," Jacque said again as the group looked towards the injured woman and a man walked out of the front door of her house behind her. "She is lost."

Edward watched, devastated, as the cruel man walked up behind her, pulling his knife from the back of his waist belt.

"You can't get there in time," Jacque said. "And the others are too close. Edward, we can make the drain but not for long."

"How can they be so cruel?" Edward whispered, watching a moment longer. "Okay," he said, finally. "Let's go."

Jacque squeezed his shoulder and crept further up the side of the road in the darkness then darted into the street towards the drain as Edward caught up behind him and tried to ignore the renewed shouts of the men only a stone's throw away. The young Frenchman crept wide and unseen through the shadows then wriggled into the darkness around the drain opening. He was almost invisible to Edward but the space was too small for the both of them as Jacque worked to release the bars that blocked their escape.

Instead, Edward looked back to make sure they hadn't been seen. He felt his stomach drop at the sight of the man behind the injured woman kneeling with his trousers dropped, tearing the nightdress from her unmoving body while his friends roared in laughter. He caught Jacque's eye as his friend observed the same and felt the burn of his gaze as he shook his head slowly in the dark.

He was right, Edward knew. Nothing could be done. She appeared to be dead and similar acts would be occurring far across the city. He ground his teeth and turned back to his friend.

Jacque nodded with satisfaction and turned back to the bars. He wiggled the three of them free without issue then set them gently on the ground by the opening.

Edward watched as Jacque slipped feet first into the hole and was almost entirely lost in the darkness. He took a breath and glanced up once more, seeing the men cheering around their companion as he worked in embarrassment to harden himself behind the still body of the woman beneath him. He tried and failed to shake off his rage and set into a crouched run through the shadows across the street, keeping his eyes ahead.

He skidded down into the shadow next to the drain and felt Jacque's hand in the darkness.

"There is a drop on this side," Jacque whispered. "Feet first."

Edward spun onto his stomach and worked his way into the hole. He squinted in anger once more at the crowd on the street as the group cheered and the kneeling man sat up to waggle his reluctant erection. Edward paused and grit his teeth with his eyes shut.

"Ed, we need to go," Jacque said. "She's dead, let it go."

"How do you know?" Edward replied, looking again.

"I saw and so did you."

"She moved," Edward said suddenly, looking more closely as the man lowered his weight onto her, cock in hand. "Her arm, it moved."

"She's dead," Jacque said again with urgency as Edward watched the man guide and thrust himself into her violently, making her lift her head and scream in pain and terror.

"Bastard," Edward growled. "Bastard!"

Jacque saw the back end of his friend shift his position in the darkness and pause a moment before an explosion rang out beside him with a flash of light and silence hung over the empty street. He heard the groan of a dying man followed by an eruption of voices as Edward slipped down into the hole pulling the three iron bars with him.

"They heard me but didn't see where I was," he whispered as he put his back to the wall and tossed one of the two-foot long iron bars to Jacque. "They were all looking away."

"One is saying he saw a flash," said Jacque, listening to the men, "But he can't say where from. That wasn't clever, Edward."

"I got the bastard in the face though," Edward replied, not seeing Jacque's grin in the darkness. He moved his feet on the soft mud beneath him as Jacque's made a louder, splashing sound. "Are you in water?" he whispered.

"Yes, it is deeper in this direction," Jacque replied, flattening to the wall as the voices grew loud directly outside the hole. "They haven't seen the drain," he whispered. "They are passing."

The two men waited, their hearts thumping as the voices spread to different areas outside their hiding place then drifted further away. After a slow count of twenty, Edward made to move as a shuffle sounded outside the hole.

"Qu'est-ce que c'est?" said a male voice, quietly. "Paul? Paul! Merde, où est-il allé?"

Edward stowed his spent pistol and pulled his dagger from his waist, holding an iron bar in the other hand. He waited as the shuffle came closer and a head popped into sight through the hole.

The man's unadjusted eyes were no match for the two men standing in darkness and Edward struck him hard on the head with the pole, causing him to drop close enough to drive his dagger into his throat and hold him steady until his weak struggle came to a stop.

Edward and Jacque tried to pull the body into the hole but as a large man laying flat on a surface too high for a strong pulling position, they had no choice but to leave him in place.

"Come on, before they return and see him," Edward said, pulling Jacque with him. The two men trudged through the shallow water made deeper by the soft mud beneath it and did their best to avoid making too much noise each time they passed the dim light of an entry point.

Urgent voices sounded on occasion as the hunt continued but it wasn't until they'd turned a long, sweeping corner that more decisive words rang through to them from behind.

"They found their friend and the hole," Jacque said, hearing their shouts echo behind them. "We need to move."

They broke into a run through the mud. As they reached another sweeping corner, the sound of voices hit them from ahead as well as behind.

"What do we do?" asked Jacque, as Edward stopped and loaded his snaphaunce pistol once more in the darkness.

"If we go for those behind us, we will have to fight through both groups. If we go forward, we may be able to fight through and get out of this tunnel before those behind us catch up." Edward met Jacque's eye in the darkness and nodded as the voices moved closer. "There are no splashes ahead," he said. "The ground must rise. Let's go."

They pulled their blades and ran around the remainder of the corner, their splashes and footsteps giving them away as they met the dark outline of three men blindly readying themselves to fight.

Edward felt the ground rise and the sound of their footsteps disappear as they closed the final gap in silence. He drove his short blade into the chest of the first object, taking it by surprise, then felt the breeze of a club that narrowly missed his head as it was swung wildly in panic. He pulled his blade free then ducked down and lunged forward towards the spinning mass, stabbing it multiple times in the trunk and feeling it drop as warm liquid washed over his hand.

He heard another thump as Jacque's opponent felt to the ground and he nodded at the shape of his friend in relief.

"Come on, we can get out," he said, as he began to

run once more, though he jogged on the dry ground for a few moments before feeling the absence of footsteps behind him. "Jacque?" he said, turning.

"Edward," he heard in a faint whisper.

He jogged back to the shape of Jacque now kneeling on the ground and felt emotion rise within him.

"What are you doing?" he asked as the sound of at least eight splashing feet grew closer in the distance. "Jacque, are you hurt?"

"He caught me in the gut with a blade," Jacque replied weakly. "I thought he just hit me so I cut his throat but then I started to bleed."

"No, no. Come on, I will carry you. When we are in the light I can fix you."

"I can't, Edward," Jacque replied. "I have lost feeling in my leg. I cannot walk. I won't make it to the coach house and I certainly won't make it to Rome. Go on without me. You need to get there. For our Queen."

"Don't be ridiculous, I won't leave you."

"You must. Give me the pistol, I will surprise them and you will get away."

"No."

"Yes, my friend."

A shout sounded from around the long corner and Jacque took hold of Edward's shoulder.

"We don't have much time. I am here in Paris for you, to support you and Francis in your mission. I have been wounded for our mission. If we both die now it is all for nothing. One of us has to get out and it cannot be me. If we hobble along, we could both die. Let me slow them."

Edward shook his head in thought, unsure of what to say.

"Edward!" Jacque growled. "Now."

Edward nodded and hugged his friend. He passed him his pistol and explained in a whisper how to cock and fire it.

"Goodbye, my friend," said Jacque with determination. And at that, he turned and limped his way back towards the threat that closed in on them noisily.

Edward watched him for a moment then turned and ran against his instincts. He listened as he jogged silently and heard nothing but splashes until an eruption of voices sounded at once. He had no idea what was said in the frenzy but no gunshot was heard. He closed his eyes in pain and stopped, knowing the pistol must have jammed and his friend would be torn apart. The voices fell silent and he waited, indecisively, pulling his blade ready to run back. Then calm, male voices began to speak and Jacque could not be heard.

Edward sighed as the splashes began to move in the opposite direction and turned on his heels to keep moving. Light could be seen ahead as the tunnel met the outside of the Parisian walls. He would escape, then get to Rome and then London as quickly as he could. He felt his throat lurch at the thought of Jacque, Amelie and everything he had seen, and he swore to himself. He would never let such a massacre happen in his homeland. Never.

PART TWO

Chapter Sixteen

<u>Spring 1573</u>

Edward grinned as he climbed the ropes of the ship he had called home for weeks and watched the familiar pandemonium of London's quays ahead as men and boys sweated under the midday sun with the cargo of a hundred countries from Asia to the New World. He glanced up at the White Tower looming behind the familiar guarded walls and smiled at the castle he had come to love. He was glad to be home and was more than glad for a spring that warmed his bones.

Rome had been tricky. After leaving Jacque and passing the walls of Paris in the unguarded sewer, Edward had stolen a horse and ridden South East with all the speed he could muster. But with exhausted beasts and the late summer heat above him, he could not outrun the word of the massacre and some cities had already erupted in copycat violence before he could reach them. Sticking to small towns without horses to exchange and with no knowledge of Francis' safehouses on the way, Edward had managed to slide unnoticed into a tense but safe Saint-Etienne, and again into Nice before finally crossing the border into Italy.

He'd learned to play Catholic well in his time in Paris and managed to remain inconspicuous as he trod the endless sun-baked miles to the capital city.

The man he'd gone to meet turned out to be one William Parry, an Englishman with a history and suspicion that Edward could neither decipher nor manipulate. With the required information gathered and autumn closing down for winter, the thought of rambling a thousand miles of icy mountain range and wildlands had turned Edward to the sea, and he had embarked at the Port of Civitavecchia, choosing to work the deck despite paying his fare. The camaraderie built through the days of work and nights of gambling had been profound and when Edward stepped onto dry land at Barcelona, he took with him the returned cost of his passage and the personal recommendation of a sailor in San Sebastian who would take him without cost right through to London.

Again, Edward had enjoyed his time at sea and mused at the true work of his friend John Hawkins, at sea in the New World, taking the Spaniards for all they were worth. There was an apparent nobility in piracy when it served a greater good, or at least the right purses. It made Edward chuckle and he glanced down as the gangway was placed against the ship and men beckoned for him to disembark.

Travelling himself, he moved as fast as a letter would have done if he had sent word of his return home and he hoped William Cecil would be present in London to provide his information to. He felt warmth inside him when he looked up at the Tower and spotted the flags that indicated his Queen was present. As he bid farewell to his shipmates and climbed down onto the wooden planks of the dockside, he headed straight to the side bridge and gate of the castle, coin in hand.

"*Your majesty, Edward Rothwell here to see you,*" said the hushed whisper behind the door as Edward waited outside the queen's chamber, deep in the Tower. A silence followed, accompanied by a shuffle of feet and then the door opened, revealing the mess of red hair and beaming smile of his petite queen.

"You're home, my wolf," said Elizabeth, surveying him and his sun-darkened skin. "Soldier, fetch William Cecil at once, please. He is in the castle somewhere." Her eyes never left Edward and she stepped back to let him through the door as the soldier nodded his head and darted away to find the Lord Burghley.

"Your majesty," Edward said, as he stepped inside and knelt.

"Edward."

He looked up, spotting her smile and grinned himself as he stood.

"It has been some time," he said. "You look well."

"As do you," she replied. A knock at the door and hurried voices told them Cecil had arrived already and Elizabeth rolled her eyes at the end of her devilish moment. "Come straight in, William," she bellowed, again keeping her eyes on Edward and smiling.

"Rothwell!" Cecil beamed as he entered. Edward nodded in return and allowed the older man to embrace him briefly. "Come, you must fill us in immediately," Cecil added, indicating to the upholstered stools by the window.

They sat and Edward told them of France. Of the build up of tension, the wedding, the assassination attempt of Coligny and then the eruption of chaos as they threw the man from a window and the city fell apart. They sat spellbound as they took in the first eye witness account of what they'd heard about.

"And with Jacque sacrificing himself for me to get out, I got under the walls and stole a mount to head south."

"It makes me shudder, Edward," said Elizabeth. "To think of the lives lost and the bloodlust of those in frenzy. We received word from Francis early on as the king awarded escort to each of the ambassadors in Paris, but we haven't heard much since. We assume communications are down across the north of the country."

"Please tell us of Rome," pressed Cecil.

"Indeed," Edward continued, nodding to acknowledge his queen before answering Cecil. "I took a safe route south, avoiding cities until I met the coast at Nice and crossed the border. From there it was straight forward but the intensity of belief is strong, as expected. I had no choice but to feign Catholicism and join in their rituals. Still, I made it in good time and before the weather turned."

"Who did you meet?"

"William Parry," Edward said, with a frown. "He was odd to say the least. I wasn't satisfied, shall we say?"

"Well your judgement is correct," said Cecil. "Though I do believe he reports true." Elizabeth's expression showed disagreement but it was lost on Cecil who spoke on. "His father was one of the guard of Her Majesty's father, Henry, but when he died he left a rabble of thirty or so children behind, of which William was one. He's been with us in one way or another for a few years after the master he served died, but he is in and out of debt and while his volatility makes him unreliable, his dependence on us does not."

"He is a liability, William, and I don't trust him," said Elizabeth.

"That is true. But he is somewhat expendable and he operates on the periphery; as a gatherer, I guess it could be said. He is rarely trusted."

Elizabeth pursed her lips, drawing a smile from Edward.

"His master, is that Earl Herbert?"

"Yes, William Herbert," said Elizabeth. "He was the guardian to my brother as a result of his marriage to my stepmother's sister, but his loyalty swung like the manhood of an overzealous colt. His son had married into the Grey family but he forced an annulment after my sister, Mary, returned and took the throne. Then he entrusted himself to both her and Philip, that foolish Spaniard, becoming one of their most persistent warriors. When Mary died, he turned to me, thanked God for the return of the true faith and pledged his sword and his coin to my rule."

"The queen is ever trusting, as you know, Edward," said Cecil.

"Naive according to some," she said, with some disdain, but allowed a smile to reach one side of her mouth. "Nevertheless, the privy council removed him from my court when they said he showed support for Mary Stuart's marriage to my cousin, though it wasn't my decision. People believe I suspected him but it wasn't the case at all."

"And then he died," said Edward.

Elizabeth nodded.

"Either way," Edward continued. "Parry was a little too open about who he worked for and seemed excited about the advances he had made in establishing himself in the circles of the Vatican. And he would not stop going on about Herbert."

"Talking fondly of him?" Elizabeth asked.

"No, talking about his death. It was like my being there gave him an outlet for his frustration. He offloaded his woes onto me and I had to endure him in order to find the answers I needed. Even so, it was a strange tale and I am never one to rule out conspiracy." Edward paused but was met with only silence, nudging him to continue. "He said his death was not natural. Working it out, apparently there were men investigating him throughout the time we were looking into De Spes and Ridolfi but with him suspected of supporting Thomas Howard's marriage to Mary Stuart, I would have thought it would be Shadows or Wolves watching him; we weren't. I knew every move we made in that investigation and I have never even heard of Herbert, not even as a peripheral sympathiser. And the way he was watched was odd. It wasn't a team and there was nothing overt. Parry kept speaking of a white haired man who would appear in all manner of circumstances and ask completely irrelevant and unrelated questions. Questions about who Herbert knew and what he did. Parry thinks Herbert knew something he shouldn't. It disturbed him so deeply that he shook with agitation as he spoke of it."

"And there is one particular conspiracy you think he knew about?"

"Maybe," said Edward, answering his queen. "I don't know. Maybe. I will bear it in mind as we have other things to discuss."

"We do. What did he tell you?" Cecil asked. "William Parry is in a few deep holes and is known to raise the alarm over very little in pursuit of reward."

"I could tell. Nothing grave, but concerning nonetheless. He said there is a conspiracy to smuggle priests into England. Many have already arrived and more are on their way. There are powers here that have facilitated passage and while it took one contact initially to receive them over here, there is now a network to aid the infiltration. I'll admit, the energy in Rome was high. News of catholic advances in the cities of France has triggered a new lease of life and they are driving their efforts towards us."

"Do you think they plan to enable secret access to worship?" asked Elizabeth.

"If not incite riots similar to Paris," Edward said, gravely. "I can work on it. I will re-establish my communication lines here and start to dig deeper."

"Yes," said Cecil, with a change of tone. "I'd like you to do so as part of the Shadows."

"The Shadows? You want me to go back to the streets and investigate with the teams? Do my activities as a wolf disappoint you?"

"On the contrary, we want to make good use of your skills."

"You mean you still feel I put the queen at risk."

Elizabeth looked down.

"Partly, yes," answered Cecil. "But in addition to that, Richard Wellesley has a new officer. Marcus and Rutherford are still providing the queen's protection and Wellesley has asked that you provide a service to him upon your return, teaching his new dog to hunt."

"I see."

"Please don't be disappointed, Edward," added Elizabeth. "It will be fun, I am sure, and you can flush out these priests for me with the resources of the Shadows at your beck and call. You're still a wolf, just a wolf on loan."

"They know not of this news yet, of course," said Cecil. "You can brief them when you get there, though it goes without saying the source isn't to be common knowledge."

Edward nodded and stood, reading his dismissal.

"Thank you, Your Majesty. It is good to see you," he said with a bow and a smile.

Elizabeth grinned.

"You too, my wolf," she replied.

Edward looked up, as he always did, as he passed under the lightning-damaged yet still enormous spire of St. Paul's cathedral. The building dominated the London skyline and the afternoon sun that had warmed his face throughout the mile walk from the Tower to the Newgate of London Wall illuminated the southern side of the massive structure in warm colours of orange and pink.

The crowds were as busy as ever inside the wall that

housed the Newgate Prison with its passage into the Old Bailey, and the yard that led to the office of William Cecil's Shadows was teeming with life.

"Something happening?" Edward asked the familiar stable-hand, Lewis, who had grown a foot taller and added the shoulders of a man since Edward had last seen him.

"Usual race to capture contraband and cargo," he replied. "Good to see you, Mister Rothwell."

"And you, Lewis. Wellesley here?"

"In his room. Go through."

Edward clapped the young man on the shoulder and stepped into the cool corridors of the Shadow Headquarters within the fortified wall.

"Rothwell!" called Wellesley with a smile as Edward walked into his office. "Welcome back."

"Good to see you, Sir," Edward beamed.

"Nice to meet you, Edward," said a bald man in the office, standing to shake Edward's hand and revealing a large, shining scar running from his temple to his jawline.

"And you..." said Edward, holding the man's gaze as in question.

"Scammell," the man added, breaking the silence. "Eoin Scammell."

"Ah, an Irishman," smiled Edward. "Does Owen have an illogical spelling, like other Irish names?"

"Ha, you know us well. E-O-I-N," said Eoin, smiling. "But it makes perfect logical sense to me."

"I guess it would! And I am glad it does. It could come in handy."

"Before you ask, my family are Catholic. But I, am

not."

"I wouldn't mind if you were," said Edward. "It doesn't make you a bad person. It's what you do with it that counts."

"Indeed it is," said Eoin with a smile that didn't reach his eyes.

Edward smiled back and finally let go of his new colleague's hand.

"So, Sir. I hear you have requested my presence and services?"

Wellesley smiled and sat down.

"I have indeed. Eoin here was a recommended addition to our clan and after stringent testing, some of which he was often not aware of, he now wears the cloak and bears the coin. Some of our more seasoned shadows have gone on to perform other duties and I need someone who can show him how things are really done. I asked William Cecil for your services, if you ever should return, and here you are, out of the blue, back on London's streets."

"Well I wasn't planning on being back on the streets, as you say, but I am here and I suppose I should keep busy.

"What have you done so far?"

"Nothing," replied Eoin. "I have just finished training."

"Right. Well, we have some new work to get stuck into. There are plots from Rome ongoing as we speak."

"The priests being smuggled in?" Wellesley asked.

"Exactly," said Edward with a frown. "I didn't know that would be common knowledge just yet."

"Ha, we have our sources too, Rothwell," Wellesley

beamed. "It was actually Eoin here who unearthed it. Training taught him to pay attention and he tells me he heard about it in the markets."

"Which markets?"

"In the Borough," said Eoin.

"You live in the Borough?"

"No, but I was walking that way."

Edward nodded, pensive.

"What did you hear?" he asked.

"That Rome are smuggling priests into England to rebuild the Catholic network. I heard it said in Irish," he added. "I didn't see who but I heard it in the crowd."

"Very well, we have a place to start then."

Chapter Seventeen

Edward took a breath as he sat at one of the desks in the office of The Shadows and readied his quill with ink. The parchment looked excessive for the handful of words he could frame in his mind and he rubbed his eyes as he considered how to start.

"Dearest Amelie..." he began.

He decided to let his heart do the talking and emptied his mind as he scribbled out his first letter to her and told her of his return to London.

He marked the letter with the address of The Tower for her reply and smiled as he rolled the scroll and sealed it with the non-descript print of the Shadows' office.

"Eoin, I will pass this to Lewis the stable hand to dispatch it and we can be on our way," he shouted across the room.

"No need, Edward. Allow me to take it as I am ready and heading out," Eoin said. "You have travelled far. I'll drop it out while you ready yourself and I will meet you out there."

"Thank you," Edward smiled. "Don't read it, mind. The secrets of ensnaring a beautiful woman are written down on those pages."

"Ha, I wouldn't think of it," Eoin chuckled. "Anyway, you know I don't need any help."

The man laughed to himself as he left the room and

Edward smiled at the feeling of home.

Edward and Eoin stood in the same doorway in Southwark that Edward had once found himself in as he hid from his angry landlord moments before he had gone to see Robert Baxter and begin a path that would change his life forever. He smiled at the memory of how he first collided with the Shadows on the job Baxter put him on, and the chase he then put them through as he raced through the secret stairwell of an upper class house in The Strand and led them through London's deserted streets until he had nowhere left to go and turned to face them. He regretted the death of one of his would-be colleagues at his very own hand but the chance encounter had since led him across Europe and made him one of the Queen's most trusted agents.

"So how did Wellesley come across you?" he asked.

"How do you mean?"

"I know he said you were recommended but there is always a story with Wellesley. I bumped into them by chance on a job and had to fight them until Wellesley decided to recruit me. Others I know were found and recruited under all sorts of circumstances. What about you?"

Eoin shrugged.

"You know, similar to that," he said.

"Who recommended you?"

"I don't know, but apparently I was tested beforehand without my knowledge and had what Wellesley was looking for."

"You must be connected to someone important

then. Where are you from?"

"Oh, just a village outside Dublin. My family were connected to things here in London."

"Did they ever tell you what you were tested with?"

"No, didn't say a word."

"And you weren't curious once you found out?"

Eoin shrugged again.

Edward frowned. A refusal to give information could be frustrating but understandable, yet the apparent lack of any information at all was odd and made his skin prickle.

"Listen, if we are going to work together, we must trust one another," he said.

"I know," Eoin replied, glancing over as though he hadn't noticed a thing. "We do trust each other."

Edward nodded and kept his thoughts to himself. He looked out and surveyed the crowd.

"You said they spoke Irish?" he added. "There are many Irish in Southwark and I can hear all sorts of languages."

"I am listening. I will know when I hear the voice."

Eoin watched the crowd until he heard a loud Irish voice among the sea of languages and smiled.

"John, tá cúig scillinge i gcomaoin agat orm," it said.

"That's it," he said to Edward, watching the crowd. "The same voice and someone just mentioned the priests."

"Where?" pressed Edward, craning his neck.

Eoin moved into the crowd and followed the sound until he drew up next to a short man and turned to face Edward.

"Him," he mouthed, indicating the short man.

Edward looked at the familiar, angular and malnourished frame as it turned and the toothless face atop it came into view. He turned his head to avoid being seen.

"Follow him and get him out of this busy street so that we can pull him," he said. "I know him. The little shit bribed me right there in that doorway the day I met Wellesley."

Eoin nodded and followed the grubby Irishman Edward knew as Simon and Edward tailed close behind. Simon had traditionally made it his business to be involved in the daily lives of everyone in the Borough, and more often than not with the intent to create opportunities to bribe and scrape together a few coins to spend in the stews. Edward watched as the moth eaten clothes and greasy hair wiggled through the heaving market, paying attention to the pockets of the unwilling here and there but never actually crossing the line. Eventually, after it looked as though he may engage with a group of equally lice-ridden young men, Simon slipped to the side of the market and took shelter at the mouth of an alleyway to spot his next prey.

"Now," Edward whispered, prompting Eoin to dart forward and grab Simon by the throat, cutting off his ability to shout and pulling him down the alleyway that he had occupied.

Only a handful of those not used to the violence of Southwark Market looked over at the commotion, until they were set back on their way by the stern glance of Edward from under his hood. He watched them turn back to the street sheepishly then turned again and revealed his face to Simon.

"Up to your usual tricks?" he demanded.

The look of relief washed over the smaller man as he recognised the tough but friendly nature of his old acquaintance.

"Thank fuck for that," he said in his usual, scrappy Irish accent, mixed over time with the tones of a dozen nations. "I thought you were someone else. I wouldn't be able to speak now if you were."

"Don't feel so confident yet, my old friend. This isn't a social visit."

"Ha, I'd not taken it for one, my *friend*. What came of you anyway? One minute the Borough's best fighting man, street born and on his way to fame. The next, you do a job for the local crime lord, the fat bloke dies and you're never seen again. Now here you are with a clean face and, what's this?" he asked, gripping Edward's cloak. "Fucking silk?"

"I've been busy," Edward shrugged. "Now listen up, we're looking for some information."

"You know better than to ask me for information without a coin in your hand."

"As I said, it isn't that kind of visit, so you're going to need to answer. We need to know about some priests coming in from Europe."

"Priests?" Simon laughed. "What in God's name do I know about priests? Other than where they find shiny arseholes to screw and young balls to cradle."

Edward drew his dagger.

"I'm not joking," Simon exclaimed. "I don't know why you'd ask me."

"Tell him, Eoin."

Eoin looked at Edward for a moment before the instruction sank in. He nodded. Then turned to Simon and spoke in Irish. Edward watched the exchange closely and saw the genuine confusion in the dirty man's eyes. They spoke back and forward for a moment before Simon squeezed his eyes shut and shook his head, turning back to Edward.

"Honest to God, Ed. I haven't got a clue what he's on about. I haven't spoken of any priests…"

Edward was listening and beginning to believe him when Eoin interrupted and quickly began speaking Irish again.

Simon looked back and forth between them as the conversation went on and his expression began to change. Edward was convinced he saw a flash of excitement and greed in Simon's eyes before it disappeared again and was replaced by a feigned look of sadness. Simon listened as Eoin spoke on then nodded gently and turned to Edward.

"Ok, I did say something," he said, looking down. "I didn't want to say, as it will come back and bite me in the arse."

Edward glanced at Eoin who only shrugged in reply.

"Tell me what you know," he said.

"I heard it from Baxter."

"You're bribing Baxter now too?" Edward laughed.

"No, but I do odd jobs."

"And?"

"And I don't know much. But priests are coming in from Europe and Baxter is getting decent sums to ensure certain doors stay open so they don't get held up."

It made sense to Edward. Robert Baxter would do

anything for coin and certainly had the capability that made him approachable by upper tier conspiracies.

"Where are they going?" he asked.

"That's all I know," Simon replied. "You'll need Baxter for more."

Eoin nodded subtly at the exchange, though Edward spotted the movement.

"Alright," he said. "You can go."

Simon looked between them again.

"And my payment?" he asked, to which Edward simply laughed and walked away.

"Let's see what Baxter says first," he called over his shoulder.

"He lives in a fighting arena?" asked Eoin.

"In a house attached to one, yes. It's mainly animals, bear baiting and similar, but they have men fight there too. It isn't far from where I lived."

"Did you ever watch?"

Edward glanced at Eoin as his mind flashed through the many occasions he both delivered and received bloody beatings in the sandy pit of Baxter's arena below the heaving crowds of Southwark's filth and London's more seedy men of wealth.

"Something like that," he replied. "Now watch for Baxter, he's slippery and he knows the Shadows well enough to try to take what he wants from a conversation."

Eoin nodded as they walked up the path towards the house and the ever-present doormen turned to face them.

"Well there's a blast from the past," said one of the heavies in his thick, woollen tunic as he turned to watch Edward approach. Another opened the door to stand next to him and grinned at the man who refused to go quietly.

"Gentlemen, I am here to see Robert," Edward said as he arrived at the door.

"Ooh, Robert now, is it?" one of them chuckled. "I see wherever you have been has gone to your head. You and that poncy cloth you wear. Does Mister Baxter know you're coming?"

"No," Edward replied, ignoring the tease. "But he won't say no."

The doorman looked over Edward in thought before his accomplice nudged him in the side.

"He's not in," he said, finally.

The accomplice rolled his eyes.

"Come in, Rothwell. He's out the back. You know the drill, no knives, nothing dangerous." He paused to look at Eoin, his eyes narrowing and his face twisted.

"This is Eoin," said Edward as he emptied his pockets and handed over his dagger.

"And the nature of your business?" asked the first doorman.

"To see Robert Baxter."

The second doorman put their daggers on a shelf and opened the door wide to let them in.

"To the back and to the right, near the dogs. He's interviewing a fighter," he said.

Edward nodded his thanks and stepped inside, feeling Eoin walk closely behind him, avoiding the gaze that followed them.

"Ignore them," whispered Edward over his shoulder. "They're big, but they're clumsy. You're here for the queen, be confident."

Eoin nodded.

"He did look at you oddly though," added Edward. "Do you know him?"

"No, never seen him."

"Is he likely to know you?"

"I'm not sure how he would."

Edward nodded again and turned into the covered yard at the rear of the building where he had both prepared for fights and been hooded and bound under the kidnap directed by the master of the house.

"There he is," shouted Edward at the tall, finely cloaked figure at the far side of the room. Dogs growled savagely somewhere behind closed gates and Robert Baxter turned to reveal the freshly trimmed beard and the face that lost its obvious handsomeness to the misplaced, arrogant sneer that replaced it.

"Well well well," said Baxter, smiling and squinting at once. "What do you think, Rothwell?" he asked, turning to present a short, bull-like man with close cut hair and a neck that seemed to reach up wide behind his ears. "He has the strength of several men."

"He certainly appears to. But can he move?"

"I can move, little-man," the fighter retorted in an accent that Edward thought was one of the North.

"He can indeed," said Baxter. "Though not quite as you did. Mitchell, Edward would tie you up in a handful of heartbeats," he added, addressing the question in his fighter's eyes.

Edward shrugged, leaving Mitchell to simply smile in reply.

"We are here for business," Edward began. "Can we speak privately?"

Baxter rolled his eyes and nodded.

"We will get you on the books for a fight next month, Mitchell. I know just the opponent and think you'll do well."

The fighter thanked him and walked away, pumping his fist, while Baxter led the Shadows into a small room.

"Ever get the urge to get back in the pit?" he asked.

"Not really," lied Edward, feeling exactly that urge. "I miss it occasionally though."

"You could've really been something."

"I did become something."

"You know what I mean," said Baxter, waving his arm. "A gladiator of the modern age. The beatings you took without falter and the way you could turn it around and bring down serious opponents. Even the best I had. I hadn't seen anything like it before."

"I did what I had…" Edward broke off as he looked around the room they had entered with its dirty, handcuffed chair in the centre . "I know this room."

Baxter laughed.

"Indeed," he said. "Though you had such a dizzy head I am surprised you do."

"Robert's men kidnapped me and pretended they had my girlfriend to get me to do a risky job for them," Edward said, bringing Eoin into the conversation."

"You *had* created the vacancy yourself, and killed another of my men on your way in here. Anything for that girl, eh? All the talent but easy to manipulate."

"Yes, well, we know she is gone now, don't we? So I have nothing to be manipulated with anymore."

Baxter laughed.

"We will see, young passionate Edward. That was also the night your life changed forever."

"It was. It was the night I encountered the Shadows," Edward added for Eoin.

"What a lucky coincidence for you."

"A coincidence, indeed. Though I often wonder if you knew Marcus was going there and saw it as a way to kill me as you'd failed yourself."

"Think what you like," Baxter shrugged. "But I could've slit your throat while you were bound in this room."

"That's not your style. You have too much pride to stoop so low. You'd be losing anyway and it would eat you alive."

"Don't confuse me as the one of us with pride. Anyway, what brings you here?"

"Business, Robert. We need to talk about priests."

"Priests?" smirked Baxter. "I wondered when you would catch up. You know me, Edward. Where there is a coin to be made."

"So what do you know?"

"I know that there are priests being smuggled into the country, some from exile and some from Rome, and they are here to continue to spread God's word and sway the tide back to the Vatican. Or some kind of holy babble rubbish."

"And your involvement is?"

"Nothing, really. I have trade coming in with ships. For a few coins, my logistical connections have poor vision and forget how to count."

"And risking trial for treason is acceptable to you?"

"I would've gotten away with it."

"Would have?" asked Eoin.

"If it had happened," said Baxter.

Edward frowned.

"What do you mean?" he asked. "There are no priests here?"

"I am afraid not. There have been blocks at every turn. Communications cut off, messengers disappearing, a handful of priests slaughtered. And not by the hand of the law. At first I assumed it was your people, but it doesn't seem so."

"It isn't us," said Edward. "What else do you know?"

"A surviving messenger said the men who intercepted him spoke with structure, deferring to others as though part of an organisation."

Edward felt the familiar prickle in the back of his neck. A feeling he had learnt to accept and act on coolly.

"What kind organisation?" Eoin said suddenly.

"Oh he speaks again. I thought you were asleep, boy."

"Answer the fucking question," Eoin shouted.

Baxter's face dropped in shock at the sudden outburst and he turned to face Edward who shrugged in amusement. The neat beard curled into its own sneer.

"What happened to your face?" he asked, grinning at

the angered Shadow. "Did you sleep with your wife's sister or did you fall over in a blacksmith's house?"

Edward watched as Eoin grew red with indignation and turned to him, his mouth open. He nodded gently and gave a reassuring look that told his new colleague to calm down.

"Ask him again, Eoin," Edward said. "He will answer this time."

Baxter shook his head.

"I don't know," he said with a sigh. "They talked about a man who led them, some kind of weapon was all the messenger could remember, and that they were part of the preservation."

"And not the hunt," Eoin whispered to himself in thought.

Edward's heart began to beat at both Baxter's words and Eoin's response as memories of the Black Axe's men in Madrid flashed in his mind.

"Was his name an Axe?" Eoin asked, making Edward's head twitch towards him and Baxter's eyebrows rise.

"An Axe? What kind of man is he, a Danish mercenary of the past?"

"The Black Axe," Eoin pressed again. "It is a name I know."

"I am sorry, I can't help you there. Some kind of weapon," Baxter replied. "Now that really is all I know, Rothwell. Do you need anything else?"

"Yes, who is your contact? For the priests?"

"Again a messenger. Once a week. He pays me, gives

me news and tells me what he needs from me. That's it."

"When?"

"Tomorrow night. Always a Friday. It gives me the weekend to send my orders. North of the city through the Cripplegate. In the village of Islington. There is an inn called Angel's Road. As it heads North, I guess. He will be there, alone, at dusk. Looks like a monk in woollen cloth but wears a moustache on his upper lip. Most unusual."

"That will do nicely. Thank you, Robert. Your attempts at treason will go unpunished but try not to repeat them. We now know and will put a stop to it."

Baxter shrugged and looked over his shoulder as two enormous and orangey-brown, muzzled dogs with heads as round, wrinkly and bulbous as Edward had ever seen led their handler out into the room, their chains struggling to hold the force.

"Ah, my new French boys. The people will love you. Are they ready?"

The handler nodded and Baxter turned back to Edward, his arms stretched out wide and the canine muscle straining noisily either side of him.

"Whatever you say, Rothwell," he said.

Chapter Eighteen

Edward and Eoin slowly walked the mile or so from the Newgate Office to London Wall's Cripplegate and out into the village of Islington. Edward couldn't shake Eoin's reaction to the possible mention of the Black Axe and he watched him closely, considering the best way to bring it up.

The small town outside the walls was bustling as the sun went down and the market sellers on their stalls promoted their end of day bargains with over-zealous shouts and laughter. Dusk was falling later each day in the unexpected mid-spring warmth and Edward tried to focus on the task at hand while his heart pulled him in the direction of Amelie, romantic walks in the Parisian sun, and of the Black Axe.

"Angel's Road," Eoin said suddenly, shaking Edward from his reverie and nodding at a weather-beaten sign swinging over a small, non-descript doorway under a couple of floors of cramped housing.

"And I would call this dusk," Edward replied. "We will look first, get a drink, sit down and observe. When he leaves, we follow and take him. Be subtle," Edward added as Eoin nodded. "Don't stare. Let's go."

They crossed the busy street and ducked through the low doorway. Edward coughed gently at the acrid air from the badly ventilated kitchen flue and side-stepped through the crowd of tradesmen and merchants, supping their ales and shaking off a hard day's work serving the travellers heading to and from the North of the country.

"What will it be?" he asked Eoin as he approached the wooden bar and one of the young men pulling wine and ale from casks behind it.

"Just an ale for me, please."

"Two ales please," Edward shouted over the din, dropping a coin into the young hand. "Any sight of him?" he asked Eoin quietly.

"He's here. Sitting at an upturned barrel near the door. We must've walked right past him."

"Sure it's him?"

"Ragged tunic, shaven head and moustache. Looks like it. He's finishing his drink. Looks like a goblet of mead."

"He'll likely be over for another in a moment then. Be subtle."

"Yes he's standing, but he's pulling on a robe. Looking like he's getting ready to leave."

"Why would he leave? Baxter isn't here yet. He doesn't know us and it's barely dusk."

"Would Baxter tip him off?"

"I doubt it, it wouldn't be worth the trouble. And if he did, why would monk-moustache turn up?"

"He's leaving."

"Now?" said Edward. "Fuck. Start heading out, I'll be behind you. As soon as he clears the door get out quick and we will tail him until he's off the street."

Leaving his ale, Eoin moved through the crowd instantly, keeping an eye on Baxter's contact without showing his movements. Edward stayed close behind him and nudged him in the back each time he moved too slowly.

As the messenger slipped out of the door, bearing left, Edward whispered for Eoin to hurry but the new shadow was already pushing his way through the crowd like a bull, earning angry shouts in reply that bounced back on Edward tailing behind.

Eoin reached the door as Edward was shoved hard in the shoulder by a burly, bearded tradesman with the dark skin of the Mediterranean.

"Where are you running to, little man?" the man shouted as Edward fell onto the table of another four men and was pushed roughly back to his feet with a shout.

He looked around, cursing as he saw Eoin dive through the door, and turned back to face the hot, ale-laced breath of his new bearded adversary.

"I'm sorry," he said as the man grabbed him by the collar. "It wasn't me, it was the bloke in front."

"He's your mate. You can take the beating," said the deep, rich accent.

"He's no mate of mine. He just stole my purse. I was chasing him out."

"We'll see about that," the big man said, feeling him to see if he still carried a pouch himself. His fingers closed around the handle of Edward's dagger through his tunic and their eyes met.

"Don't do it," Edward whispered.

The big man grinned and Edward rolled his eyes as he lost more time and Eoin roamed alone behind their target.

"Fine," he said, slamming his knee into the big man's

crotch then cupping the back of his head with his left hand. He dropped the same elbow down across his chest to control him and drove his right thumb into the left eye that had squeezed shut against the pain. Edward hooked outwardly to pull on the bone of his eye socket and the man screamed, dropping to his knees as noise erupted all around them and a heavy tankard full of ale crashed down on his head. Edward turned quickly, feeling movement, and threw his elbow into the face immediately behind him before arms grabbed his neck and pulled him backwards.

The noise was shocking as almost every man present began to fight and yells of rage joined those of laughter as the rabble did what they did best. The inn erupted into mayhem and as Edward twisted off the arms around him and drove his forehead twice into the face of the man holding him, he found himself standing alone among the pandemonium and was able to slide out towards the door. He emerged drenched in ale and used a water barrel to rinse the blood from his hand and face before breaking into a run with a curse in the direction Eoin and the monk had headed.

"Where are you? Where are you?" he said to himself as he ran along the road outside the inn and ducked into an alley with no sight of them ahead. He turned two corners until he heard shouting nearby and ran towards the noise.

"Tell me about him. Tell me where I can find the Axe!" he heard Eoin shout in his Irish accent. The sound came from just around a corner ahead and Edward pulled his dagger as he skidded around it and burst into a courtyard with his arm raised.

Eoin was nowhere to be seen but several men *were*

present, and they surrounded Edward, grinning and holding blunt weapons. Edward could hear Eoin scream in the distance as they closed on him and he lashed out, feigning ahead and then whipping his blade wide at the man to his right. The tip caught the man's throat with a spray of blood as Edward's arm collided with the club and knocked both his dagger and the heavy bat to the floor. He felt the throb begin in his forearm immediately as he picked up the club from the man who writhed on the floor with his fingers in his neck and spun outside the attack of another, swinging back himself to bring the weight of the tool down on the back of an exposed head. Another, smaller, mallet-like weapon landed on his shoulder from a third man, knocking him to his knee and deadening his other arm, and he jumped up numbly and weaponless inside the arc of the second mallet and sunk his teeth into the face of its wielder, pulling his arm tight around the man's head and tearing the flesh of his cheek bone free in his mouth.

They crumpled to the floor and Edward turned only to see the fourth man drop his weapon and run away.

Edward turned back to the bleeding man beneath him and spat out the piece of flesh, roaring in his face.

"Where did you take him?"

"He must be silenced."

"What do you know of the Axe? Give me answers," Edward growled.

"You told him about the Axe," the man whispered. "Everyone you have told must die."

"He knows nothing, I've told no one. Where is he?" Edward roared again.

The man simply laughed and then grimaced in pain.

"They will all suffer, even your girl."

"My girl has already died at the hand of that bastard."

The man shook his head.

"Your new one. Your French girl."

Edward grit his teeth and let out a shout of rage.

"Who the fuck are you people and what do you want from me?" he said, readying his fist as he heard Eoin scream in the distance.

He looked to the sound and back to the man beneath him, his face bloody and torn. He could taste the blood in his mouth as the cry of agony carried on. He knew he couldn't leave a new, inexperienced shadow in danger for the sake of his own endeavours and cursed in frustration.

"Fuck!" he shouted again as he slammed the man's head into the floor and got up to follow the sound.

His arms were returning to normal as he turned every corner, each one bringing nothing but empty alleyways and dead ends. He searched on and on before winding his way back to the courtyard to find it empty. He roared in rage at his lost friend and failure as a mentor.

He could do nothing but get help and he set into a run back to the London wall and on to the Newgate office of the Shadows.

Edward jogged back in the darkness to the Cripplegate and passed through into the city without issue. He sped up as he hit the streets south of the Barbican and crossed past the top side of St Paul's Cathedral to Newgate

Prison and into the quiet yard beneath the wall.

"Rothwell," greeted the guard as Edward ran in and bounded down the corridors towards the office and bedroom of Richard Wellesley.

"Sir, it's Eoin," he said as he threw open the door and found both Wellesley and Eoin sitting calmly together in the office. "What are you doing here?" he asked.

"I came straight here when I couldn't find you," Eoin replied. "I followed the contact but he led me through a narrow path and surprised me at the end."

"A funnel and trap," said Edward. "He knew what he was doing after all."

"He asked me what I wanted and I did my best without you there. I didn't want to reveal who we were so I said I was had been sent by Baxter to get updates."

Wellesley nodded at Eoin's tactics.

"And?" asked Edward.

"And, he said he came to say there were none. That the current operation is ceasing until they can shake off what is disrupting them."

"Anything else?"

"No."

"You didn't say anything else?" Edward pressed.

"Nothing. He said he would get word to Baxter and he left. I looked for you everywhere and couldn't find you so came back."

"Bullshit," said Edward, suddenly.

"Bullshit?"

"Edward," said Wellesley. "You don't believe Baxter's contact?"

"I don't believe this Irish cock."

Eoin went to stand as Wellesley laid a hand on his arm.

"Edward, I don't know where this is coming from," said Wellesley. "But you left an inexperienced shadow to work alone and it sounds to me like he got answers without showing out."

"I left an inexperienced shadow? He pressed his way through a heaving inn, angering the drinkers and leaving me to fight them without looking back. He then caught someone and screamed at them about the Black Axe while I was ambushed by four men with clubs and had to leave two of them dead in order to get free. I then looked high and low to save his arse while he was sitting back here with you."

"What Black Axe?" asked Eoin.

"You know full well what Black Axe," said Edward. "You reacted at Baxter's and then again in Islington while I was attacked by men who told me you knew about him and had to die. What do you know?"

"Edward, this has to stop," said Wellesley. "This nearly got you killed or kicked out of the Shadows once before. Why do you still have this mysterious, passionate vendetta?"

"I don't," Edward lied. "But *he* does and I want to know."

"You don't have to answer that," said Wellesley.

"It is ok," said Eoin, quietly. "I did react at Baxter's. When I was a child, my father was a soldier, a good soldier, who undertook operations away from the battlefield. To bring down regimes, kill those who couldn't be reached, and destroy the plans of enemies before they could occur. Ireland has been a place of unrest for my entire lifetime. When I had seen maybe 8 or 9 summers, my father returned home in panic and whispered to my mother about a man called the Black Axe. I overheard them speaking and he said he had stumbled onto something he shouldn't have and men were looking for him. My mother took me to my uncle's house to keep me safe and my father was killed in our home that night. Weeks later, they found my mother too. She was hanged from a tree outside the village.

"So when I heard of a man named after a weapon, I reacted. I am sure you would if you were me."

"That is a devastating story, Eoin. Is yours anything like that?" Wellesley asked Edward.

"Nothing of the sort. I have no story. There is nothing I seek and I am sorry for your loss, Eoin."

Eoin nodded.

"But that doesn't solve what happened tonight and why I nearly lost my life while you screamed for answers and yet claim you said nothing."

Wellesley stood up.

"Eoin, you may leave. Go home for the night. You did well."

Eoin nodded and stood. He looked as though he may say something to Edward but then thought better of it, dropped his head in disappointment and walked out.

"You need to calm down," Wellesley said to Edward. "He's new."

"Something isn't right, Sir. He acts strangely, won't talk about who he is and he suddenly starts reacting to the mention of this Axe."

"Sounds familiar, don't you think?"

"It is different."

"Is it? Give it time, Edward. I'll keep an eye on him too. Just carry on and we will see how it turns out."

Edward nodded his agreement.

"Is there anything you want to tell me?" Wellesley asked. "Your face said a lot when he was speaking of his parents. I've often wondered of your past."

"There is nothing. His story is tragic and nothing like mine. The Black Axe is not related to my concerns. It was just an interest of mine once as I had heard the name. That is all."

Wellesley nodded.

"Very well. Get some rest, we will alert you when word comes in on the priests."

Chapter Nineteen

Once more, the seven men gathered and greeted each other in the secret meeting room used only for the purpose of one discussion. The oldest, a white-haired man known as Silver, looked around at those with him and when they had settled, he indicated to the one they knew as their leader, the Black Axe, to begin.

Black let out a cough and caught their attention, bringing their conversations to a halt.

"Gentlemen, we meet again and have some pressing issues to discuss. Let us begin without delay and start with the preservation. Green, tell us of the activities surrounding the Vatican."

"Quiet at present, Black," a dark skinned man with a rough, London accent replied. "As you know, they are taking their time with a peaceful infiltration of priests to work on the culture of the people and restore Catholicism from underneath. William Parry is sniffing around, we believe under the direction of the privy council, or at least one of the queen's closest advisors. Either way, he isn't much of a threat. Unless he revisits his questions around the death of his master, Herbert."

"He still shouldn't get far," said Silver.

"He speaks of a white-haired man who often spoke

to Herbert and asked questions."

"Yes, well, that too can be covered. The way it was spun, he backed Norfolk and Mary against the queen. As far as I am aware, she holds him responsible as one of the traitors. Please carry on."

"Otherwise," Green continued. "Phillip of Spain remains vocal but as far as Cartez in Madrid has informed us, he has planned no violence since he was duped by Hawkins' man Fitzwilliam ahead of the landing with Alva."

"Fitzwilliam, who we believe was Rothwell?"

"Likely, according to the description put up by Cartez."

"And did Cartez ever admit what he leaked to Rothwell in believing him a messenger of ours?" asked the bearded man known as Blue.

"He remains firm that he said nothing other than revealing that Black would be heading to Spain himself. And that the man we believe was Rothwell had mentioned Thomas Cobham."

"Cobham," said Silver. "The name that seems to materialise in every conversation I have."

"Indeed," said Black. "Still, we know where we are with him at present." Silver nodded. "And Red, tell us of France."

A ginger haired man with a tight beard, ironically known as Red, blew through his cheeks.

"The massacre was devastating. They think more than fifty thousand were butchered in Paris and as word spread to other cities, Catholic mobs copied them under the belief the King had told them to. Thousands more have been killed since."

"Never pleasant," said Black.

"And far from expected," said Red. "Who would've thought a wedding would have such an effect?"

"It was a perfect storm. The king's mother, Catherine, intentionally steered towards escalation but it was the careless shot at Coligny that started the bloodlust."

"I had cultivated protestant power in multiple cities across the country under your direction. Was pushing Henry of Navarre into a position of power worth this pain?"

He caught the eye of Silver watching him and looked down.

"He was an obvious choice after they were humiliated by the Aragonese," said Silver. "The Catalan and Basque regions of Spain have been head to head for as long as I can remember and a breakthrough for the Navarrese would have truly balanced the religious power in Europe. The king was too easy to manipulate as he forever fears a take over from his illegitimate half brother and after a quick nudge, the wedding was underway and all was moved according to plan."

"Until his mother got involved" said Black.

"Yes, Catherine," Silver mused. "She was in hand and had little influence once the union was in motion. But then the king confided in Coligny and the old man became suspicious. He had no idea what an ally he had been to our cause but the decision was out of our hands. When the first shot missed, I visited him to blame it on the Guises of France and see if he could be persuaded to join us but he had none of it. His integrity for duty was unwavering despite religious commitments and he saw straight through me. So I triggered the mob I had waiting to cover our tracks and it seems it was all Catherine needed to swing the pendulum the other way."

"You didn't tell me you were in Paris at the time of the massacre?" said Red.

"Did I need to? I left after Coligny was butchered."

Red shrugged and waited to ensure Silver had stopped.

"And despite all of the headway we have made in La Rochelle," he finally added. "She besieged the city behind her son's back and slotted Henri de Valois in place, taking back that major seat of power and restoring the port to catholic influence."

"And now the threat from Spain is alive once more," said Black, drawing nods and murmurs from the men around him. He too waited for further reply but read the silence and moved on. "Keep us informed, Red, and use all of your resources to restore La Rochelle and quell the pain in Paris."

Red nodded.

"So, the hunt," said Black, raising his voice further and turning to White. "Enlighten us, please."

"It is progressing," White replied. "He has not opened his mouth yet but it is only a matter of time."

"Are you sure he trusts you?" asked Silver.

"He risked his life and beat four men to save me?"

"This is Rothwell we are speaking of. He would save a bear from a baiting pit while dogs hung from his balls."

White nodded.

"He has had his suspicions and called me on them," he said. "I gave him a close to home cover story and in the weeks since then he has not mentioned it again.

"Ok, well make him mention it. We can't sit around while you run wild thinking you're an investigator," said Black. "Don't forget what you're doing. If the queen knows, then she has kept quiet but if the truth gets out now, we risk losing everything."

"Surely even though Rothwell knows we need him dead, he doesn't know why?" asked White. "How would the queen know?"

"We don't know what he knows," said Silver. "How could we? The queen trusts him a little too much despite his blunders and misdirection for him to have not told her something. She has a thing for the man but not enough to treat him as she does. No, she knows something and we need to know what. If she has to go, she has to go, but not without reason. Her very presence supports the preservation, which matters above all. We need to find out who knows and sink that bastard before his next birthday."

"It will be done," said White. "I will not delay.

"Good," said Black. "Then none of us should. Safe travels, all. Meeting adjourned."

Chapter Twenty

Summer 1573

Lost in thought, Edward tripped on a raised stone slab as he walked through the corridors of the Tower on his way to see Thomas Cobham. He shook his head and grinned back at the Tower soldier who attempted to hide his amusement, and walked on towards the large wooden door of the luxurious holding cell provided to Cobham.

A month had passed without another mention of the Black Axe from Eoin and despite spending day after day together in pursuit of various criminal adversaries, Edward's subtle conversation teasers hadn't coaxed his shaven headed colleague to open up. Something didn't sit right with Edward and he had growled in frustration from the floor in Albert's room as he tried to explain his concerns to his old friend and his lady. It had actually been Agnes, the landlady from the local inn by London Bridge and Albert's late-in-life lover, that had given Edward the idea of approaching Cobham. 'Someone must know him,' she had said. 'Whatever his story, someone will know him. You work for the queen, Edward. You must know someone who is privy to all of the darkest secrets.' Edward had grinned as she said it and jumped up, kissing her on the cheek. Only Thomas Cobham knew the undertone of each and every conspiracy in London.

Imprisoned in the Tower almost two years prior, following his involvement in the plot to marry Mary Stuart to the Duke of Norfolk, Edward hadn't visited the cunning conspirator since he had confronted him and discovered that he too sought the men of the darkest conspiracy of all, the Black Axe.

He waited while another young guard unlocked and pulled open the heavy door and then stepped inside as it was closed behind him. From where they were in the castle, Edward assumed the view of London would be spectacular if only the small window could be reached at the top of the high stone wall. Even so, the light it allowed in was bright and Thomas Cobham sat watching him with interest from the comfortable chair next to his desk.

"Edward Rothwell," he said, surprising Edward with his healthy appearance and apparent cheer.

"It has been a long time, Thomas," Edward replied.

"It has. I am still waiting for that pardon you promised."

Edward opened his mouth but his words dried up and he simply shrugged.

"I did suggest it," he finally said. "Cecil was open to it in support of your brother but I think our queen prefers life when she knows you're tucked away. I assume that's why she treats you so well here."

"Who knows, but forget it. I knew it would never be in your power to achieve. What brings you back?"

"Your uncanny ability to know everything and see everyone," Edward replied, sitting on the end of the bed and raising his eyebrows at the soft, comfortable surface.

Cobham spotted his appreciation and smiled.

"That's certainly the first time my overzealous interest in the political shadows has been described with compliment. I have often wondered at the progress of your endeavours and imagined you hadn't returned for more information as you were dead or tied up in Newgate Prison."

"I've been close."

"What do you need to know, young Rothwell?"

Edward took a breath and considered where to start.

"I have been working with a man and I don't trust him. He came from nowhere and has mentioned the Axe. One evening I was attacked by men who mentioned the Axe while I could hear him screaming in the background. I lost him and when I returned to the office in shame, there he was, sitting unharmed. I feel like I am being set up."

"You think he's working with the Axe?"

"No, of course not. I think I am being set up to change my course and be hung out to dry for choosing my own objectives over the queen's."

"His name?"

"Eoin Scammell."

"Owen Scammell? Never heard of him."

"Neither had I. Spelled E-O-I-N. He's Irish."

"Irish? He is unlikely to be with the Axe then."

"Why?" asked Edward.

"Because he is probably Catholic."

"And?"

"And a part of me believes they protect the queen as she is a Protestant queen. King Henry tried so hard to have a boy and those he did were stillborn. Suddenly the notion arises that he should divorce and so begins the departure from faith as we knew it. As far as I know, no one protected Queen Mary. Our one Catholic monarch since. She had phantom pregnancies and died young. How did you stop the plot to put Mary on the throne?"

"With difficulty."

"With unknown help, I would guess. Why are the smuggled priests not here now? Why has that fallen short? The entire continent is upside down in this holy war."

"It is indeed. A Catholic mob just mutilated thousands of Huguenot and Protestant civilians in Paris because of the royal wedding."

"They did? I hadn't heard. What wedding?"

"A Protestant Navarrese prince to the Catholic French princess."

"An unusual union. But unlikely to cause a mob."

Edward shrugged.

"My man in the castle believed the king had been persuaded to put on the wedding and the mob was triggered by the assassination of a man called Admiral de Coligny. I was there. I was chased."

"Coligny was killed? And the king was influenced to break his Catholic realm. But Coligny was a powerful Huguenot. While I wouldn't put it past the power of the Axe to set up the wedding, they wouldn't kill Coligny if my theories are correct. Unless he knew something he shouldn't."

"I don't know. Either way, none of it helps me with my current problem."

"Then set him up."

"Set him up?" Edward coughed.

"Yes, set him up. Admittedly, I've landed in prison for doing just that but it's the only way and you're certainly not averse to walking the murky line. If you want to flush out a loose tongue, you leak incorrect information. If you want to discover a bad egg in your team, you put them to the test."

"I couldn't. He's supposed to be on my side. It would be treachery."

Cobham raised his eyebrows.

"It depends how much you want to know," he said.

Edward thought for a moment.

"Wait," he frowned. "I assumed you had your ear to the ground when you mentioned the smuggled priests. But you don't know of Paris? How do you know of the priests?"

"I needed to flush out the Axe and prove my theory. And it worked. I put the wheels in motion and someone somewhere knew of it and stopped it, while your lot were still in the dark."

Edward's mouth dropped open.

"Parry thought it originated in Rome."

"*William* Parry? Overtly, it did. But I am afraid England's greatest fool misjudged where the notion began."

"So it seems. Parry is extremely paranoid at present. Obsessed with the murder of his master, Herbert."

"Yes. Herbert. Another mystery. He'd been married to King Edward's protector and had a son marry into the Grey family until Mary took the throne. Then somehow he became the trusted ear of Mary and Phillip. After Anne Parr though, he married the daughter of the Earl of Shrewsbury. Old George, his father in law, had been one of the greatest warriors of both the queen's father and her grandfather. And *he* was instrumental in King Henry's divorce from Catherine. Herbert was immersed in conspiracy, alright. But on which side I have no idea."

"You set up the smuggling of the priests to test a theory?"

"Don't judge me. Just test your own theory," Cobham said, confidently.

"I would need a blessing."

"How can you? Who knows who is involved in setting you up, if it is indeed to catch your immorality and misjudged priorities. This *Owen* came from nowhere, as you said. No, I would guess there is no one above you that you can trust."

"There is one," Edward said, standing up. "I have one."

Cobham smiled back.

"Then go and find out. And let me know how it goes," he grinned.

Edward took a deep breath as he approached Elizabeth's chamber directly from Cobham's cell in another part of the Tower. The guard announced his arrival as he always did then opened the door for Edward to enter at the command of his queen.

"Your Majesty," he said, kneeling briefly and then rising as he saw her bored expression.

"Edward the Wolf," she said as he rose. "What brings *you* here?"

"I came to seek your counsel, my queen."

"Did you now? And have you ever just visited without a reason? Just to see how I am? Have a good catch up? Tell me about your day?"

Edward blinked silently.

"Nothing to say?"

"I am sorry, Your Majesty. I just. I never assumed I was welcome as a casual visitor."

"Really?"

"Truthfully."

Elizabeth sighed.

"Of course you're welcome. In fact, I spend most of my time wondering if anyone will ever visit for leisure. It is a lonely life, the life of a royal. Especially a solitary royal with no kin. Surrounded by people day and night and yet not one of them will be themselves around me. 'Yes, Ma'am.' 'Certainly, Your Grace.' 'Why thank you, Your Majesty.' Never has any person simply said, 'Shut up, Bess, you're rambling on.' Or, 'Liz, pass the sweets.' No, instead I sit here day after day, year after year, even, without an honest conversation, a moment's romance or even an argument to regret."

Edward watched his queen open up to him and felt his heart burst at his own lack of judgement.

"Well you're certainly rambling on now," he said, feeling his heart race at his words.

She looked up at him in shock then quickly let a smile creep across her face.

"Am I indeed?" she said, playfully, standing up and walking towards him, her chin pushed forward defiantly.

"Oh yes, you're actually giving me a headache," he said in reply, sticking out his tongue and laughing at her expression as her mouth formed an 'O' in shock.

"Well maybe I should have that aching head chopped off then?" she said, poking him in the chest.

"Well it wouldn't be pleasant but I'm sure it would do me a favour in comparison to this racket."

She laughed and bit her lip as she pretended to punch his chest. Then she let her hands fall softly onto him and fell silent herself, looking down at her fingers.

"I couldn't chop off that beautiful head of yours, you frustrating man. What would I have left to marvel at?"

"I frustrate you?"

"Not intentionally," she replied, turning away with a sigh. "Your French lady wrote to you."

"My French lady?"

"Amelie, is it?"

"It is. I asked her to address any reply to the Tower."

"Which means it comes to me," Elizabeth added. "You never told me about her."

"It just happened so quickly. I met her in the strangest circumstances, we met and walked a few times, and I kissed her. She was...beautiful."

"I imagine she was, to have captured you."

"I didn't expect her to reply. I wasn't even sure that she was alive after Paris."

"Well apparently she is, and she misses you," Elizabeth added, holding out a scroll for Edward to take.

"Thank you, Elizabeth," he said, holding her gaze.

"That is ok, my Edward," she said. "I didn't read far.

After all, it is not my business. So tell me what it says."

Edward laughed and opened the scroll.

"It says she is coming to me. That she has permission to leave her home and is travelling to London. She is excited to see my home and all else that Southwark has to offer."

"She wants to see Southwark? You must offer her a better time than that, Edward."

"I guess as I live there and she knows no better. Although, I never told her where I live."

"You must have slipped it out. Regardless, you came here to seek my counsel. While I would appreciate a leisurely visit, I won't deny you my thoughts when you need them."

"Thank you, Ma'am. The new shadow, Eoin. I don't trust him."

"I see," she said. "Do you feel he is incompetent? Or worse?"

"Worse, I am afraid."

"Corrupt?"

"Maybe even worse. It sounds strange but I feel like he is attempting to tease me into losing my way, to follow the Axe."

"The Axe? You have told him your secret?"

"No. Though he has told me his. At least, he pretended it was his, though it did not seem genuine. He hasn't mentioned it again but something isn't right."

"And you do not wish to call him on it?"

"I don't think so," Edward mused. "I mentioned my feelings to Wellesley but he was content. It does force me to wonder if it is a test from above. After all, why call me back."

"Edward, Richard Wellesley chose you to join his

team and put you through his most stringent test. It is with you that he is content."

"Then why will he not listen to me regarding Eoin?"

"Because he trusts him too. He trusted you when no one else did, remember? He is arguably the very best judge of character that we have."

Edward shrugged.

"I guess so," he said. "Though I'd like to be sure. To test my theory."

Elizabeth looked at him closely.

"That doesn't sound sensible, my wolf. Do not do anything you will go on to regret."

Again, Edward shrugged.

"Edward, you have a look in your eyes and I feel you must quell this fire," she said. "Distrust is one thing but to double cross your own is another. I cannot protect you if you cross that line and set up another within the company that you serve. I give you this wisdom at least. Take your time and let the answers come out on their own. Wait for your Amelie and keep safe. It is not worth it."

He looked her in the eye and waited.

She shook her head gently.

"It is not worth it," she repeated.

Edward nodded eventually and lifted her hand to lay a kiss upon it.

"Thank you," he said. "I will not delay in returning…for leisure."

"I do hope not," she said, smiling at his words but frowning at his expression.

He backed to the door, bowed once more, then

turned to leave and headed out to the corridor.

"You," he whispered to a small guard further down the corridor. "The queen's protection, Marcus and Rutherford. Are they here, in the Tower?"

"Of course," the guard replied. "If she is here then they are here."

"Good," Edward replied. "Go to Marcus for me. Tell him to meet Edward at his Aldgate apartment tomorrow an hour after sunrise. We have a secret mission and I need his help."

Chapter Twenty One

Edward felt the cold drizzle patter against his hood in the darkness and smiled at the memory of the last time he sat nervously in the Strand outside a large house that he was about to force entry into. He looked across at Eoin sitting next to him and remembered Hurley, the cocky oaf who had been forced to join him on a kidnap job for Robert Baxter only to be killed by the Shadows on the night they had recruited Edward. He had given them a fight that spanned from the Strand to the Fleet River and they were about to kill him too until Wellesley had spared his life.

He took a breath. Wellesley *had* spared his life. And he *was* a good judge of character. And now here he was, ignoring his leader's word in order to trick his trusted colleague and expose him as a traitor. He had a witness in case he was wrong and had Baxter's men involved both in the ruse to trick Eoin, and to pull Edward out if things went dangerously sour. Even so, it did not feel right.

"How long shall we watch for?" Eoin said, suddenly, shaking Edward from his thoughts.

Edward looked up at the giant residence opposite them from where they sat hidden on a balcony across the road.

"We need to see signs of life," he said.

The looming house was one of the largest in what was arguably the most prestigious street in the city. From their lofty, diagonal vantage point, Edward looked at the three storey home with its corner turrets and beyond, into the enormous gardens that disappeared in the gloom out to where they met the Earl of Bedford's Covent Garden fields.

"I feel like we are being watched," said Eoin, glancing around. "I don't like it. We are not alone."

"This house is abandoned," Edward lied, looking around and smiling at where he knew Marcus was sitting, completely hidden from view.

They returned their attention to the manor and fell silent only to hear whispers in the rain below them. They both glanced over the balcony's edge and saw a mass of men congregating outside the house.

"What are they doing?" Eoin whispered.

"Be quiet, they've just stopped for a moment," Edward replied.

"What is taking so long?" moaned a voice below. "Are we going in or what?"

"Hang on," said another. "The deadlock is as stiff as your mother."

"It's the stiffness of your father's cock you remember in your nightmares, my friend."

The group of men chuckled and the shadowy men on the balcony shared a glance.

"It's not abandoned, is it?" said Eoin.

"I guess not. Looks like a safe house."

"Belonging to whom?"

"God knows," Edward grimaced, having flashbacks.

"We better get out." They turned and stayed low as they crossed the balcony towards the open window and heard the door finally open below.

"About bloody time," a voice shouted. "Let's take it upstairs and get the fire lit. The flue is cracked down here and will choke us. I'm soaked through and need to warm up."

Edward spotted the fireplace inside the room and put his hand on Eoin's shoulder to stop him going in.

"There is only one chimney and one upper floor," he said. "They'll be coming in here."

"Shit," Eoin said, appearing to panic.

"Don't worry," Edward replied, watching closely. "There is an iron drainpipe there. Let's go."

Eoin nodded and climbed over the edge of the balcony. Edward looked over the side and watched until the last of the men were in and the front door was closed, then nodded to Eoin to begin his descent. Edward followed behind and slipped over the edge just as candlelight filled the room through the large glass window.

"There," he whispered as he shimmied down. "Signs of life in the top window."

Eoin looked up and saw the pale light and shadow in a window overlooking the street.

"That's our cue," he replied, and stood back so that Edward could jump the last few feet and join him on the floor.

They crossed the road and were surprised to see another group of men walking towards them on the path.

"I thought you said no one was about," one growled angrily. "Oi, you two. Where are you going?"

"Just having a walk," Edward replied as he nudged Eoin forward and sped up in the opposite direction.

"At this time of night in the bloody rain?" the voice called back again. "Wait there."

Edward pushed Eoin harder.

"What are you doing?" Eoin asked. "It's not like you to run. And who do they think they are? They don't own The Strand."

"It's not about pride or fighting tonight, Eoin. We have a job to do. And we can't be seen here."

"Oi!"

"Run!" Edward said.

They darted forward past the large house they had been watching and another, ducked into a side alleyway and tracked around the back to get back to their target.

"In here," Edward whispered, ducking into a bush and putting his foot in a deep puddle. He shook his head at the night's uncanny resemblance to his memories.

They waited quietly as more men than they had seen filled the spaces around them, searching.

"You let them get away, you fucking idiot," a voice said.

"Bollocks," said another. "You should've gotten closer before you shouted."

"Look, they're gone and were nothing anyway. They ran straight past the house and had no idea. Let's go inside over the road. I can see the fire through the window."

"Not a chance. In fact, go and get that lot out here too. The Axe is upstairs and when the Axe is in, we take no chances. None. Ever."

Eoin stared at Edward in the darkness.

"The Axe?" he whispered, barely restraining the volume.

Edward nodded.

"You said it was a real job," Eoin said.

"It's true. This house is one of the Black Axe's. And he is here."

"How did you know?"

"Because when I found out who he was, it was easy to work out his whereabouts. And here we are. We have to kill him, Eoin."

Eoin blew through his lips. He looked excited. Nervous, but excited. Edward looked around and saw Marcus slip through the men and into a hidden position behind him, then he turned back to Eoin.

"Ready?" he asked.

"And the Axe is home?" Eoin replied, looking nervous.

"We can take him. We can get in without being seen and take him."

Eoin nodded.

"What happened with you, Edward?" he asked. "With the Axe? What did he do to you?"

"Don't worry about me. I did this for you. The intelligence came in and here we are."

"Truthfully? It was for me? You seek him too. What was it?"

Edward looked at Eoin and sighed. He was about to betray the man and have him locked away for treason once he named the target and Eoin agreed to kill him. The man was hell-bent on killing the Axe even if it meant crossing his monarch and her closest advisors. He made a decision.

"Fine," he said. "He tried to kill me once too. Or his men did. That is all."

"There must be a reason?" Eoin replied.

"I guess so. It was a long time ago. In France. My family died but I survived."

Eoin smiled.

"What is funny?"

"Nothing," Eoin said. "You just want him as much as I do."

Edward grinned back.

"Hang on, I recognise this house," Eoin said, looking confused.

"It's Burleigh House," Edward said, solemnly. "The Axe is William Cecil."

"It is Cecil? We are going to kill Cecil?"

Edward nodded gravely.

"He is the Axe, Eoin. We are."

Eoin nodded.

"Does the Queen know?" he asked.

"That Cecil is the Axe and we are going to take him out? No."

"Does she know about the Axe at all? And about you? Does anyone?"

"No," Edward replied.

Eoin nodded again and Edward led the way towards the door once he had confirmed the path was clear. He crept up the steps to the grand porch and slipped the spare key Cecil had given him months before into the lock. He turned and nodded to Eoin then opened the door gently only to receive the full force or a leather-gloved palm to his face, hammering him from his feet as he stepped through. He landed on his back with a thud, feeling the cold marble echo through his body.

He cursed at the over-zealous role play as he was hauled to his feet. He held up his hands to stop the charade when he noticed he didn't recognise the guards. He looked around as more approached from the road and garden and frowned as he looked for the men he had tasked.

"I knew you were a traitor," said Eoin coldly beside him. He was unguarded and standing tall with a sneer across his face. "It took time to set you up but you fed into it perfectly."

"Set *me* up?" Edward cried. "This is *my* plan to test you!" He craned his head against the grip on his hair only to see Marcus get dragged up the steps, his face bloody and his arms limp.

"Both of you disgust me. To slay the queen's most trusted man over a twisted obsession. Your own friend and mentor."

Edward shook his head in disbelief. He looked around again for Baxter and his men, his only hope, and saw the bearded villain watching him with a smirk.

"You of all people know where my loyalties lie, Rothwell," he said, swinging a purse of coins. "Come on."

His men followed him and Edward turned back to Eoin.

"You are under arrest by direct order of the queen," the scarred shadow said. "She is heartbroken, I hope you are content. Putting you to death is her greatest regret."

Edward opened his mouth to speak only to have a hood pulled over his head and his legs kicked away from behind. The floor collided with him once more, stealing his breath, and he was dragged away by his arms.

"I'm sorry, Marcus," he said. "I'm sorry."

Chapter Twenty-Two

Edward felt pain shoot up his leg as his foot collided with something hard and he was hauled out of a cart by an arm around his throat.

"Delivery!" a voice shouted, next to his ear. "Got two special guests for you."

Edward heard a man laugh and begin to mumble in reply as a thud sounded next to him and Marcus was heard to groan somewhere near his feet.

"What are they?" a gruff voice called from further away.

"Just a couple of traitors," the voice in Edward's ear said again as Edward was pulled backwards and was forced to hurry his chained feet to keep up.

"Traitors? We don't take traitors here. Why aren't they in the Tower?"

"Because these are different and Marshalsea is the right place for them. You'll see, they're no more important than a couple of debtors and thieves. In fact, put them with the rapists to keep them occupied."

"Ok," the voice said, wearily. "Bring them into the holding cell and take your restraints off them. We will book them in but be warned, we are far over capacity and there is sickness in the cells. It's not going to be comfortable."

"Perfect," the voice said. "I'm told someone will be along later for interrogation. For now, they can wait and rot."

Edward heard a heavy, metallic lock scrape against its housing, then was hit with a wall of noise.

"You weren't joking," the voice said in his ear as he was hauled once more and just about held his footing as he backed into a hard, stone step. "In you go," the voice said again as he was turned around and shoved forward.

The noise around him was deafening, like the roar of the crowd when a declawed and muzzled bear was finally taken down by the mastiffs and bulldogges in the fighting pits. Terror mixed with rage, which mixed with excitement, which mixed with agony. The sound of human suffering, with the scent of all that came from it.

Edward's arms were held tightly by large hands as his bounds were released and the chains were removed from his legs. He was walked backwards and forced down onto a hard bench before the hood was finally removed and the dimly lit room came into sight.

"Don't even think about trying for the Master's Side," said the same voice from his ear, only this time it wore a red beard that framed stained teeth and sat below piercing blue eyes. "The guards are under strict orders that it is the Common Side for you and you'll face the cadavers and rats of the Strong Room if you even ask."

Edward nodded to the cloaked man.

"Are you a Tower Guard?" he asked.

"None of your fucking business."

The man turned away and Edward looked around the room. Another seven men sat broken around him, waiting to be admitted to one of the heaving cells of Marshalsea Prison's Common Side, one of whom was Marcus having his shackles removed. The Shadow's head lulled towards Edward as his hood was removed and Edward's stomach boiled with anger as their eyes made contact and the state of his best friend's face was revealed. Through the blood, Edward could see the torn flesh that spanned from the man's ripped eyelid and barely contained eye ball, through what looked like claw marks on his cheek and an upper lip ripped through so that the side hung grotesquely and the gaps of the now missing teeth were revealed.

"What happened?" Edward mouthed, filling with emotion.

Marcus said nothing but another dirty face filled the space between them.

"The silly prick fell over as the cart moved away and stuck his face under the wooden wheels. We were all surprised his head didn't burst open. The skid marks are impressive though."

He chuckled and moved away, leaving Marcus in view, torn to shreds and broken inside. The men who arrested them left the holding cell and headed out through the front door as the gaolers walked in.

"In the name of God, Marcus, what are you doing here?" one of them said.

"Job gone wrong," Marcus replied with slurred speech, wincing at the pain. He smiled as new blood seeped over his chin.

"I'm sorry, Marcus," Edward said.

Marcus waved a hand loosely.

"Why? He *is* a traitor. It is plain as day now," he mumbled.

"You think?"

"He's a traitor and so is Baxter. They're connected, it's clear, and it's not through work with Wellesley. I don't know why or how but for whatever reason, Eoin and Baxter are together and it isn't for the health of our queen."

Edward let his head fall back against the stone wall. Eoin and Baxter. In all his suspicion and insight, he hadn't for a moment considered the possibility of Eoin and one of the informants being linked.

"I've always known Eoin was corrupt," he said. "But what for? I assumed to get close to Elizabeth? He said he chases the Axe too but that was all a ruse to put me here."

"Maybe it was you he was after," Marcus slurred with a shrug, turning his good eye to Edward.

Edward frowned in thought.

"I have wondered, but he's had ample opportunity to take me out. He must want more and with me out of the way, he will go after the Queen."

"And Baxter?"

"Hired by Eoin. He will do anything for coin if it suits his purpose and carries no risk to him. He chose a side."

"Treachery against the Queen is not a low risk path, my friend."

"No, Marcus, it isn't. But helping to catch apparent traitors is not the same."

Marcus swore under his breath.

"Bastard," he said.

"Someone recommended Eoin to Wellesley and he

gave him a shot," Edward continued. "Someone with enough clout to pull it off has inserted a traitor into Elizabeth's own secret unit to remove her close protection and move in. She's in great danger and we need to get out."

Marcus nodded.

"How?" he asked. "The queen's own men saw us in the act of targeting Cecil himself. Just to be there with such organisation, the operation must have gone far enough up the chain. There must have been enough intelligence submitted by Eoin for us to be suspected all the way up. Maybe even by Elizabeth."

"Where though?" Edward said, leaning forward and gathering speed. "Where did the intelligence go? Who organised the operation?"

"Anyone could have?"

"Anyone with which men? They weren't Tower Guards. They weren't from Greenwich or Windsor. I don't think they were soldiers at all."

"There is no way Wellesley or Cecil *or* Walsingham or any of them would execute an operation like that and not use soldiers or shadows. And they were not shadows."

"Who said Wellesley, Cecil or Walsingham sent them?" said Edward.

Marcus' head snapped around and Edward nodded.

"Eoin is a traitor and he used Baxter on the job. There was no one else of authority there," he added.

"But they were inside Cecil's house?" asked Marcus.

"And he wasn't there. I used an old friend, Peter Burntback, to move that light around."

Marcus watched him for a moment then turned and

faced the guards.

"Guard!" he called, leaning forward and feigning illness. He made eye contact with the guard he knew and the man came over, crouching by them.

"Adam, did you recognise the men who brought us in?" Marcus asked, nodding as the guard shook his head. "I don't believe they were soldiers at all," he continued. "I need you to get to Rutherford. Tonight. Now. Tell him Marcus and Edward have been arrested and are in Marshalsea, Eoin and Baxter are not to be trusted and the Queen is in danger. Now, make your excuses. Go."

Adam, the guard, nodded and disappeared as a handful of other gaolers entered from the side and gathered up all of the prisoners. Edward and Marcus were encouraged to their feet and were pushed together towards the heaving noise of the common side cells.

Edward opened his eyes with a squint as he felt a hand on his shin that woke him from his sleep. He looked into the sweaty, soot-blackened face and woollen rag shirt of one of the prisoners crouching over him.

"Head," the man whispered. Edward looked at him confused. "Head. It's time. I'm ready to come. Head!"

Edward aimed a punch at the man's face but his arms couldn't move. The hand shook his leg again.

"Head!" the dirty man said, urgently. "Quick, I'm coming!"

Edward was completely paralysed. His eyes glanced around the dark cell at the sweaty bodies everywhere. The noise was deafening and the odour of urine and vinegar was intense. Standing, sitting, laying, moving, men were all around him but none were facing him. None but the man with the hand on his immoveable leg. He tried to speak but nothing left his mouth, then he felt a hard slap to his face despite the man not moving and the room changed in an instant as he found himself looking into Marcus' unbandaged eye.

"Ed, it's time. They've come. They're going to take us for questioning. I heard them. Quick, they're coming."

Edward snapped to and sat up from where he had slept. The cell was crowded with men but this time those around him turned to see why he was startled. Scraps and tussles had broken out in places but the violence was surprisingly low and the other prisoners appeared to know better than to try their luck with the two mysterious traitors.

"Clear the way!" a voice shouted as the bored men parted and a burly guard in Marshalsea uniform came into view. "You two. You're wanted."

Edward glanced at Marcus as they got to their feet and followed the guard out of the room under the gaze of at least sixty curious eyes. As they stepped into the corridor, they found themselves facing a man Edward did not recognise. Tall with close cropped hair and a short but thick, dark beard, the man wore a long, high quality black cloak and a squint that assessed Edward from top to bottom. His hand popped out of his cloak and flashed a coin that Edward knew only too well. The Shadows.

"Who are you?" Edward asked.

"Good start," the man said. "I'll ask the questions

though. Let's get on with it."

Edward glanced at Marcus as one of the guards grabbed his arm and pulled him roughly behind the mysterious Shadow along the dark corridor. Marcus shook his head slightly in a way that Edward assumed suggested he didn't recognise the man either, and was taken in the other direction by a guard alone.

The remaining eight cells roared with taunts and jeers as they passed them and Edward watched the door to the Strong Room, housing the deceased bodies and faeces of the prison, loom ever closer as they walked. He'd once seen a man thrown to his death to land in the slop among the rats and cadavers, only to have his scream cut off as the iron door was shut and he was left to join the bodies around him. He was probably still in there. Edward felt his heart beat faster and the taste of vomit fill his throat as they approached the door, only to turn right into a darker corridor as they got there and finally into the interrogation room where he had first seen the use of thumb screws and had gone on to solve a crime by showing pity and recruiting his first informant.

He was thrown roughly into a wooden chair and shackled as a large table was dragged over in front of him and the Shadow sat down.

Edward held the man's gaze in silence as the guards left the room and the door was shut behind them.

The man opened his hands in gesture and waited, eyebrows raised, for Edward to speak.

"What?" Edward asked.

"Speak."

Edward frowned.

"I don't recognise you," he said. "I thought I knew all of the Shadows."

"The Shadows?" the man chuckled. "I'm not a Shadow."

"Then why do you brandish the coin like you are?"

"Oh, it is my coin, but I am not a Shadow. Don't assume you know everything, Edward. I work in…a different unit. For William Cecil directly. And have been sent here by the man himself."

"A different unit? I know of no such unit."

"You didn't know about the Walsingham Wolves until you became one either, did you? And yet I know of them despite not being one. I guess that tells you something. In fact, what it should tell you is that you know very little and only what they, and we, want you to know."

"But the queen…"

"The queen keeps you where she needs you and you do what is expected for her. At least, you did. Until intelligence suggested otherwise. No one thought the operation would catch you in the act though."

"So it was a job."

"It was a job."

"I don't believe it. The queen knows me. She will vouch for me. Even to Cecil. I have witnesses."

"Witnesses who saw you conspire to murder the Lord Burghley. Oh the queen will not vouch for you. She only now feels safe for the first time since your radicalisation in France."

"My radicalisation?"

Cecil's man nodded, his eyebrows raised.

"Walsingham watched you turn as your woman came into your life. Always a woman, for Rothwell."

"What woman?" Edward asked, knowing the answer and feeling his heart quicken at the personal knowledge the man was showing.

"The woman in Paris who turned you. *'She knows my feelings underneath,'* you said. You were groomed once more by the stupidity of your cock and now you're here, an inside man, attempting to take out the queen's closest advisors and put the blame on others. We have been onto you since you left France."

"There was no woman in Paris," Edward replied. "How can you say I was radicalised? You didn't see what I saw."

"I didn't see what you *survived*. What *you* survived that no one else could. What your aide couldn't survive despite being in your company."

"Do not speak of Jacque! And Francis survived."

"Walsingham survived by staying in a safe house until he could arrange escort as an English ambassador. You and your aide ventured out and guess what, the aide didn't make it. Yet you not only survived, but you made it out of the city and went straight to Rome, meeting a suspected traitor."

Edward opened is his mouth to speak and closed it again. The allegations were infuriating but his interrogations had taught him just how easy it could be to incriminate yourself when desperate.

"Carry on," he said, instead.

Cecil's man smiled.

"You got out and while you were in Rome,

Walsingham came home and told the queen all about your time in France and your woman."

"The queen knows the truth."

"Well, the queen didn't believe it either, until your French agent turned up herself."

Edward's head twitched to the side a degree and his interviewer grinned at the emotional infiltration.

"I still don't know who you mean. What did this agent do?"

"She spoke to the people you spoke to. Looking for you. Saying she escaped France and came to you for safety."

Edward took a breath.

"And who did I speak to?" he said.

"The queen, Cecil, your man Marcus, soldiers. You probed into Eoin's vulnerabilities and tried to plant a seed of doubt in Wellesley's mind. Oh we have been watching you."

"Anyone else?"

The man squinted.

"Of course, you're a busy man," he said.

Edward took a moment to think. He had not mentioned Thomas Cobham, who Edward had seen only in the privacy of the Tower. As Cobham's idea, he could have been part of the trap, but no one knew Edward would approach him and Edward just didn't think it was right.

"It matters not, Rothwell," the mysterious man continued. "You have committed an act of treason and intelligence suggests you were working your way to set up the shadows for an assassination of the queen." Edward closed his eyes, feeling the words and being powerless to stop them. "The evidence against you from Walsingham, Eoin and the plot at Cecil's house are conclusive and as a foreign threat on English soil, the agent with the legend of Amelie has been arrested and held for execution without trial."

"No!" Edward shouted. "She is not an agent. She is innocent."

"You know this Amelie then?"

"Yes. Yes, I know her. She is innocent and knows I am from London. I told her my real name."

"And you told her of your past?"

"What?"

"Your past," the man said. "The ghost you chase. Walsingham said he has always wondered if your past would come back and whether it was closer to home than they thought. That you intend to kill the queen."

"No one knows of my past. Not Amelie, most certainly not you. Only a woman knew of my past, Maggie, and she's dead."

"And yet the queen knows all about you, you said. 'She knows the truth', were your words. I assume you discussed this with the queen, and that is why she has protected you all this time."

"The queen knows nothing of my past."

"Nothing?"

"Nothing."

"She knew you had lived in France. Cecil himself knew. She knows you chase the ghost of some memory and it corrupts you."

"She doesn't know why."

The man let a smile hit one side of his mouth.

"*She doesn't know why*," be mimicked. "Tell me why."

"Fuck off!" Edward laughed. "Tell you about my past?"

"It may be the only way to clear your name."

Edward stared back in silence.

"So you have worked your way in to the tightest circles of the English monarchy," the man continued. "You have repeatedly swayed and caused suspicion, twice you have worked with women who have worked against us, and yet you have not told the queen of the ghost you chase."

Edward shrugged but again, stayed silent.

"Then it only confirms what the queen fears. What I was indeed sent here to confirm myself."

"Which is?"

"That this black axe you name and chase is the queen and you intend to kill her."

"No."

"That you coordinated a *chance* encounter with Richard Wellesley, became a Shadow and then played on the edge of the rules in order to elevate yourself to the next level and get close enough to the queen to set up the Shadows for the assassination."

"No!" Edward exclaimed.

"You have been tested for a long time, my friend. Wellesley trusted you, Cecil trusted you. Walsingham is not so easy. You worked to stand out with your mock rogue attitude but you had no idea of the wolves. No, when Walsingham heard of you he set you up for the ultimate test. And you didn't disappoint. Hawkins, Spain, Howard, Ambush, Paris, Rome, Eoin. Teasing you all the way with mention of this Axe."

Edward shook his head. He didn't trust the interrogator in front of him but the man knew only what a genuine agent could know. He had no idea how to deny the allegations. He closed his eyes.

"I only feel sad for your friend Marcus who must now also perish for doing no more than trusting a traitor with a good story. But your French woman, it is a shame such a pretty face will be forever left in anguish by the squeeze of a rope."

"No!" Edward shouted again and tried to stand up. "Leave her alone. Leave her alone! Allow her to meet the queen. The queen will see. She is innocent."

"Put a deadly foreign threat in front of our monarch. Splendid idea and a fine last ditch attempt to succeed. Goodbye, Edward," the man said as he stood and turned to the door that opened for him. "You got close, I'll give you that. Now your path will end. And no one will ever know you existed."

He turned and disappeared, leaving Edward silent in shock as the heavy door clattered shut once again.

Chapter Twenty Three

Once again, Edward was woken by Marcus tapping his leg.

"They're here," he said.

Edward looked up at the broken and sorrowful face looking down at him and felt his emotions rise at the pain he had put his best friend through.

Edward had been left, sweating, next to a roaring fire for hours after his interrogator had left, and he was eventually dragged back and laid next to Marcus who sat with his head bowed, looking at his strapped hands. '*Thumb screws*,' he had said, quietly, without looking up.

The cage door opened and Adam, the guard Marcus had spoken to upon their arrival at the prison, walked over to them.

"It's time, I think, my friend," said Adam.

"Did you find Rutherford?" Marcus slurred.

"I did. In the markets by St Paul's. He looked pained when I told him but was being watched and told me to get away as quickly as I could so that I wasn't followed. The last I saw of him, he was moving through the crowd but there were men behind him and their faces said it all. I don't know if he made it but no one has given us word to release you. I am sorry."

"Thank you for trying," Marcus said, looking at Edward with grim acceptance.

"What is happening now?" Edward asked.

"We are moving you."

"Moving to where? Out of the prison?"

"Not exactly, we just have orders."

"What's going on?" a deep voice shouted from the back of the cage near the door. "Shackle 'em and pull 'em through. Hurry up, Adam."

Adam the guard pulled heavy shackles from his belt and clamped them onto both of the men's ankles and wrists.

"You'll have to move slow but use each other for balance," he said.

"Adam, I need one more favour," whispered Edward as they stood.

Adam glanced at Marcus who nodded in reply.

"Go on," he said.

"I need you to get a message to Richard Wellesley. It doesn't matter how, it just must happen. Tell him that Marcus and Amelie are innocent of all things. Tell him that he must convince Cecil to let Amelie go. It is my fault she is tied up in this and she knows nothing. And Marcus, he must be honoured, not shamed."

Adam opened his mouth to speak then closed it again. He nodded.

"Thank you," Edward mouthed as they reached the door and were pulled along more roughly by other guards.

They were marched slowly and noisily away from the tired din of the other, packed cells and down a corridor towards the Master's Side of the prison, as Edward had once been shown. He felt his heart beat in relief as they walked the long corridor past the small open windows that looked into the dark courtyard but felt it quicken once more as they were stopped in their tracks and the guard in front slid a large iron key into the courtyard door. It opened with a squeaking, rusty grind that seemed to pass through Edward's soul, and the men were pushed out into the dark, cold air.

Edward caught Marcus as he stumbled and they stood there in ragged clothes as the door was shut and bolted behind them. They glanced at each other and then Edward looked up at the sky. He had no idea what time of night it had become and wished he'd paid attention on his sail from Rome as he looked at the stars in the perfectly clear sky that let the chill reach into their bones.

"I guess it doesn't matter what the time is," he said, as he looked down at his wrists and the heavy iron cutting into them. The wrist cuffs were chained to the ankle cuffs and both sets were separated by a foot long bar that prevented their limbs from moving in any free direction. "What do you think is happening?" he asked, knowing the answer.

"Well, based on the position of the stars, the mathematical angle that separates the four walls of this courtyard and the exact weight of that door aligned to the speed in which it was closed, I'd say we are…well…fucked," Marcus replied, making Edward laugh.

Another grinding sound caught their attention as a bolt was slid across a large and solid iron gate on the far side of the courtyard.

Rutherford took a breath as he slipped on the red tower-guard tunic of the man he had just rolled into a bush behind him. He had no idea if the man was rogue but after speaking to Adam, the Marshalsea guard, he had heard Wellesley order Eoin to select two men to carry out an execution within the prison. 'Make it silent, remove the bodies and cover it up,' he had said. 'I cannot believe I have to give this order.' Rutherford had seen the sorrow in his eyes from where he stood out of sight, but the relish in Eoin's had told him all he needed to know. He knew his best friends were innocent and after watching Eoin order a man that he didn't recognise, he had then followed that man for hours until he stood where he did now, waiting for another to join him at the back gate of Marshalsea. Rutherford had hung back around the corner until a second man approached and had sprung from the shadows, silently taking him down, suffocating him until he slept, and then taking his tunic before binding him and rolling him, shirtless, into the cold mud beneath a bush.

He straightened his clothes and walked into the torchlight of the Marshalsea back gate.

"Who are you?" the man said.

"I was sent, who are you?"

"I was expecting someone else."

"Well, then I guess we are both in the dark. Eoin sent me."

"Keep that name down!" the man whispered harshly. "But fine, if White sent you, I guess we are good to go. What were you told?"

"Just that we are here to execute two prisoners and need to keep it quiet."

"Tower guard?"

Rutherford nodded.

"Ever done anything like this before?" the man asked.

"No. Been a guard a long time though and worked a few interrogations and executions. Why does it need to be kept quiet?"

"These two are Shadows who work for the queen."

"Ah," Rutherford nodded, with a sigh. "The men with the coin. Well, it's come from the top, so I guess they deserve it. They always seemed shady to me anyway. Put on a uniform and fight fair, I always say."

"Quite," the man replied as he turned and slid back the large, rusty bolt on the gate.

Edward watched the large iron gate slide open with a groan as two men stepped into the gloom from behind it. One wore the red tunic of a tower guard while the other was cloaked in darkness. They stopped for a moment and faced Edward and Marcus silently.

"Ready?" the cloaked man said, pulling a long dagger from his hip.

"No," said the man in red, stepping into the light and making Edward's heart leap as the blonde hair of his friend and colleague came into view. "Shadows are the queen's men. They should be tried, not executed."

"I knew you wouldn't have it in you. Stay here then,"

said the cloaked man as he turned to dart towards Edward and Marcus.

"No," Rutherford replied again, grasping at the man's shoulder and pulling him back. He grabbed the moving dagger-arm as the cloak whirled and the blade thrusted back towards his stomach. He managed to stop the stab with a grip on the tight and unyielding sleeve, but his other hand gripped only a loose cloak and the man beneath it moved freely.

"Imposter!" shouted a voice as a stone hit Rutherford in the back of the head and an undressed and partly bound man staggered into the darkness of the courtyard.

Edward watched the moments in horror as Rutherford turned in distraction and the sharp dagger was driven into his gut above the navel.

"Die, bastard," the cloaked man growled as he held the blade still and Rutherford gripped it, slicing his fingers on the edge.

He grimaced as he moved his hand to hold the cloaked arm still and dropped his other from the man's shoulder only to return it to drive a short blade into the bared throat.

"You die," he said, through pain, as he watched the eyes facing him open in surprise and glaze over in an instant. He dropped the body, forgetting the dagger, which was pulled agonisingly from his stomach by the falling hand, and looked up at Edward and Marcus as the bound wrists of another were slid over his head to pull on his throat.

"Let him go!" Edward roared as he dragged his chains across the courtyard to the men, struggling in a heap on the floor. He dropped onto the undressed man, driving his forehead into his face and feeling his nose crumble beneath him with a grunt. He lifted his head and struck again. Then again. Then again. And continued as the sound of the man's voice below him gave way to silence and the splattering of a wet and crumbled face.

"He's dead." said Marcus, causing Edward to pause and look down at the pulp below him. It groaned.

"He isn't."

"Rutherford, Ed. He bled out. He's dead."

Edward cleared his eyes with his heavy, chained arms and looked down into the face of his friend. He felt emotion rise inside him at the peaceful expression on the face that had once scorned him yet still saved his life time after time. The face of possibly the hardest and most trustworthy man he knew. Killed, like everyone else, because of Edward's own selfish, personal mission.

"I'm sorry, my friend," he said.

"He knows," said Marcus from where he sat, half-broken. "Of course he knows. That's why he came. But we need to move. We can mourn him later."

Edward nodded and looked up in fear as the door to the courtyard opened once more. Adam's face appeared, took in the scene and sagged with relief.

"It is Rutherford, Adam," Marcus said, quietly. "Take care of his body and when we have cleared this up, we will have him collected.

"Rutherford? Fuck." Adam said, checking the corridor then stepping out into the cold darkness and quickly unshackling Marcus before moving on to Edward and releasing the cuffs on his wrists. He gave him the key.

"Take their clothes and put yours along with your chains on these two. I will take Rutherford into the Master's Side once you have gone and take care of it until you return. Leave the key on Rutherford, close the gate on the way out and look after Marcus."

Edward nodded, holding the key.

"Thank you, Adam."

"Just make it worth it."

"This one is still alive," he said, looking down at the broken face of the undressed man and feeling the dried blood crackle on his own brow for the first time.

"The strong room will finish him," Adam said, looking down at Rutherford, closing his eyes for a moment and then turning on his heels to head to the door. He helped Marcus to his feet as he passed, then disappeared silently back into the prison corridor.

Edward worked to strip the bodies, throwing the cloak over Marcus while the broken man did what he could, then slipped on the red tunic of the corrupt tower guard. He pulled their clothes onto the bloody bodies and finally attached the heavy shackles to their ankles and wrists, falling back with an exhausted sigh once the work was done.

He slipped the key into Rutherford's pocket and held his hand for a moment, thanking him silently for saving their lives. Then he hauled Marcus up and together they hobbled out into the street.

Chapter Twenty Four

Edward pulled Marcus in tighter to help the man make his final steps up to the old, wooden door in the shadows of Southwark's back streets. He turned the handle and for once the door was locked.

"Albert," he called, tapping his fist on the door. "Albert, it's Edward, please open up."

The sound of a lock slid back behind the oak and the door crept open to reveal Albert in a nightgown and the warm glow of a gentle fire, reaching the end of its life in the hearth.

"Jesus Christ. Come in, lad," he said, pulling back the door and nodding as Agnes pulled the bedsheets over herself.

"Thank you, my friend," Edward said, stepping into the warmth. "Evening, Agnes."

"Hello, Edward. Bloody hell, what's happened to him?" Agnes replied, pulling on her own cotton gown and rushing over to help Marcus to a seat.

"We were set up, Albert. The Shadows set us up. The new lad, Eoin, is corrupt and while exposing him, he turned the men against us and we were arrested. We've been in Marshalsea and escaped a silent execution by the skin of our teeth. Rutherford didn't make it."

"He was arrested with you?"

"No, he saved us. Marcus shouldn't have been there either."

"Leave it, Ed. I made my own choice and was right to be with you," Marcus replied from the floor. "The fight against corruption that endangers our queen is exactly what we do and we don't know who to trust. We will sort this."

"What will you do?" Albert asked. "You know what I'm going to say."

"Calm down first?"

"Along those lines, lad, yes. But I can see another urgency. What is it?"

"Amelie. They have Amelie."

"What's she doing here?"

"I assume she came to see me and they took her. Cecil thinks she is a spy and that I am corrupt and the queen believes him. She's going to be executed. I must get to the queen. She is in the Tower at the moment."

"And do what, lad? If you're a wanted man, you can't just walk up to the queen's house and knock on her door. And you're wearing a Tower uniform, if I'm not mistaken? That tells me somehow they are not happy with you."

"I have no choice, Albert. I lost Maggie. I won't lose Amelie."

Albert opened his mouth to speak and thought better of it. Edward was not in panic. The fire spoke for itself. He nodded and Edward nodded too in reply.

"Are you going to wear the uniform to get in?" Agnes asked as she tended to the filthy and infected wounds on Marcus' face.

"I don't think so. They will know I'm not a guard and may even be looking for their missing colleague. No, I will act like a shadow and use our namesake to my advantage."

Edward felt the cool brick against his cheek as he looked around the corner of the empty riverside warehouse opposite the entrance to the Tower. Sitting at the western end of a small moat-bridge that approached the main gate, Edward noted the single guard looking bored at the gatehouse and then scanned the top of the looming wall that sat behind it and curved around to where it disappeared into the dark water and the boat entrance in the distance.

He had no idea if he would be recognised but for the first time had no faith in his coin as he approached the royal residence. He pulled his hood right over his face and sauntered towards the guard.

"Who comes there?" asked the guard, with confidence.

Edward opened his hand and let his coin catch the light so that the guard would at least not call for reinforcement.

"Let me see your face," he asked again. "Oi, pull back your hood."

Edward took another few steps and then pulled back his hood, holding his coin in front of his face as he watched the guard's movements. The soldier's confidence did not match his posture and appeared instead to stem from youthful arrogance.

Edward waved his coin as the guard squinted in the

gloom and then dropped his hand and stepped forward quickly, moving inside the range of the young man's weapon before he could react. He pulled the unsuspecting head forward with his left hand and struck its face with his elbow on the right. The guard's knees buckled as his nose gave way and he let out a distant groan as Edward's hands followed him down and crossed over, locking his tunic into a tight strangle, pressing his wrist against his throat and cutting off the flow of his carotid artery until he was unconscious.

Edward was careful to let go before the young man's unconsciousness became lifelessness, then gagged and bound him before dragging him out of the gatehouse and rolling him down the grass hill into the dry moat.

He gathered himself and looked across the bridge. The top of the wall was clear. He stepped forward, sliding sideways through the heavy iron door, left ajar, and then passed under the sound of more guards at the top of the curved staircase. He exited the wall into the street and slipped along in the darkness towards the inner gate that would open onto the White Tower where the queen would be sleeping.

The lack of alertness was both reassuring and disappointing to Edward as he neared the inner gate and stepped out of the shadows suddenly, showing his coin to the surprised guard before driving his knee into his groin, covering his mouth and stepping behind him to encircle his throat until he too was silent.

He dragged the limp form into the shadows, using the man's own belt to gag him and left him sitting upright so that the blood would return to his head more slowly. Then he stepped through the door of the inner gate and stopped to take stock of the final challenge ahead.

"Who the fuck are you?" asked a voice to his right as he watched the door of the White Tower. He turned in shock, only briefly seeing the frowning face that disappeared as a heavy glove struck his cheek.

Edward stumbled backwards, muttering that he was a shadow, as the guard looked around the corner for his absent friend and came back into view with his hands held high.

"Intrud…!" he shouted as he leapt at Edward, only to have his voice cut off by a short jab to the throat that left him gasping and distracted long enough for Edward to shove him through the gate door and pull it closed.

"All ok?" A voice rang out from atop the inner wall. "Rob? Robin? Soldier!"

Edward clung to the wall and moved along in the shadows as the calls went out above him.

"David, confirm what is happening!" it called again.

Edward looked around, gauging his options as the guard on the doorway to the White Tower followed orders and left his post to run over to the inner gate. The door was left wide and Edward's heart began to beat as his opportunity was revealed. He looked at the empty darkness inside the doorway, up at the wall once more, back at the door and then broke into a sprint.

"In the street!" a voice roared, making him jump.

"Stop!" shouted another voice from the direction of the guard who had left his post.

Edward heard the sounds erupt around him and set his sights on the door, driving his knees as hard as he could and hurtling towards the giant shape of a man that appeared suddenly in the doorway just as Edward's body collided with it.

"Fuck," the man said as he was knocked backwards into the wooden stairwell behind him and the two men stumbled to the floor. Edward jumped to his feet moments before the large guard could react and he slammed the door shut with his foot, hearing the noise outside disappear and turning just in time to duck the swing of a blade that would've severed his head.

He closed the distance on the outside of the man's huge shoulder and wrapped his arms around him, putting his heel in the back of the guard's knee and pulling them both to the floor in a heap.

The guard's muscle was far beyond Edward, who did his best stay to low, blocking the outside of the sword arm and putting on pressure until his head was pressed into the man's neck and he could slide his leg over the large belly to move on top and again drive his forehead repeatedly into the jaw and neck of his adversary.

The guard was unconscious after several strikes and Edward fell back, panting and looking up at the gentle flickers of torchlight on the stone ceiling. He listened for movement over the calls for action outside the door and then leapt to his feet, forcing himself to move on as he scaled the staircase one floor at a time and burst into the queen's chamber past the guard who was looking out of the window for instructions.

Edward slammed the door shut again and locked it against the panicked calls of the guard outside, then turned to find his monarch sitting up in her bed, looking at him in the gloom through narrowed eyes.

"Your Majesty," Edward said, sheepishly.

"If you fancied a cuddle, Edward, you only needed to ask," she said, making him smile. "What the hell are you doing?"

A side door burst open and two armed guards stepped in only to be stopped in their tracks by the roar of the queen.

"What are you doing, Sergeant?" she said.

"Intruder, Your Majesty," the man replied, turning to Edward and pointing his sword at him angrily.

"Do you know who this is?" she asked. The man shook his head, surprising Edward. "This is one of my shadows, you stupid oaf," she continued. "Get out and find the man who arrived from France. Send him to me."

The men left and repeated the orders to others outside, eventually leaving Edward and Elizabeth in silence.

"Your Majesty, it is not true. There is no need to call Francis," he said, as the queen's eyes narrowed. "I was set up, Amelie is not a spy, and I beg your forgiveness for all I have caused."

"Francis?" she said.

"The man from France," Edward replied. "I am not a traitor and Amelie is here only for me."

"Apparently so."

"Please," Edward continued. "I would never betray you."

"You work for me, Edward, I do not own you," Elizabeth replied, mournfully. "I do not see it as betrayal, you may court whomever you please."

Edward looked at her confused.

"Then you will release her?"

Elizabeth laughed.

"You really think that much of me? That I would lock away a woman for stealing the heart of the man who holds mine?"

Edward twitched his head, though his mouth stayed open.

"But they said she was a spy?" he asked. "Cecil had her locked up?"

"Well he hasn't told me and William knows better than to meddle with the affairs of *my* heart without keeping me informed. Amelie is a pleasant girl. And she suits you. But what are you talking about? A traitor for what? Edward, what is going on? Look at you, why are you hurt?"

Edward pinched his nose for a moment and looked back at Elizabeth, stepping closer than he should but pulling nothing but curiosity from the eyes of his queen.

"I was taken," he said. "Against your advice, I wanted to test our new Shadow, Eoin, as I knew he was a traitor. And he is, I have proven it. But he set us up, Marcus and I. We were arrested and taken to Marshalsea. The man who interrogated me. He knew things. He must work for the crown. He said Amelie was arrested as a spy and was to be executed, and that you and Cecil had decided I was to be killed as a traitor with no trial. They came to execute us in the prison courtyard but Rutherford saved us. He was killed."

Elizabeth listened with her eyebrows raised.

"I know nothing of this, Edward," she said. "Set up

indeed. If Cecil knows of this, I will have his head and I do not jest. But I do not believe he does."

"Walsingham then?"

"How, he is in Paris."

"He is in Paris? Then who arrived from France? And if she is not under arrest, how have you met Amelie?"

A French accent sounded in the corridor outside and Edward looked at Elizabeth.

"The raunchy little aide with nine lives, of course. Though the Parisian bloodbath certainly hasn't robbed him of his confidence."

"Edward!" the voice roared as the door opened and Jacque walked in and embraced his friend.

"Jacque, you're alive!" Edward chuckled, then frowned. "You're alive?"

"I am."

"How did you escape the tunnel?"

"With French charm and Parisian arrogance, my friend. *My* French charm, and the arrogance of *those* idiots. I had heard them call each others' names and when I went back, I held out the pistol in the dark but it jammed. Luckily they didn't hear or see me attempt to fire, so I spoke instead. I said that you had escaped and that their friends, who I named, were looking for you and said for us to turn back. I showed them your gun and said you dropped it so it didn't work. I let one keep it and we made our way back."

Edward shook his head.

"What did you do?"

"I had to join them. I cheered them on but they didn't do much before I found space and disappeared. I managed to get back to the white house."

"And Amelie? How is she here?"

"Well, it was Francis' orders to make sure you got through and I did what I had to do. When I got back, he made me a Wolf and set me to work. I still had two of the women in the palace tending to the king's mother so I used them to get close and listen to her."

"We have since blocked every recess around my chamber," Elizabeth said, with a smile. "Tell him what you heard, Jacque. The part that Francis said he would want to hear."

"I heard Catherine talking about Coligny and what she described as 'some men called the Black Axe' who had set up the union for the royal wedding. After someone else tried and failed to kill Coligny, she had him finished and used it to kick off the mob across the city without any comeback. She was furious with Charles for sending word that other cities should not follow suit and sent her own men ahead of them across the country. Including La Rochelle."

"La Rochelle?"

Jacque nodded.

"When I heard her orders for Henri de Valois to besiege the city, I got back to Francis first, convinced him to let me take word there and travelled as quickly as I could. I beat the army but no one believed my warning, other than Amelie's father. Luckily I got there before the siege took hold and, having barely survived Paris, he was all too eager for me to get her out and bring her here, to you."

"She is under my protection, Edward," said Elizabeth. "For her father, and for you. Though Jacque, here, may now have beaten you to become my favourite."

Edward looked between them, unsure whether to laugh or cry.

"She is here and she is safe," he whispered. "Where is she?"

"She is staying here in the Tower but she was not pleased that you didn't write to her," said Jacque. "I blamed the violence but she…"

"I did write to her," Edward said. "She wrote back."

"I remember," said Elizabeth. "Jacque, why did you not tell me she was saddened by this?"

"I didn't think it important," said Jacque. "I should have said, really, I know you love a romance."

Elizabeth laughed as Edward was once again astounded by the Frenchman's confidence.

"One day I will remove his tongue, Edward, don't worry. But he's useful for now.

Jacque grinned and bowed his head.

"Wait," Edward said, shaking his head from the distraction. "She wrote to me, she knew I lived in Southwark…"

"When you hadn't told her," said Elizabeth.

"Right. And she said she was looking forward to seeing me." He closed his eyes and smiled. "Eoin dispatched my letter for me. Then he set me up and had me think I was arrested by Tower guards at the Cecil House while William waited upstairs. Marcus' man said Rutherford knew nothing of our arrest but the man who interrogated me brandished a coin and said he was neither from the Shadows nor the Wolves. He knew all about Amelie but didn't describe her and then he questioned me about my past. But I see now, he was neither a Shadow nor a Wolf. He had Eoin's coin and they knew of Amelie only by my letter."

"Why?" asked Jacque.

"Because Eoin is part of something bigger. Something outside of our organisation. He didn't set me up to have me killed. He set me up to question me. Put me under pressure using Amelie. He knew of the Axe. He told me some cock and bull story of his own hatred of the Axe. That was what I tested and it was in that test that he turned it back on me."

"So the Black Axe organisation is in the Shadows?"

"Well, Eoin is."

"But how?" asked Elizabeth.

"They were in Cecil's house."

"No," she said. "William has been away for weeks."

"Then they broke into his house. I am such a fool. And to trust Baxter who saved his own skin and left us to be taken as well. Not my best work," he said, looking at his queen apologetically.

"So these men," she said. "One of them has infiltrated my own ranks. Do they threaten me?"

"I do not think so," said Edward. "No, the questions. They were all about my past. What I chased, who chased them with me. Whether the Black Axe was the reason I was a traitor and who else followed, including Amelie. They could've killed me any time and they asked nothing of how to get to you. I thought nothing of it as I assumed I was believed a traitor, but that was not it. And Eoin had asked the same while we worked together. No. They wanted to know who I have told. That is why I have not yet been slain in the street."

"Are you that much of a target that knowledge of their intention to kill you is dangerous to them?"

"No, Your Majesty. There is something else. I've heard of both the preservation and the hunt. If I am the hunt then something else must be the preservation. There is a theory, that they fight against Catholics. That they orchestrated your father's reformation, got rid of your sister and even went as far as to set up a Protestant husband to the Catholic Princess of France."

"You believe they seek to preserve me?'

"The protestant crown and therefore, you."

"Whose theory is this?"

"Thomas Cobham's."

"Thomas Cobham," Elizabeth mused. "The man who fights for me and fights against me at the drop of a hat."

"And now you know why."

Elizabeth squinted.

"Yet we do not know why you are hunted."

"But to keep me alive in order to find out who I have told? The preservation must be more important than me."

"Until now," said Jacque. "They tried to kill you. Which means they have decided they know enough of who you have told. My guess is if they don't know you are still alive, they will now take out anyone you are close to."

"Amelie is safe," said the Queen. "Is there anyone else, without your Margeret?"

Edward turned to face her.

"Albert," he said. "I must go. Jacque?"

"About time," Jacque replied.

"Find out why!" Elizabeth called as the men ran through the door and left her alone once more.

Chapter Twenty Five

"Albert! Shit!" Edward shouted as he rounded the final corner on the approach to the home of his oldest friend and saw the door ajar. Readying his dagger, he glanced at Jacque and ran into the oak, slamming it open with his shoulder and baring his teeth ready to meet whatever faced him inside. Instead, he found the bloody remains of the old man and his woman, lying face up with terror fixed upon both of their expressions.

"No," Edward whispered, kneeling next to Albert and closing his eyes. He felt Jacque's hand on his shoulder and stood to face him.

"You can mourn later," Jacque said. "They are near. How do we find them?"

"We don't even know who they are," Edward replied, glancing again at Edward as his eyes burned.

"It was Eoin," said a weak voice from the floor.

"Marcus!" said Edward. "You are ok. What happened? Were you able to fight? Albert is dead."

"I know," Marcus replied sadly. "The door went in and the two of them were dead in seconds. Albert and Agnes were standing, seeing to me, when the door was forced. One man asked where you were, Albert said nothing and then a sword came through his back from the other side. A man I don't know cut Agnes' throat in the same moment and I was unable to stop them. With them dead already, there was no sense me showing out, here in the corner, out of sight. So I listened and watched and hoped you'd come."

"I understand," said Edward. "I am glad you are not harmed and it was a wise decision. A senseless death is worth nothing and now we know who." He glanced at Albert once more and squeezed his eyes shut.

"Who else?" he asked as he opened them again, still looking at his old friend.

"Eoin. And Baxter."

Edward's head snapped around.

"Baxter? he asked."

"Baxter. And others."

"So Baxter *is* with Eoin. He didn't just take the easy side. He is his man."

"He is more than that. They spoke of the Axe. Baxter is closer than Eoin is and has been all along. He said the Axe is safe while he is at Baxter's place."

Edward nodded.

"He's here," he said.

"He's here," Marcus replied. "And Baxter is as close as we have known anyone so far. Go. And kill them all."

Edward nodded and stood.

"You will be ok?"

"Of course," Marcus replied.

"I'll send help. Jacque?"

Jacque nodded and ground his jaw.

"Let's kill these *bâtards.*"

Edward nodded, looked at Albert, stowed his dagger

and led the way through the door and out into the dawn sunlight.

The two men jogged in silence through the stirring Southwark streets and the distant sound of the morning market coming to life. Edward kept his breath steady as he prepared himself for what he intended to be his final fight, whether he died with the Axe or finally freed himself from the burden that held him. Either way, he would avenge his family and his poor beloved sister. He glanced at Jacque occasionally and saw the Frenchman watching him throughout. A steady eye, always aware.

They rounded the corner to the front of Baxter's array of buildings and jogged straight up to the lone doorman outside.

"Wait, what?" the heavy man said, suddenly, seeing them approach and completely failing to respond.

Edward slammed his dagger into the man's throat, dropping him silently and rummaging through his cloak pockets to pull a key, a knife and a knuckle duster from within.

He tossed Jacque the blade and put the duster on his empty hand ready to open the door. He nodded once, turned the key and entered quietly, cutting the throat of a sleeping bouncer sitting in a chair before Jacque could even step inside. He held his hand over the gargling mouth until the large man fell silent and still, then dragged the body into a dark recess and turned back to Jacque.

Calm voices told them men sat inside the closed

room to the right hand side, and with a point from Jacque and a check up and down the corridor, they readied their weapons as Edward kicked open the door and ran into the warm room, connecting his knuckle duster to the first face that opposed him.

The owner of the crumpled face dropped to the floor and the remaining three men reacted in panic, jumping to grab their own weapons and scrambling as shouts sounded elsewhere in the building. Edward spotted and headbutted Baxter straight away, knocking him backwards into a wall next to the large, lit fireplace, then turned to an older man, pushing him against the wall with his elbow and readying his blade to stab. His heart beat faster as he looked into the face that struggled against him and recognised the features of the man who had commanded men to kill his former woman, Maggie. They had called him the Axe.

Their eyes met in surprise as it dawned on Edward who he finally held and Eoin's voice roared in protest as the man attempted to escape and impaled his stomach on the sharp blade held frozen and out of sight between them. Edward looked from the terrified eyes to his hand and back again as his dagger sunk up under the ribs of the older man and his expression glazed over.

"Not the Axe!" Eoin shouted from the floor as Jacque slowly pushed his own knife into his chest from above. He gurgled in the sudden silence of the room and turned his eyes to his killer, watching him in disbelief as he too slipped quietly away to nothing.

Jacque leapt up and shut the door, locking it as voices came close outside but went about their business, unaware of what had occurred or the presence of the men who came to kill them. He kicked the still form of the man with the crumpled face but he was out cold. Edward looked down at the Black Axe lying wide-eyed and bloody beneath him and felt emptiness throughout his body.

"And that's it?" he asked Jacque. "How can that be it? This man. This *myth*. Half of my life. I killed him but I have no answers."

"What about him?" said Jacque, looking at Baxter.

Edward looked around, remembering his troublesome acquaintance and finally understood the man's sway in the city.

"You," he said. "You've known all along."

Baxter sat folded against the wall and looked up at Edward, his neat beard caked in blood from his nose and his eyes harsh. He shrugged.

"I need answers, you bastard," Edward growled, hauling him to his feet and holding him against the wall with his blade at his throat."

"I am not scared of you, Rothwell." Baxter said. "I never have been. You were but a task for me. To see if you really were the one and to flush out what you knew. But now it's over. You are who you are and you will die along with everyone who has ever been close to you."

"No, Baxter. Your precious Black Axe is dead. It is over for *you*."

"Ha!" Baxter laughed. "Is it arrogance? Optimism? Just plain stupidity? You think this is about one man?"

"What then? What is it about?"

"All you need to know, my friend, is that you must

die. And now it is clear you will never know why. It will come, you cannot escape. We are in the very lifeblood of this continent and we are here, for you."

"I have survived this long."

"You have been allowed to! Yes, you have been oddly helpful in the preservation of our queen but you have been our pawn, *my* pawn, since the beginning. Do you think you became a Shadow by accident?"

"You're in the Shadows? Who?"

"Not a person, Eoin was lucky. But who do you think gave them the merchant? And who put you there the same night? It is some of my best work. I knew what you would do. You'd either die, spill your guts and tell them everything, or based on what that fool Marcus had told me about the leadership, impress them and be recruited. With which I would have endless opportunities to test you."

"So why wait? Why not kill me with each of those opportunities?"

"You surprised me a number of times. You surprised me but those surprises all gave you away. Westminster Abbey, your diversion to Spain, your actions in France. Oh yes, we know about France. But some things didn't add up and it was why I still had questions. You knew we protected the protestant crown. But how? And why? Have you always known?"

"I'll ask the questions."

"And why suspect your woman, Margeret?" Baxter added.

"Don't speak of her. You killed her. She did nothing."

"On the contrary, she crossed you. She recruited you, she tricked you, and she got you to open up."

"She stood by me."

"Eventually. Who can predict the twists and turns of a woman's heart?"

"It matters not!" Edward shouted. "I am not here for conversation. Why do you hunt me?"

Baxter shrugged.

"Your Axe is dead!" Edward growled again. "It is over!"

Baxter's indifference then gave way to laughter.

"That was not the Black Axe, Edward," he said, laughing further at Edward's expression. "Oh don't look so confused. Yes, the idiot Eoin said so. And yes, many thought so. But of course, the Axe is not quite that slack. *Black*, as he was known, was only a cover. Only a handful know who the real Black Axe is."

"Do you?"

"No."

"You do. Tell me!"

Something heavy hit the door, though no voices were heard.

"Tell me!" Edward roared again.

Baxter looker him in the eye.

"No," he said.

The door slammed again.

"Edward," said Jacque, readying his two blades. "We don't have long, the wood has cracked."

Baxter smiled.

"They're coming."

"And I'll kill them. But I'll torture you. Believe me, I've had practice."

"Yes, I've heard. The nauseous interrogator," Baxter sneered.

Edward grit his teeth in anger as Jacque suddenly shouted and dropped to the floor, holding his knee. Edward turned to see the man with the crumpled face scramble to the door and open it. Edward was too far away to stop him and as it unlocked, the door burst open, hitting the man in his face once more and knocking him backwards to be trampled by four large men who stormed into the room.

"Edward!" Jacque shouted, throwing a small but heavy vase from the floor, just missing Edward and striking Baxter's head.

Edward ducked the short-clubbed swing of the first man who entered and turned to see Baxter drop the knife he had pulled from his cloak to clutch his bleeding head. The man with the club dropped his tool and grabbed Edward, pushing him backwards to the floor. Edward held on as he fell, pulling the man down with him and pushing his foot up under the man's crotch. He felt the heat of the fireplace burn his ear as he fell close and watched in shock as the man he took with him pivoted up onto his hands and was pushed by Edward's foot to land deep in the hearth. Sparks hit Edward in a wash of burning ash and the room erupted into deadly screams as the man caught ablaze and leapt out of the fire in panic to fall again into the upholstered furniture of the room and set it alight.

Jacque had stabbed a man in the groin from underneath and had climbed to his feet to repeatedly stab another who clung to him in his own desperate bid to survive. Edward watched Baxter escape the room through the door as the last man assessed the mayhem around him, watched his burning friend fall silent as flames engulfed him, and left the room, dragging the man with the crumpled face to his feet to exit together.

Edward screamed for Baxter and jumped to his feet, batting away smoke and burning ash from his clothes and pulling Jacque from under the man who had died on top of him.

"Baxter," Edward said.

"Let him go, Edward. The fire. We need to go," Jacque pleaded.

Edward said nothing but hauled Jacque up and shouldered him through the door and into the hallway. He spotted what he assumed was Baxter's blood against the wall in the stairwell as he got Jacque to the front door and let go to nudge him outside.

"I have to get him," he said suddenly, from the doorway.

"No, no no," Jacque said desperately, holding his balance and limping painfully in a circle to face his friend who had disappeared back into the smoking building.

Edward heard Jacque call his name as he ducked low under the black smoke and climbed the stairs past the bloodstained walls and into a maze of rooms. He kicked the doors in and searched each one, returning to the landing each time to find the smoke thicker and eventually flames beginning to lick the walls around him.

He finally kicked in a door at the front of the house

and found Baxter in the room, clutching his head and bleeding eye, and gasping for breath from a window he had opened.

"Fuck off," the older man growled at Edward. "You'll get nothing from me and we will both die in this heat."

"I need to know, Robert. I need to know," Edward said, approaching him slowly.

Baxter circled away, around a bed that sat in the centre of the room and back towards the blazing hallway as Edward found himself next to the window.

"Please," he continued. "I just need to know. If we both die now, it matters not. Who is the Axe?"

"That, you will never know," Baxter grimaced.

"Then why? Why me?"

Baxter looked at him sincerely then for the first time, with confusion and pity in his eyes.

"You really don't know who you are? Who your parents are?"

"My parents are dead."

"They weren't your parents, Edward. They hid you on the orders of…"

He began to cough.

"Who?" Edward roared.

"The crown, of course. You do not know who you are?"

Edward blinked. He had no idea what it meant.

"Tell me," he pleaded as the floor began to groan.

Baxter looked at him and shook his head.

"No," he whispered, sadly.

And with his last word, the floor gave way with a loud crack and both Baxter and the bed fell into the roaring fire of the room they had fought in directly below.

Edward watched in horror and turned to grab the window sill as the floor disappeared beneath him and he was met with blistering heat and the brightness of flames that stretched the height of both floors.

He ignored the pain and pulled himself up to the window, stretching his arm out and pulling himself through.

"Edward!" Jacque called from beneath. "Edward drop! The floor is even!"

Edward turned himself to hang on to the window, then dropped to the floor, landing hard on his ankles and falling backwards into a heap. He rolled away from the heat of the crackling building and clambered away with Jacque.

"You have way too many lives, my friend," said Jacque.

Edward sighed and nodded.

"But my answers died with my last one," he said.

"Come on," Jacque said, quietly. "Your beautiful French lady awaits."

Edward looked at Jacque and smiled.

"It's not so bad," he said.

"No," Jacque replied. "It's not so bad at all. Life goes on, my friend."

"Thank you, for everything."

Peril of the Crown

Chapter Twenty Six

Spring 1583

"No no no!" Edward whispered to himself through gritted teeth as he slid behind a hedge and sat panting, pulling his legs in tight just in time to avoid being seen.

"He's here somewhere," a little voice said, followed by an even tinier giggle.

"Check the other side of that bush," said another, the accent unmistakable.

He closed his eyes and wiped the sweat from them with his sleeve. He heard footsteps approach on both sides and waited, looking left and right. He knew he couldn't get to his feet in time to get away and considered crawling under the sharp leaves when a face appeared at the side with a grin that touched his heart.

"Found you!" shouted the voice of his son, Albert, running into view and leaping onto him with a squeal. Edward laughed as his breath was taken from him by a knee to the chest, then jumped out of his skin as the face of his beloved daughter, Margaret, appeared over the bush with a giggle and was then swept away by the hands that held her.

Amelie then walked around the bush, laughing, and laid the tiny, wriggling form of their girl on top of the melee.

"I thought I'd made it away," Edward said, between laughs.

"Never!" said Albert, laying into him with punches only to wriggle to the floor himself as Edward tickled him back.

"They are *your* children, Edward. You cannot outrun them," Amelie said, joining them on the floor.

"Not with this hip," Edward chuckled, wincing at the old wound in his thigh.

"My Edward, the battered veteran."

Edward smiled.

"You know you love it," he said. "It has been a little while though. It has been nice to be here, especially through the winter. A couple of months wrapped up by the fire was exactly what we needed. And it has been nice to spend time with these two," he said as Albert sprinted away, chased by the little legs of Margaret. Being six years old to his sister's three, Albert loved to love and loved to tease his little sister, reminding Edward of his own childhood with his sister, Ella.

Amelie caught his rueful smile and held his hand.

"You've given a lot," she said. "I didn't think we would get you back last year."

"Oh I'd always get back to you. Just this time with a leather neck and a hobble."

Amelie smiled and punched him in the arm.

"You always said you were too fast to get stabbed again," she said, playfully.

"I would've been if they hadn't thrown acid at me!" Edward replied, grinning, before his face turned serious and he shuddered in thought for a moment. His hand went absently to the burnt ridges of his neck and throat. It still tingled when he touched it. He smiled again. "But without that, they never would've gotten a knife to my leg."

"Oil of Vitriol," Amelie said, reaching up and tracing the white scars of his neck. "I doubt I would've ever known of it without this."

"I'd only heard the name myself; never seen it. It's the sulphur in the acid that burns through. Yes, the priest hunt was quite a time. They were only defending themselves, I guess. Locked up and executed for praying and preaching to others. It's just God, after all, but it's the uproar it causes. Edmund Campion, the things he preached. After Paris, the thought of a stirring among the mob like that sends shivers down my spine. I'll be honest, I never want to see Paris again."

"I still fear for you every time you leave for work. Though I know you have no choice. I remember you saying, the Throckmorton brothers were in France, clearly up to something, and Campion had stirred a hornet's nest across the continent and was raising an underground force of the clergy right here."

"Not to mention William Parry causing headaches, though I have faith in him."

"Faith? The one you saw in prison? I don't trust him, Edward. That name, that *man,* will lead you somewhere from which you will not return, I can feel it."

"Well, he is safely in Poultry Prison where I left him over a year ago. Or at least he should be, I haven't heard otherwise. He broke into a house and robbed a man to whom he owed a debt of six hundred pounds."

"Yes he did. But worse, you believed him when he dropped in mentions of your Black Axe."

"He's not my Black Axe. Still, I find myself trusting him."

Amelie snorted.

"Don't pretend you don't love it," he said, rolling her backwards and pinning her to the floor. "Even the scars."

Her smile dropped and she looked between his lips and his eyes.

"I love that you don't chase your demons anymore," she said.

"I just love that they don't chase me," he replied. "But it did stop. Maybe that man I killed *was* the Axe. Baxter could've been saying anything. It kind of rubs on me that I don't know. I still have to look over my shoulder."

"I am afraid you do," said a strange male voice from behind Edward, making them jump.

"What are you doing?" Edward said as he turned and saw the familiar, yet aged face of the old mysterious shadow he only knew as eye-patch.

"Apologies, Rothwell," said eye-patch, his hair a full grey and a contrast to the darkness Edward remembered from ten years prior. "I bring news. How are you feeling?"

Edward blinked at the casual nature of the conversation after such an intrusion.

"Well, thank you. Recovering," he said. "The leg has been a pain, the face is simply unfortunate."

"I know the feeling," said eye-patch, grimly. "Still, hazard of the job."

"It is. What news?"

"You are needed in London. Her Majesty and the Lord Burghley require you to travel."

"Where to?"

"Paris."

Edward barked a laughed in disbelief.

"Please elaborate," he said.

"Cecil will brief you when you meet him with the queen. But we may have a rogue wanderer in our mix. Parry," he added, seeing the question in Edward's eye.

This time Amelie laughed.

"I knew it," she said.

Eye-patch smirked and fixed his one eye on Amelie who held his gaze through the falling tendrils of her red hair.

"She is vetted by the queen," Edward added. "She knows the outline of our business."

"A little dangerous, don't you think? To her, I mean?"

"I am right here, you may speak to me directly," she said, to which eye-patch nodded his assent.

"She accepts the risk," said Edward. "Still, here we are. Parry, however, is meant to be in prison."

"And he was. He was released six months ago and was sent to Paris with a mission. You were recovering so were left alone. Queen's orders. Either way, he has gone missing. Francis is in London and asked for you. The queen and Cecil agreed, and you have been summoned."

Edward nodded.

"William Parry, rogue in Paris. It couldn't be worse. Leave it with me, my friend. I will leave immediately."

"Very well." Eye patch nodded to them both in turn and set on his way.

"I am sorry," Edward said without taking his eyes of

the mysterious figure.

"Just be careful," Amelie replied, grasping his face. "And have fun."

Chapter Twenty Seven

Edward flashed his coin as he had so many times as he handed his horse over to a stable hand and crossed the short bridge into the outer street of London's Tower. He nodded to the guards and soldiers he had worked with through long, drawn out priest-hunts and interrogations and made his way into the White Tower, up the wooden staircase and into the queen's outer chambers.

"Afternoon, Ambrose," he said to the guard.

"Sir."

"Don't let him in!" a voice called from a window seat overlooking the river.

"If it isn't the old leper himself," Edward replied cheerfully, seeing his oldest remaining friend get up slowly and walk over to him. "How is your cock? Still full of the pox?"

"Worse, sadly, thanks to whatever I caught from your wife," replied Marcus with a grin that stretched the caterpillar-like scar across his face.

Edward laughed.

"Still look like a cart ran over your face though, eh?"

"You can talk, with that snail-trail across your chin."

The two embraced with a chuckle as the guard looked on, bemused.

"How are you feeling?" Marcus asked, more seriously.

"Better, thank you. The burn still itches and I doubt the leg will ever get feeling back but it gives me something to think about and I'm more than ready to get back to work. How is bodyguard duty?"

"The same. She lives a relaxed life at present and threats are unlikely to come in the form of wild solo attacks. Still, since my Mary and children died, I rarely leave the old girl's side."

"You're the best she can ask for."

"She treats me well and I live here now, or wherever she is staying. It's a good life. Got the word that Cecil needs you? He's been here since he sent for you. Where did they find you?"

"At home. I was in the garden with Amelie."

"Did he sneak up on you?"

"Old eye-patch? Yes."

"Ha, he does do it so well."

The men laughed as the main doors to the chamber opened and Edward found his petite queen looking up at him quizzically from under her mess of bright hair.

"Are you ready, Edward the Wolf?" she asked. "Or are you going to stand around here all day with my chambermaid?"

Marcus' chin almost hit the floor as Edward barked a harsh laugh and followed Elizabeth inside, looking over his shoulder to grin at his stricken friend.

"Good to see you up and about, young man," Cecil said as the queen turned abruptly in front of Edward and examined his scars.

"They suit you, you know," she said as her mouth froze in an open position and her eyes crossed slightly as she looked closely. "What you did for us in the hunts, Edward," she added, still tracing the scars with her eyes. "I am so grateful. I know you put yourself at risk. The sympathisers in those hidden villages. They are fierce and I heard you were often outnumbered by those who fought to hide and protect the hunted."

"It was hard," he replied. "But it needed to be done and I had some good men with me. I just didn't expect…you know. This."

"I know."

"Please sit, Edward," Cecil interjected, breaking the mood once more. Elizabeth rolled her eyes and indicated with her head for Edward to sit as she did the same.

"I hear you need me in Paris?" Edward asked.

"I know it isn't your favourite place," said Cecil. "Though we thought you might want to see your friend, Jacque. He works hard for Francis in the city over there and reports in via the current and soon to be ambassadors, Sir Henry Brooke and Sir Edward Stafford. Jacque and Stafford have lost track of William Parry and we need him found."

"Carry on."

"Parry went to France six months ago holding a letter from Francis to Brooke that said he was to reinfiltrate the most influential catholic conspirators and become privy to their plans."

"But?"

Cecil smiled.

"But, he disappeared and is allegedly now in Italy rubbing shoulders with the highest level that exists outside of the Vatican."

"And you feel he has turned?" asked Edward.

"It seems so, does it not? He may be following a trail but why not report in?"

"It isn't always that easy. Maybe he has been swept up and is playing his part? He may not have had a chance to update his handlers before they left and now he can't get word out if his letters could be read."

"I would suggest we usually train our agents well enough to find a way."

"You do, but not William Parry. He's been useful and you set him to work. He's no agent. I doubt he has many ideas at all. Who is Henry Brooke?"

"Sir Henry Brooke. Brother of Thomas and William Brooke, alias Cobham, as you know them."

"He's a Cobham?"

"Yes, though don't look so suspicious. All but one has been more than trustworthy to our monarchy."

"All of them now then, with Thomas' demise."

"Indeed. A shame. It saddens you?"

"He was useful. As is Parry."

Edward paused and noticed his queen watching him. He glanced at her sideways.

"Your Majesty?"

"What is your judgement of William Parry?" she asked. "You seem to trust him."

Edward frowned in thought.

"I do," he said. "I believe William Parry is a legitimate

servant to you, our country and our church. But I also believe he is another Thomas Cobham. I feel he has an agenda that makes it appear as though he is crossing the line, but he is working hard and probably risking his neck."

"Edward, he not only walks a fine line, he is an out and out criminal. Robbery, Edward. He is dishonest."

"I am not convinced," Edward replied. "The last time I saw him was in Poultry Prison over eighteen months ago after the robbery. He opened up and he went deep. He still speaks of his master, Herbert's, death. And still believes there was more to it. He believes people were after him and set him up to look like a traitor. He tried to help and was steered to Southwark where a local crime lord, who I believe was the deceased Robert Baxter, managed to swindle him into debt. Herbert then died and Parry was convinced he was killed by people who protected you, Your Majesty, based on the questions and insinuations about Herbert being involved with Norfolk and Mary. It was the white haired man who had asked all the questions and he thinks it was all a set up. A short time before the robbery, he heard the name Thomas Brooke continually popping up and came to England without informing you to speak to him. Thomas, he discovered, was indeed Thomas Cobham who had been charged with piracy the year before and left the country. Parry said he kept digging into places that Thomas had been and it got him noticed by men in cloaks."

"The shadows?" asked Cecil.

"Probably," said Edward. "If he was sniffing around Cobham's activities, then it would make sense."

"Either way, Cobham died a few years ago. Five years

ago now."

"Indeed, except Parry believes Thomas approached him in Paris in the year after his supposed death. Fifteen seventy nine. It makes little sense but he said it was Cobham who told him to write to you and apologise for betraying your trust."

Cecil frowned.

"But he came back and he did what he did," he said. "As your queen said, 'robbery, Edward'."

Edward shrugged.

"Maybe." Then he noticed his queen smile and continued. "He went for Hugh Hare at the Inner Temple as he was indebted to him and Cobham had told him that Baxter was involved with the Black Axe. Having been told by me, of course. So he went for Hare, broke into his lodgings and confronted him for answers. Hare fought Parry immediately when he mentioned the Black Axe and the noise must have alerted the guards. Parry was stopped and arrested by the white haired man who was the head of the cloaked men."

"Indeed. Richard Wellesley arrested Parry."

"Right. Well Parry had been convinced that man was involved in the conspiracy until he turned up and arrested him. He had been the man who questioned Herbert. Then he found out who the cloaked men were and therefore why Wellesley was questioning Herbert. He found out they were linked to you and now he knows they are not part of the conspiracy. Which we know, as they are the shadows. It is the dead end he finds himself in now which must inspire this rogue behaviour. He is chasing leads. Not against you, but for his own purposes. Much like I did."

"Why did you never tell us, Edward?" asked Elizabeth.

"He asked me not to. He felt you must have been after him all along and he knew he went too far. He felt it was better to take a conviction for robbery and then return to work than to reveal himself as rogue in any form, despite the innocent intentions."

"And do you trust him?"

"I do."

"Very well. In that case, we have a start and can take a steady approach. We need to know. If he is even remotely split in his loyalty, we cut him off now. Remove his privilege and banish him from returning on pain of death under my orders if he does. If it becomes so that he is a traitor, I ask you to execute him on the spot. On foreign soil where he belongs. And if he is loyal, sort him out. He needs to walk a straight path or he is finished."

Edward nodded.

"Good luck," she continued. "I know you will choose what is just."

Chapter Twenty Eight

Summer 1583

Edward shivered despite the heat of the sun as he gently wound his way through the streets that he had last seen bloodied and torn by the crazed mob. He steered his mount with his knees and watched the bubbling city around him, alive with excitement at the new summer and warmed to cheer by the long days and wealth that came with it.

The crowd thickened and grew in boisterousness as he approached the famous Les Halles Market for the first time since his teenage years. His spine had tingled when he first heard the name mentioned but Cecil had told him it was the surest of ways to find Henry Brooke. The man allegedly maintained a rigid routine in order to make himself findable by any that needed him. As a former bodyguard, Edward recoiled at the thought of presenting such an easy target for threats, yet he appreciated the sensible approach as he too sought the wisdom of the man who called Thomas Cobham brother.

The crowd parted to let him through and a number eyed him suspiciously as he disrupted the throng of business and banter that occupied their lives. Finally his eyes fell on The Market Tavern, as it was named. Henry would be present between one and two in the afternoon to sup ale and meet any that approached him, though Edward was assured by Francis Walsingham before he left that Henry was not well known to those that did not directly discuss the affairs of their country and he would not be busy. Edward had arrived in Paris just after midday and finally approached the tavern at the end of the second hour of the afternoon.

As he reined in to dismount, a proud looking man in his mid forties emerged from the dark doorway, an ale-induced sway to his stance but his eyes sharp as stone. He adjusted a tight and high ruff around his neck that seemed to hold up a neat chin strap beard topped by a sharp and well oiled moustache, and surveyed the space around him coolly. He was as described and Edward remained in his saddle.

"Sir Henry," he called. "Mister Brooke."

The din of the crowd drowned him out and he tutted in frustration, kicking in his heels a little as Henry turned away. "Cobham!" he shouted again as loud as he could, stopping the man in his tracks. Edward felt the assessment of his gaze as the man turned and set his eyes on him. "Sir Henry," Edward followed up. "I am here to see you, dispatched by the Lord High Treasurer."

Henry eyed him further.

"He sent you personally?" he asked.

"He did."

"And his name?"

"The Lord Burghley?" Edward asked as he drew up next to the man. "William Cecil, though that is hardly a difficult question." He watched Henry chew his lip for a moment and then subtly flashed his coin. "I am here on business," he said.

Henry let his chin lift in acknowledgement then glanced around briefly before looking back up.

"Your name?" he asked.

Edward raised his eyebrows and waited patiently.

"Very well," Henry conceded. "In private." He dipped his head back towards the doorway of The Market Tavern and smiled at Edward. "Come on," he said. "I'll be up on the balcony. Mine is a strong ale."

Edward smiled as the man strode inside and shook his head, jumping down from his saddle and tying the reins of his horse to a post with a clove hitch knot. He entered the noisy tavern and was surprised at the lack of revelry, the noise instead coming from a multitude of intense, semi-hushed conversations that he could only assume were related to the business that could not be discussed in the open forum of the market. He wove between the many occupied tables towards the landlord who stood, wiping out and stacking wooden cups.

"Two strong ales, please?" he said before catching himself in the frown of the barman. He held up two fingers and pointed to a cup of ale sitting half drained in front of a sleeping man.

"Cochon anglais ignorant," he said, turning his back and filling two cups from a jug. "Deux deniers," he said, smugly.

Edward smirked at the extortionate price, equal to a full days wages for a labourer or indeed a market worker in Les Halles. He reached into the pocket in his cloak and dropped five minted deniers into the hand of the landlord.

"You're welcome," he said, turning without

acknowledging the man's surprise.

He made his way up a rickety, spiral staircase and found Thomas Cobham's younger brother watching him from a table on the outdoor area of the balcony overlooking the busy market.

"Well that shut him up," he said. "Not the friendliest but he serves good ale."

"It better be," Edward said, sitting down and placing a cup in front of the nobleman. "Edward Rothwell," he said, meeting the unasked question of his host.

Henry raised his eyebrows and smiled.

"Well I didn't expect this," he said. "Your reputation precedes you; from many sources."

"How so?"

"Well, Francis speaks fondly of you, as does William Cecil. I hear the queen favours you also. Though I am most intrigued by the account of another."

"Thomas?"

"Thomas," Henry replied.

"I was sorry to hear of his passing."

Henry paused though his expression said little. Edward silently applauded the man's poise. He was well trained.

"So what brings you here?" Henry said.

"William Parry. I hear he is missing?"

"He appears to be, yes. What do they think back in London? Do they feel he has gone rogue?"

"They do, yes. I have been sent to find him."

"And do you agree with them?"

Edward watched Henry for a moment as they judged

each other carefully.

"No, I don't. I think he is following a trail."

"To?"

"To what your brother sought for many years."

"Which, I believe, is the same as yours."

"Once," Edward replied. "Mine came to an unanswered conclusion. William now chases ghosts, I feel. What once was, doesn't seem to be so any longer."

"And do you honestly believe that?"

"I think I have to."

Henry watched his cup for a moment.

"And how would you feel if I told you that was, in fact, not the case?" he asked, without looking up.

Edward shifted in his seat.

"I would be intrigued," he said. "Do you know something I don't?"

Henry nodded. He leaned in close before something or someone in the market caught his eye. Edward followed his gaze and saw a red haired man watching them from the crowd. He indicated that he would join them with his hand and then began to weave towards the door to the tavern.

"That is Sir Edward Stafford," said Henry. "He will be my replacement here as ambassador when I leave as I have been recalled to England but Francis doesn't trust him. He has a gambling habit and maintains an unhealthily friendly relationship with some less desirable powers here in France. He has Cecil's protection, however, and believes he is untouchable as his mother knew Elizabeth well and his wife, Katherine, is one of Elizabeth's best friends."

"He is Katherine's husband? I have met her."

"He is. She, however, also walks a fine line and is close with Catherine de' Medici here in Paris. A woman who remains at the height of power with her third son to be on the throne still heavily influenced by her whim." Henry looked over the balcony and watched Stafford near the door. "I must tell you quickly before he reaches us. He will purchase a drink on his way up so we have a moment. William Parry came to me with a letter from London requesting he re-infiltrate the English Catholics who are thought to conspire here. Though when I pushed him of his time in prison to gauge my own levels of trust, he told me of Herbert and of his suspicions. And thus I told him of my brother. Edward, Thomas is alive. He is in Milan where he believes the men in this mystical organisation seek to remove the Pope and sabotage the catholic church. He believes they intercept communications between The Vatican and Madrid and do so in order to disrupt catholic plans to attack our queen. William's information would be news to him and I care for my brother a great deal. So I instructed William to integrate with the English Catholics here and then bought him time to travel to Milan to see Thomas. He should return in good time, if not imminently, if all is well."

Edward blew through his cheeks.

"Thank you for telling me," he said.

"Staying for a few extra I see, Henry," said Stafford as he walked out onto the balcony and pulled over a stool to join them. "Hello, Henry's companion," he added as his eyes took in Edward.

"Afternoon. Edward Rothwell," Edward replied, holding out his hand.

Stafford's eyes lit up in a way Edward couldn't decipher.

"Edward Rothwell," he said. "Well I never."

Edward looked Stafford over and couldn't help thinking he agreed with Francis. The man was younger, maybe thirty at most, and kept a neat red beard to match his hair. The air of arrogance that emanated from him matched what Edward had been told and he decided he was the last person he would feel comfortable confiding in.

"Well, Rothwell is no stranger to secrets, so I assume I can speak openly," Stafford continued. "The Spanish ambassador would like to meet you again before you leave, Henry. To ensure there is nothing left unsaid before you rejoin the politics back home."

"What could possibly be left unsaid?" asked Henry. "We have had a number of conversations and our countries do not align but we all wish for a stable relationship."

"He feels you do not respect him or his position here in Paris."

"Well, my two well-meaning visits to Madrid were met with ignorance from all including the ambassador and he has been no better here. He also opposed Francis and I in our representation of the League of Amity in place of Medici's suggestion of a marriage of her youngest son to Elizabeth and quite frankly, I do not like the man. In fact, Stafford, I have very little idea as to why you *do* enjoy his company so much."

Stafford pressed his lips together then turned to Edward.

"For what do we owe the pleasure, Rothwell?" he

said, ignoring Henry's glare.

"I am here to find William Parry," said Edward. "Cecil and the queen are concerned for his loyalty and seek both his whereabouts and his justification."

"Yes, Parry. He has indeed disappeared. He had tasks given under our friend Henry here and then made his way south without a word. We only believe he is in Italy as my employee, Jacque, overheard some of Parry's supposed targets, or dare we say associates, talking about it."

"Really? Who? And what did they say?"

"That he had gone to Italy."

"Where is Jacque now?"

"Working, I presume. How is Richard Wellesley?"

"Wellesley?" frowned Edward. "He is well, why do you ask?"

"He is a friend, as is William Cecil, who I assume you have met." Stafford looked out over the crowded market and laughed at a scuffle in the distance among the masses. "This city, always a treat," he said. "Have you been back since the massacre? It is as good as forgotten here now."

"What makes you think I was here during the massacre?"

"Oh, Jacque mentioned it when I got here."

"I see," Edward replied. "No, I haven't been back. I don't have fond memories of that visit. It was a hard time."

"It was. I lost some close friends around that time also. In England, though. Attacked in their home. It was hard to take."

Edward nodded, unsure of how to interpret the man.

"I am sorry for your loss. Is there anything else I

should be aware of while I am here in Paris?"

Stafford shrugged.

"Only the Throckmortons," said Henry, barely restraining his disdain. "Sir Francis Throckmorton," he continued, seeing Edward's question at the name. "He and his brother Thomas arrived here some time ago. They are from a known catholic family; their father, in fact, presided as senior judge over Queen Mary's will. Their arrival was noted but not concerning, and their meeting with our well known catholic exiles Charles Paget and Thomas Morgan was even to be expected. But then they met the Spanish ambassador also," he said, eyeing Stafford, who seemed to ignore him. "Their activities have been unusual since and there have been correspondence sent between here and London in their hand, though we do not know who to. I suspect it may have been to the Spanish ambassador in London, Bernardino de Mendoza, though I hope it was not, of course. We are keeping an eye on them but nothing has turned up just yet."

Edward nodded his thanks again, then turned to Stafford, who was looking out at the market once more.

"Thank you, both of you," he said. "I may not see you again before I leave the city, so Sir Edward, good luck in your work here; and Sir Henry, have safe travels back to London when you depart."

"You too," said Henry, gripping his hand firmly. "Good luck."

Edward stood, nodding his thanks and left the men behind as he began his next adventure, though where to begin, he had no idea.

Chapter Twenty Nine

Edward traced back his escape path from the city ten years earlier, seeing both the repairs and the scars of the damage he had witnessed. Not for the first time that day, he recalled the expression of the helpless woman, pushed from her upstairs window and brutally abused by marauders on the street below before Edward had fired the shot that betrayed Jacque and his position. Her expression had been a daily vision for many years following the ordeal and returning to the scene only resurrected the flashbacks all the more vividly.

He walked through the gardens of the Tuileries Palace towards the river and looked into the distance at the white house he had stayed in with Francis Walsingham before the massacre. Clean and non-descript, it still had an air of mystery about it as it gazed over the green expanse of the gardens, though to all who saw it, Edward knew, it was but a normal house with a view.

He decided to make the Latin Quarter his first port of call, as it had once been before, and he smiled as he met the foot of the bridge and his eyes fell across his friend.

Jacque casually browsed the wares of one of the street vendors at the apex of the bridge while keeping watch on a small group of men on the far side. He managed to hold animated conversations without losing sight of the men and as they moved a little further around a corner, Jacque's conversation moved seamlessly to the next vendor without a hiccup. He never lost sight of them, Edward saw, yet never once appeared out of place or preoccupied.

Edward slowly slipped up the side of the bridge behind him and too began to browse the pottery of a street seller.

"Maybe the limp slows you down, my English oaf," said Jacque without turning or losing sight of his target.

Edward chuckled quietly.

"You're good, I'll give you that."

"It's been a long time, my friend." Jacque said, indicating with his head slightly and leading Edward between two covered stalls, where he could speak out of the hearing of those on the bridge yet appear to stand alone. He offered his hand behind him without breaking focus and Edward shook it. "It's so good to see you."

"You too," Edward replied. "Who are you on?"

"Throckmorton. Francis, that is. There with the long hair. He's been here for some time and we have been monitoring him but when Henry heard he'd met the Spanish Ambassador, we got closer. I do believe there is something afoot. An Oxford law alumni, Throckmorton is a member of the Inner Temple and it appears it was he who helped Campion and his peers spread their Jesuit propaganda throughout your country. That same year, he left England and began to meet known English Catholics across France and Spain, eventually arriving here and whispering with these two.

"The older two there you must recognise?"

"Thomas Morgan and Charles Paget."

"Indeed. Morgan in the hat and Paget with the moustache. Both are still agents of Mary Stuart. Paget flicks between Paris and Rouen while Morgan has been here since he left the tower and exiled himself. As you know, they have done Mary's bidding since before the plot to marry her to Thomas Howard."

"And here they are with Throckmorton. Who is the fourth? On his own to the side?"

"Throckmorton's brother. Another Thomas, known as Tommy. He tends to stay back and observe their surroundings. He has also met William Parry a number of times, though very briefly."

"Parry? That is why I am here. I hear he has left the city and I am due to leave for Italy as soon as possible."

"Save your energy, my friend. Parry is here in Paris."

"He's back?"

"He is, and he is due at this meeting. In fact..." Jacque tailed off and indicated with a nod. Edward's eyes followed along the river bank and he saw the fresh face and wispy dark beard of William Parry approaching the group.

Tommy approached Parry as he neared him, only to be ignored as Parry stepped past both him and his brother and shook hands with Morgan and Paget. Francis Throckmorton looked on with a frown as Parry appeared to commandeer the conversation and then end it, taking something from Morgan, which he stowed in his pocket. He was the first to leave and the others dispersed immediately after.

The Throckmorton brothers were left standing and speaking to each other as Morgan and Paget disappeared into the Latin Quarter and Parry began to cross the bridge.

"What are your plans?" Edward asked, slipping backwards out of sight while watching Parry.

"My brief is Throckmorton, not Tommy or the others, so I will watch him from here until he returns home and then I will move back to base."

"Where is your base now?"

"The white house, of course."

"Still?" Edward beamed. "Wow."

Jacque nodded.

"Right, I will intercept Parry once he is off the bridge and I will see you at the white house this evening. Does anyone else reside?"

"Just the housekeeper. Henry lives elsewhere and thankfully Stafford seems to have no interest."

"Just as well," Edward chuckled, grabbing Jacque on the shoulder and falling in behind Parry as he bounced down the slope of the bridge to the north eastern side of the Seine and turned left along the bank away from the gardens.

"What are you doing here?" Parry asked after a while from around a corner, making Edward smile. "Are you losing your touch?" he added, smugly. "I spotted you three times, you know."

"Did you?" Edward replied, feigning shock. "Oh. I guess you must've seen me behind you as you stood looking in the apothecary window?" he said, making Parry frown.

"Or as you left the overhung alleyway and watched me from your hiding place behind the old cart? Or, I guess, as you stopped to offer an empty hand to the confused beggar while looking over your shoulder at that interesting brickwork?"

Parry opened his mouth to speak and then closed it again, stumped.

"It is good to see you exercising your tradecraft," Edward added. "You saw me when you were meant to see me and you led me the right way to clean your route. But your observations were a little obvious."

Parry smiled.

"Very well, I will practise," he said. "So, what *are* you doing here?"

"I came to find you, William. Or at least, I was sent to. Cecil and the queen are a little unsure of your intentions, disappearing as you did without a word. And I must say, even with the candid briefing I received from Henry Brooke, your relationship with Morgan and Paget appears to be stronger than expected. Talk to me, William, for London isn't happy."

Parry closed his eyes.

"They're going to kill me one day, Edward, I know it. Elizabeth just doesn't trust me. I don't know what I can do to ease her mind."

"Perhaps don't disappear to rub shoulders with the opposition."

"I am a spy, Edward," Parry whispered, harshly, glancing around. "I went to Milan and proved I am a good, faithful Catholic."

"Yes, without telling anyone or keeping in touch with your handlers."

"Henry knew. Why he didn't cover me, I don't know."

"Because Stafford reported back to London without his knowledge, that's why."

"There is something about that man," said Parry, his eyes narrowing. "Yet he seems to stay in favour with the queen and her closest advisors. Maybe I need to do something impressive to gain her trust."

"Just stick to your briefing for now, William," said Edward. "All will be well. I will speak for you. Now tell me of Milan. Tell me of Thomas."

Parry glanced sideways at Edward before looking away and slowly releasing a breath.

"Thomas managed to escape the country after his charge for piracy, knowing his last chance at pardon had come and gone. He fled to Flanders where he managed to meet William the Silent, William of Orange, who was yet to be declared an outlaw. There he learnt of such men watching communications between Rome and Madrid, who William did not know but had used to his advantage. Thomas received sponsorship to travel to Italy and report back on what he found. Though, of course, he had his own agenda."

"And what has he found?"

"Not a great deal, though he discovered that King Charles here had been talked into the royal wedding of his sister by a dark skinned man with an English accent from Rome via a young, red haired man to whom Charles was compelled to listen. Thomas sent me to Rome to find out who that may have been."

"It has been ten years."

"It has. Though alas, I could not find safe passage as I was stopped at every turn by a force I could not identify. In the meantime, I have returned to operate from here and see what comes to light. And in doing so, I have become closer with our catholic friends, through whom I plan to show Elizabeth just what I am made of."

"Are they planning something?"

"They weren't. But I planted a seed and now they are moving. It will return me to a favourable standing."

"Not through agent provocateur, it won't, William. Believe me, I have tried such things in the past."

"I have no choice. I must see who responds, to further our less obvious inquiry, and I will cover it as a successful investigation."

"One foot wrong and they will kill you. I am under orders to do the same, if I feel you are not faithful."

William turned to Edward, his mouth open as though his words were stolen from him.

"But you don't plan to?" he managed to utter.

"If I do not and you are implicated in a plot that you cannot control, what will happen to me? We will both be for the gallows."

"Edward," Parry pleaded. "You must not. You know I am loyal. You *know* it. And you know why I am doing this. What your reasons were, I do not know, but mine are clear and are not simple enough to turn away from."

"The Black Axe once hunted me relentlessly. Why I am still alive, I have no idea, but I discovered things worth living for. I understand your reasons but it is not a simple task. If you do this, you do it right. You must not be implicated, do you understand?"

Parry nodded.

"You know enough to help cover it. Smooth out rough edges. Make it plausible. For our cause."

Edward shook his head and laughed.

"Our cause? You are beginning to sound like them," he said.

"Here," said Parry, passing Edward a stamp. "It is Morgan's seal. He passed it to me so that I could legitimise my communications with the catholic elite. Use it instead. If you need to, cover us with communications from Morgan. Make me out to be innocent. You know you can."

Edward twisted his mouth in thought.

"Tell me of Throckmorton," he said, accepting the plan.

"He is in the way," Parry sneered. "He thinks he is a conspirator because of his family's connection to Mary but he cannot operate at our level. Paget mocks him."

Edward raised his eyebrows.

"That could make him dangerous."

"He is not," Parry laughed.

"Which is exactly why he could be. Your disdain could make him reckless. What does he plan?"

"It is not completely clear, though I believe he plans to facilitate a Spanish backed invasion of England, led by the Duke of Guise, dethrone Elizabeth and replace her with Mary, who will marry Guise."

"Sounds original," said Edward.

"Like I said, Throckmorton is an amateur. All the ideas."

"Yet he has managed to speak with the Spanish Ambassador and has travelled across France and Spain. Does he speak to anyone else in the French royal house?"

"I don't know, though he boasts that Mary trusts him with her letters and that he has established the delivery route through the French to Morgan and the Spanish Ambassador."

"He must have French contacts in England. Perhaps in the embassy. We need to take him seriously, William."

"Well, he plans to leave for England tonight."

"Right," said Edward. "Then I shall join him. I have fulfilled my mission here in Paris anyway. If I back you, Parry, do not let me down. Or I will kill you myself. Understand?"

Parry nodded.

"And do us both a favour; check in with Henry Brooke and Stafford. Farewell and good luck," Edward added, turning on his heels and walking away.

He turned three bends before he looked both ways and caught a glimpse of red hair in his peripheral vision. He looked in the distance and saw Stafford, busying himself with his waistcoat. Edward nodded and approached the man who seemed to notice him with surprise.

"Rothwell," Stafford said. "Twice in one day. What are your plans and where are you lodging until you leave? I can show you the better of the local inns, if you like?"

"I'll be leaving tonight, I'm afraid."

"The road to Italy is long, my friend. You should rest. Maybe take a day or two?"

"Why?"

"I don't know, maybe stop making us all appear lethargic with your eagerness. Unless you know where Parry is, a day or two won't make any difference."

"Parry is here," Edward replied. "I have just left him. He is working legitimately and will check in soon."

"You are fast. Did he find anything in Italy?"

"Nothing of note, though he has strengthened his appearance as a good and willing catholic."

"Maybe it is a little too close to home for him if he finds it so easy."

"He is true to his word. Still, I am sure not all Catholics are bad."

Stafford narrowed his eyes.

"Of course," he said. "Even so, if he is here, why leave so soon?"

Edward watched the man, for once unsure of his own judgement, though he knew appearances were important if he were to allow Parry's intentions to cross a murky line once more.

"Throckmorton is heading back to England tonight. I will see Jacque, obtain the details of his whereabouts and then follow on behind him."

"Good man. I will report to Wellesley and Cecil."

"No need. I will do so, though to Walsingham in the first instance."

"Yes," Stafford replied, absently. "Walsingham is best."

Chapter Thirty

September 1583

Francis Throckmorton's thighs ached, barely clinging on to his saddle as his body rocked in hysterics. Tommy, his brother, too was in pieces at the story of the Frenchman they had met on their journey. A man who seemed to be able to keep entire rooms in fits of laughter.

"And she actually asked you if *you* were ready?" he asked, receiving a nod from the Frenchman, Claude. "You truly are a master, my friend. And what about you, Robert?" he asked the Englishman who travelled with Claude. "Do you command the ladies as well as this one?"

"Alas, no," said Robert. "But then, I have never needed to. Claude leaves me the scraps and they're good enough for me."

Throckmorton laughed.

"Well I must say," he uttered, "This has been one of the most eventful journeys of my life. Thank you for your unstoppable comedy. This is where our paths separate, as we must head west past Windsor, and London lies straight ahead."

"We should keep in touch," said Robert.

"I am afraid I cannot. I have much work to do and it will take all of my concentration. When it is done, and the world changes, I will once again be free to enjoy myself."

"I have the same pressures," said Claude. "Last time I was placed in the French Embassy in London, my life was not my own. I do not look forward to it. Not with the way London treats the French. At least, the real French. I wish the King's Mother would pull her weight once and for all."

Throckmorton smiled.

"I too have business with the French Embassy. I can find you there?"

"Of course."

"Very well, we shall speak again. Farewell, my friends."

"Farewell," said Claude.

Francis and Thomas Throckmorton steered their horses away quietly and walked into the distance, suddenly laughing again at something Claude had said.

Claude watched fondly and chuckled to himself as he heard one of his punchlines repeated in the distance. He turned to Robert.

"Well, that's the Throckmortons sorted. We will bump into them again, I am sure," he said.

Edward chuckled.

"You never fail to amaze me, *Claude.* They were as much a closed book as I have ever seen. I was just going to tail them but how you got in there, it was inspiring."

"Thank you, my friend," said Jacque. "It was good to work with you again. So what now?"

"Now? You keep that line going with Throckmorton and I will brief Walsingham on what we have so far."

Jacque nodded and the two continued on their

journey towards London.

"Was that true?" asked Edward. "About the maid and the bull?"

Jacque laughed.

"No, my friend. Of course, it is true that I found her there with her head stuck between the rails. But it wasn't a cow that put her there."

Edward chuckled and shook his head.

"It wouldn't have stopped you if it had been."

Chapter Thirty One

November 1583

Edward covered his mouth in haste as the grease from a mouthful of lamb spilt over his lips and into his short beard. He'd allowed the thick hair to grow for the first time in his life and wondered how the likes of Cecil got by, eating anything with a face full of fluff. He wiped his chin clean with his rough sleeve and looked down at the glistening lamb-filled bread pouch in his hands, smiling and taking another huge bite. He'd kept up surveillance on Francis Throckmorton and anyone Jacque had pointed out to him from the embassy, and with the curious envy of the nobility, he found it easier to blend into the streets than to appear as an equal.

"Look at the state of you," said Jacque, approaching him from the side.

Edward smiled and offered a bite of his snack. Jacque laughed and declined.

"What's happening?" Edward asked.

"Walsingham is back. He's at the Newgate Office. Wants an update."

Edward nodded.

"About time. How was Scotland?"

"No idea but he's in a bad mood." Jacque laughed at

Edward's expression. "Good luck, my friend."

He tapped Edward on the shoulder and turned to move back into the crowd. Edward watched him go then rested his head against the wall behind him before shrugging and digging into his bread bundle once more.

"Rothwell, come in and sit down," said Walsingham from his seat behind the large familiar desk. "Wellesley is away and let me use his office."

"How are you, Francis? I trust your trip north was worthy?"

"The trip was fine; it's the state of the nation up there that vexes me. The Spanish Ambassador, de Mendoza, has a whole network of them ready to invade. All I can say is thank god they don't have the physical ability to do so. And if Forster hadn't found the letters on that messenger, we wouldn't even know. There are renegade priests running wild just south of the border and a Jesuit mission is trying to convince King James to invade as well. What's happening here? I hear you weren't away for long?"

"Not long, no. Jacque picked up Throckmorton's trail in Paris after he and his brother had toured most of Western Europe, rubbing shoulders with catholic nobility far and wide. We came back on the same ship as them, Jacque made friends, as he does, and we rode in from Dover with them. They know Jacque is in the French Embassy now while I keep an eye on leads he picks up."

"Get much?" Walsingham asked, curtly.

"A little. Several letters to Morgan in Paris."

"Replies?"

"On those we let through, simple acknowledgement. On those with more risk, I have been replying instead."

"Morgan is meticulous. How did you feign his letters?"

Edward felt the seal in his pocket but, remembering Parry's words, decided to leave it in there.

"We lifted the seal from one of his letters and did our best to replicate it. It's crude but the Throckmorton brothers seem not to have noticed."

"Very well," Walsingham replied. "We are on track then. And Parry?"

"He was back in Paris when I arrived. He was with Throckmorton and Morgan."

Walsingham's eyes narrowed.

"I bet he was. Tell me, did you question him?"

"I did."

"No, Edward. Did you push him? He's up to something, he's a meddling fool."

"I did, Francis. He's straight. He is working hard to legitimise his catholic connections. Morgan certainly trusts him."

Walsingham chewed his lip for a moment before nodding decisively.

"Right, well he's one of two pains in my arse at present. What happened with Somerville?"

"Somerville? I haven't heard of him."

"He was picked up on the road from Warwickshire, waving a pistol and demanding the queen's head be put on a post."

"Another one? They are coming in thick and fast."

"I know. It concerns me greatly, Edward. We can trust nobody."

Edward watched Walsingham, who merely frowned back intensively.

"Who did he threaten, soldiers?" Edward asked.

"No, but uniformed officials."

"Are you suggesting he's a credible threat? He sounds slightly off-centre to me. Perhaps his mind is not quite up to scratch?"

"I care not. He's a danger and so is his family. He is married to Throckmorton's cousin and the Catesby and Tresham children will be a danger in the future, I am sure. He is even related to some upstart aspiring writer who romanticises such drama. Shakespeare or something. He will amount to nothing."

"So what do you need?"

"Get into him, Edward. Pull him apart and find out who he works for and his motivations. And stop pussyfooting around Throckmorton. This is in the family and we need the entire family closed down before it gets out of control. Somerville, Throckmorton, Somerville's father in law, Edward Arden, or anyone else we need to cut out. Get something real, get them in and get something tangible on the Spanish Ambassador so we can expel him as well. Do not delay."

"Anything else, Sir?"

Walsingham looked at Edward, one eyebrow raised.

"Yes, have a shave and clean yourself up. Now get out."

Chapter Thirty Two

"It was like he was someone else. The anger radiated from him like heat."

"Do you think he is just under pressure?" Marcus asked, glancing at Edward.

"Perhaps," Edward replied. "Whatever happened in Scotland really riled him. It may be paranoia. He doesn't trust anyone, it seems, least of all me. He was furious."

Marcus blew through his lips as they marched down the familiar corridor towards the less prestigious holding cells in the Tower.

"We better get this right then," he said. "Guard?"

The tower guard standing nearby nodded his head and opened the cell door where they stood without a word. Edward entered first and took in the sight of the unkempt man before him.

"Don't hurt me," the man said, quietly, not looking up.

"John Somerville?" asked Edward.

The young man in his twenties finally glanced at Edward, his eyes alive despite the fear shown in his body.

"I am Somerville," he said.

"Do you know why you are here?"

"The men, they took me, but I must not delay. She

must be killed."

"Who must?"

The man laughed.

"If I don't do it, they will. They tell me I must, they hurt me."

Edward glanced at Marcus and knelt down next to Somerville.

"Tell me more, John."

Somerville laughed.

"What is there to tell?" He laughed wildly, making Edward jump, and then stopped abruptly, squeezing the skin of his thighs in his fist until it turned purple. "Leave me alone."

"I am afraid I cannot do that, John."

"Not you!" He grimaced again. "No, no, no. I will, I will. Let me see her, please," he said, looking up. "Let me see her."

"Who do you want to see?"

"The queen, of course. Let me see the queen." He closed his eyes again. "I am asking, be quiet." Then he opened his eyes once more and looked closely at Edward. "I need to see her."

"John, do you know why you are here?"

Somerville laughed again, high pitched and erratic.

"Have I done it already?" he asked, his eyes bright. "Is she dead?"

"The queen?"

Somerville nodded hungrily.

Edward shook his head.

"No, John. She is safe."

Somerville squeezed his eyes shut again and grabbed them with his hands, falling back onto the floor where he sat, his nails digging into his eyelids and drawing blood

"Calm, John. Are you ok? What is wrong?"

Somerville whispered to himself, too quiet for Edward to hear. Edward looked at Marcus, who shrugged and shook his head.

Edward tapped the young man on his shoulder, making him freeze and open his eyes.

"Don't hurt me," he said.

"I am not going to hurt you," said Edward.

Somerville's gaze settled on Edward as though seeing him for the first time.

"Don't let them hurt me," he said, before closing his eyes again. "Go away, go away."

Edward stood back and watched the broken man on the floor.

"John, why do you want to kill the queen?"

"I must kill her," Somerville replied. "They say she must die, I've heard them speaking. He speaks to my wife, Margaret. He speaks to me. He hurt me. They hurt me. Do it, Johnny, do it, Johnny. You are one of us, Johnny."

"Who does?"

"My…" he shook his head and whimpered then opened his eyes and sat up, looking at Edward. He shook his arms, writhing on the floor, pulling at his clothes. He held his breath, shaking with effort until his face was red and he exhaled with a cry. "Kill me," he said, reaching for Edward's ankle. "Kill me, please!"

Edward stood back and pulled Marcus back out of

the door, looking into the cell.

"Guard," he said. "Take his clothes, take them all right now and watch him constantly. Do not close this door. I want you watching him permanently. Handover to the next guard when your shift is done. Now!"

The guard shook from his reverie and ran into the room, pulling off Somerville's clothes as the young man screamed on the floor.

"What are you doing, Edward?" asked Marcus.

"He is broken and lost and when he gained control, he begged for death. I don't want him to hurt himself, he could strangle himself with his clothes. Is the queen in? Is Cecil here?"

"She is in her sitting room with Cecil and Walsingham," said Marcus, looking back as the guard withdrew, holding a pile of dirty clothes and leaving the naked man on the stone floor inside.

"Do as I said," Edward remarked. "If anyone questions it, send them to me, do you know who I am?"

The guard nodded.

"Good. If he tries to hurt himself, call for help and hold him still to keep him safe. I will sort this out."

"Please allow us to see the queen," Edward said to the guard as he approached the queen's chambers.

"Nature of business, please?"

"My business, now open the door," said Marcus.

The guard knocked on the oak once and opened it to announce Edward's arrival. Edward walked into the room and bowed deeply with Marcus before rising to face his queen. Walsingham frowned, looking between them.

"What do you want, Rothwell?" he asked, making the queen tut.

"To discuss Somerville, sir, Your Majesty," Edward replied to them both.

"You have racked him already? What did he say?"

"I have not, and I do not believe we should."

Cecil raised his eyebrows as Walsingham sighed and stood.

"Elaborate," Walsingham pushed, impatiently.

"His mind is broken. He may be a danger but he is no conspirator."

Walsingham barked a laugh.

"Listen to you," he said. "Have you gone soft? Or is he another William Parry that you seem to protect.?"

"Francis, listen to me."

"No you listen, Edward. This man attacked official soldiers and outwardly admitted his intention to harm the queen. Rack him so that we can find those he conspires with."

"It is not the case. Why would he attack soldiers if he intended to get to the queen? He does not conspire. I will speak to him again, but he needs help."

"Help?"

"Help to be calm. Unless he calms, he will not speak. He *cannot* speak. I need to reason with him, allow him to look forward to a safe release, where we can protect him."

"Preposterous! He is in prison for high treason, Rothwell!"

Edward glanced at Cecil and the queen.

"Do not look to them for help," said Walsingham.

"Francis, enough," said Elizabeth calmly.

"He is not of sound mind, Your Majesty," said Edward.

"And what do you propose we do, Edward," she said.

"He should not be tortured. It wouldn't be just."

"He must be tried and executed," said Walsingham.

Edward sighed.

"If he must," he said. "But not tortured, and he mustn't be tried until he is calm and has been spoken to."

"Do you truly believe he is unwell?" asked Elizabeth.

"I do," said Edward.

The queen looked at Marcus and he nodded.

"Very well," she said. "Francis, you will leave him untouched in his cell for now."

Walsingham opened his mouth to speak as a knock on the door rang out once more and it was opened by the guard.

"Your Majesty, your agent," he said.

Jacque walked into the room and bowed before nodding to Edward and addressing Walsingham.

"Well?" asked Walsingham.

"Throckmorton has been in to see the French Ambassador, Castelnau."

"And?"

"And the nature of the discussion is unknown but he carried letters from Mary Stuart and delivered them to the Ambassador."

"Your source?"

"Giordano Bruno in the French Embassy. He has been feeding me information. We have also intercepted letters from Throckmorton to the Spanish Ambassador, Mendoza."

"That will do! Cecil, please mobilise your Shadows to bring in Throckmorton and his brother immediately. Jacque, Rothwell, with me. We move now."

"Leave Edward here please, Francis," said Elizabeth. "He will join you shortly."

Walsingham's expression burned as his face grew red with frustration.

"Yes, Your Majesty," he said before turning to Edward. "And you, Rothwell. Leave Somerville to me."

He turned on his heels and marched from the room. Jacque nodded to the queen before following behind and indicating for Marcus to join them.

When Edward was alone with Elizabeth and William Cecil, he felt his queen's gaze fall upon him.

"What is it with you two?" she asked.

"I do not know, Your Majesty. He has returned from Scotland with fire in his heart and I seem to be in his way."

"He has become paranoid, Edward. He has been somewhat shaken since the attacks in Paris and the more that occurs here, the more he fears a repeat of the massacre. The mood in Scotland has put him on edge."

"I am unsure why he is frustrated with me."

"It is Parry," said Cecil. "He doesn't trust him and your faith in the man gives him cause to suspect you as well. As Her Majesty said, he is paranoid."

"And what of Parry, Edward?" asked Elizabeth.
"As before, Your Majesty. He is loyal."
She nodded and raised her eyebrows at Cecil.
"Very well," he replied.
"Very well," she said.

Chapter Thirty Three

Edward grinned at the bustle of the Shadows Office within the walls of the London Wall New Gate. The farriers and stable hands had been frantic in the yard as Edward had passed but as he stood in the doorway of the office itself, it reminded him of a market at the height of summer.

"Andrew," he said, spotting his old friend and colleague. "What's happening? You lot look ready to take on the mob! Are you pulling in Throckmorton this morning?"

"Way beyond that, Edward. We are rounding up his family. I'm after Arden this morning with Leon of Sparta, over here."

"I'm not even Greek!" shouted a dark skinned man at an opposing desk.

Edward grinned.

"Edward Arden? John Somerville's father in law? Don't tell me someone questioned John?"

"Edward, Somerville is dead. He strangled himself to death in his cell last night."

"He did what? How? I had him stripped naked in an empty cell and put on constant watch because he wanted to hurt himself."

"Yeah, well it seems someone either forgot or didn't agree as he was found leaning against the wall with a scarf between his neck and the window bars."

"This is despicable."

"It's ok, he confessed first. He was racked and gave up his father in law and some priest that Arden kept hidden as a gardener. We are going to round them up."

"Andrew, he was not of sound mind. He should never have been tortured and should not have been able to kill himself, especially after being broken on the rack. I don't doubt Arden's involvement but how can we possibly believe the account of a man like that?"

"We don't need to. Throckmorton gave up Arden as well. Arden is married to his cousin or something like that."

"Francis Throckmorton? I thought he was being brought in today?"

"Walsingham had him brought in last night and put to torture. He gave everyone up almost instantly. Pathetic, really."

Edward fumed and looked around the room. Walsingham was sitting, nestled among a group of shadows and pointing out markers on a map.

"Walsingham!" he roared, bringing the room to silence and Walsingham to his feet. "*Sir* Walsingham. What the hell do you think you're doing?"

"Pardon me?" replied Walsingham, indifferently.

"You had Throckmorton questioned? You know full well what Jacque and I went through to build that case."

"Yes, and so does everyone else now. Are we to take your loose tongue as a sign of your carefree attitude to this work?"

"How dare you question him?"

"Listen to me, Rothwell. Jacque brought the information to me, as he damn well should, and you were there. Throckmorton gave up everyone, the action worked. We don't have time to sit around and wait for you to play footsie with the queen!"

"Don't you let her hear you say that."

"What is the problem? He talked," said Walsingham. "Why rush?"

"Because he is a danger to this country, you fool!"

"Just like Somerville?"

Walsingham twitched.

"Yes, just like Somerville," he said.

"He was in a cell, Francis."

"He was in a cell because he was dangerous, Edward!"

"But he was no longer dangerous when you had him killed!"

Francis opened his mouth to speak but Edward continued.

"And you racked him?" he shouted. "You racked a man who didn't even know where he was!"

"It was necessary," Walsingham said, quietly.

"Why? Jacque gave you the information. You planned to torture Throckmorton, what was the rush? You had the whole family by association anyway."

"Not the priest."

"Who cares about the damn priest?"

"Regardless, we did not have Somerville killed."

"No but you handed him the rope. Or at least, the scarf."

"You two," said Wellesley, calmly, from across the room between the many shadow heads watching in astonishment. "I think we better take this to my office."

Walsingham pushed his way out of the room and led them to Wellesley's office where he held the door and slammed it behind them.

"Don't you ever question me in front of the men, do you understand?" he demanded.

"How could I not? When I walk into a room and find out that you have shit on my investigation, tortured an insane man and lost your mind with your paranoia?"

"Am I paranoid? Or do you nestle next to the queen while consorting with double agents like William Parry?"

"Edward is right, Francis," said Wellesley. "Throckmorton was his investigation. Though Edward, confronting the Principal Secretary of the Privy Council in front of Her Majesty's staff is somewhat inappropriate."

"Inappropriate?" roared Walsingham, though he was silenced by Wellesley's right hand.

"Edward?"

"It was," said Edward. "I apologise."

"Accepted," said Walsingham. "You need to calm down, Rothwell, but it is done now."

"Good, then let us…"

"No. You misunderstand me. You need to calm down. Take some leave. Go home. Be with your wife."

Edward opened his mouth to speak but Walsingham shook his head.

"That's an order," he said. "Get out of my investigation. I will call you when I need you." He held his chin high for a moment, mastering his emotions. "Good day," he said, finally, as he turned on his heels and left the room.

Chapter Thirty Four

January 1584

Edward shivered against the cold and watched his breath as he waited for the door to the queen's chambers in Whitehall to open. He knocked again, feeling the sting in his knuckles as the large, oak doors were pulled back and he stepped inside.

"Business with Her Majesty," he said, receiving an absent nod from the clerk, who didn't look up from his desk. He handed his cloak to the attendant and made his way through the echoing stone corridors and into the busy chamber.

William Parry stood in the centre of the room, surrounded by onlookers and speaking passionately to the queen who sat pensive at the head of the space. Her sudden gaze at Edward distracted Parry, who turned and opened his mouth wide at the sight of his friend.

"Yes, Your Majesty. Edward Rothwell was present," he shouted. "He can bear witness to my account."

Walsingham, sitting in the front row near the queen, narrowed his eyes at the statement.

"I repeat once more, Your Majesty. I befriended these conspirators and infiltrated their circle. I have managed to penetrate further than any other and return here now to deliver news."

"And yet you disappeared for months?" asked Walsingham. "Henry Brooke himself reported your absence."

"Indeed, Sir Walsingham, but I was working my cover. Stafford has seen the value in my efforts and I bring you these letters in his own hand."

"I have seen the letter," said Walsingham.

"Hold on, Francis," said Elizabeth, unfolding the parchment. "Let us see. Yes, here at the end, *'Besides that I think he hath some matter of importance that he hath kept to deliver to yourself for the good will he hath to do your service.'* Go on, William. Tell me your news."

"The conspirators in Paris were naturally distrustful of my return, so to put all men out of doubt with me, I left for Italy where I justified myself before the inquisition in Milan. I told them that I had news from Catholics in England and wished to discuss the information with the Pope himself. Sadly, safe conduct to Rome was not likely and I returned to France where I re-integrated with those I was to target. I did indeed present the notion that together we could assassinate Your Majesty and did so in order to reveal the most dangerous among them."

"And in doing so, invoked Agent Provocateur, Parry!" yelled Walsingham, suddenly.

"It was necessary, Principal Secretary. I wrote a letter to the Pope and in doing so bought the favour of Morgan, who sent me back to England to murder our queen. I have with me a letter from Como, the Cardinal Secretary of State, approving our actions in the name of the Pope."

"Read it please, William," said Elizabeth.

Parry pulled a rolled letter from his breast pocket and opened it wide.

"Very well. *His Holiness hath seen you letter of the first with the certificate included and cannot but commend the good disposition and resolution which you write you have towards the public service and benefit: wherein his Holiness does exhort you to persevere and to bring to effect that which you have promised.*' Your Majesty, as a result of my actions, we have written evidence that the Pope himself condones the death of you, our Monarch, at my hand."

Walsingham stood.

"You arrange a meeting with the Pope to deliver news in person and then you do the same with our Queen while speaking so fondly of her demise," he said.

"No, sir," said Parry. "I bring evidence. I have done my work."

Walsingham raised an eyebrow and met his queen's eyes, his decision clear. She chewed her lip for a moment then turned to Edward who shrugged and tilted his head. She closed her eyes then nodded once, looking back to Parry.

"Very well, William. I thank you for your service. Go on and return to Lord Burghley to discuss your duties onward."

Walsingham tightened his mouth and glared at Edward. Parry bowed deeply and stepped backwards until he could turn and head for the door. He grinned at Edward as he passed him and those nearest in the crowd watched curiously. Edward turned back to Elizabeth who nodded, subtly. He bowed in reply and looked to Walsingham who stood and made his way towards him as conversations began throughout the small crowd.

"You saw him in Paris," Walsingham said. "I struggle to accept your judgement with this but my hands are tied. Did you see nothing of this?"

"I didn't, Sir."

"Then he kept it from you?"

Edward worked his mouth, knowing

"Poor timing," he said. "Though I admit, he walks a fine line."

"He is rogue."

"I don't believe so. Although his desire to operate in silo is concerning, I feel he does so purely to gain your favour, and that of the queen."

"Yes, the favour of the queen, just as he did with the upper echelons of the Vatican. I just don't trust it and he is too close. Follow him, Edward. Just, don't lose him, no matter how long it takes. I want to know who he meets and how he operates. This summer will be the answer we need, then I can either put it to bed or string him up. Right now, I don't care which, as long as it is right."

Edward nodded once and turned on his heels, following Parry out of the door.

"William, let us speak," he said, as he found Parry standing gleefully in the corridor.

Edward led them out into the cold and through a series of tight alleyways until he found one of the more appropriate inns for quiet conversations.

"Why are you really here?" he asked as they sat down with a drink.

"Because I have letters from Stafford for Walsingham and the queen. Though I do not understand Francis. He still holds such distrust despite my success. Stafford says I should leave him out of my communications."

"Do not ever leave him in the dark, do you understand?" interrupted Edward. "He is a just but paranoid man and to do so would be to invite execution without doubt." Then he paused. "Stafford said that?" he asked.

"He did."

"That's interesting. He said the same to me. He spoke of Cecil briefly, asked of Wellesley and then said he should indeed simply communicate with his old friend rather than Walsingham."

"Wait, Wellesley and Stafford are close friends?"

"Apparently so."

Parry hung his head back in surprise and sagged, his mouth open.

"Does that mean something to you?" asked Edward.

"Nothing," said Parry, returning to the conversation.

"As I said, Francis is paranoid," said Edward. "He is acting wildly at the moment and anyone remotely suspected of conspiracy is hauled in and tortured. Both Throckmorton brothers, George More. He had Edward Arden brought in and pulled strings with Judge Christopher Wray to have him executed. I confronted him and last I heard he has calmed down but you must keep your nose clean."

"But I am in favour with the queen now, Edward. I must now show them what I am truly capable of."

"It carries too much risk, William."

"No, Edward. It must be now." He looked around and lowered his voice. "The Black Axe *protects* the queen. If there is a plot, they know about it. They even intercepted my letter to Como and told him I was not to be trusted. It wasn't you and it wasn't Morgan. No one else knew. It must be them. They know but are clever in putting a stop to any activity. No, the only way now is to plot again but take it right to the point of assassination. Only then will they reveal themselves."

Edward laughed.

"We must! We are on the inside," said Party. "Only we can create a plot that can leak to the Axe and yet get close enough to realisation without being stopped by Walsingham and his men."

"Are you mad? If you get anywhere near an assassination, you will be hung, drawn and quartered within weeks."

"It won't be me. I have a candidate."

"And you are actually going to *tell* another of your madness?" Edward whispered, harshly. "You think that won't get back to Cecil and Walsingham?"

"Edward Neville. Ed."

"Who?"

"Neville. He is a Government Agent but they don't trust him so he is constantly pushed aside and is disgruntled, to say the least. And if that isn't enough, he despises Cecil's son, Thomas. By marriage he took Neville's land. It is perfect."

"It is not. It is madness, William. If you follow this

path, I will not protect you. I will not be able to. The Axe is not enough to step so far over the line."

Parry shrugged.

"Very well, I will keep up communication with Morgan instead. There is nothing I cannot achieve now." He smiled smugly.

"Use your head, William," said Edward. "Use your head and get back in your box. I will not protect you, I swear to you." And with his last word, he stood and left the inn.

Chapter Thirty Five

September 1584

Edward restrained his smile as Elizabeth winked at him from between the curtains of her carriage and then let them fall, concealing her inside. He glanced around the crowd who had gathered to catch sight of their monarch as she moved from her lodgings in parliament and set forth for Windsor. Faces, both clean and dirty, clambered over each other for a view of her carriage and Edward watched Marcus at the front of the entourage, surveying every sudden move.

"So far so good," said Walsingham, moving up beside him. "Final report, please."

"Here?"

"Here. We have not had the chance to speak for some time."

"Very well," said Edward. "Between other duties, I have monitored Parry closely. He remains the same; brash, gloating, but he has acted not in any way that gives me suspicion."

"Who does he speak with?"

"No one," Edward said, watching the crowd.

"No one? In half a year he has spoken to no one?"

Edward glanced at Walsingham to find him watching him closely, then looked ahead once more.

"No one of any consequence," he said.

"Who?"

"Whores and tradesmen," said Edward. "Innkeepers, shopkeepers, blacksmiths. No one of any consequence."

"Very well. And after a summer of watching, you have no suspicion?"

"None, Francis. He is clean."

Walsingham grunted his assent and moved forward to speak with another guard, riding beside the queen.

Edward looked back to the crowd, feeling his guilt. He spotted the eyes of Jacque on the other side of the entourage, watching him questioningly. 'Ok?' the Frenchman mouthed. Edward nodded, then saw a familiar face in the crowd over his friend's shoulder.

Ed Neville watched the carriage from under a hood through narrowed eyes. He moved sideways through the masses, keeping pace, as Edward nodded once to Jacque then moved back behind the carriage to swap sides. He patted the Wolf's shoulder as they passed, then took up position in his place, his eyes not leaving the man he had seen meeting with Parry on several occasions. They had spoken once, when Edward had gotten too close intentionally in order to force a conversation and Parry had introduced them, though he had not used Edward's name. Parry's expression had told Edward immediately that they discussed his plan and yet he had not for a moment considered they would be mad enough to try it, let alone on such a public journey.

He saw Neville look through the crowd and make eye contact with a man ahead of the procession. It was Parry. No other strange movement stood out in the crowd and

Edward knew Parry's intentions would not come to fruition. The Black Axe would not be there to stop them and they would be faced with torture and execution when they made their final, desperate move. Edward had warned Parry that he could not protect him. He considered allowing the men to tie the noose around their own necks but the threat to his queen was not negotiable. Nor would be his obvious incompetence, having spent six months watching one of the would be assassins. He made his decision and handed his reins to a guard, jumping down from the saddle and moving into the crowd.

He neared Neville, who stood with his hand inside his cloak. He moved in from the side and jerked his arm free, revealing a dagger and finding the surprised face of the man inches from his own. A moment's shock gave way to panic then contorted with effort as Neville tried to pull his arm free. Edward reacted quickly, pulling it back and headbutting him as he stepped forward. A chuckle from the nearby crowd sounded as Neville fell to the floor and Edward leaned over him, bending his wrist and removing the blade from his hand.

"Parry is wrong, Neville. And he is an idiot. Your part in this is not known, now get out of here while you can."

Neville nodded in fear at the intense eyes of the scarred man who had spared him and scrambled to his feet, disappearing into the crowd.

Edward looked up and found Parry, watching in confusion as his accomplice fled through the crowd. Edward did not believe he had seen him and those around him looked back to the carriage with a cheer as he slipped through, pushing and apologising to make space as Parry's face turned back to the entourage with a look of dread. He closed his eyes in fear as Edward neared him from the side and then opened them again, pulling a large pistol from his cloak and pointing it at the carriage, pausing in hope.

Edward caught him from the side and grasped the gun, his finger tight against the flintlock hammer and holding it from the metal frizzen upon which it was destined to strike.

Parry looked around in surprise and found Edward staring him down.

"You fool, William," whispered Edward, harshly.

Parry shook his head as his eyes filled with tears.

"It was the only way," he said as he began to weep.

"The Axe will not reveal himself for the likes of you and all you have done is put us in danger of torture." Edward looked around and saw the guards watching other areas of the crowd while Walsingham spoke to Marcus at the front of the group, both of them looking ahead. "Get out of here, you idiot. Get out of here and hide. Keep low and do nothing. I am due to travel so will meet you in ten weeks today where we last spoke of your preposterous idea. Now go."

Parry nodded, tears spilling onto his cheeks and fled through the crowd. Edward watched him go then looked back through the crowd to the carriage. No one watched him, though as he moved back through the masses and mounted his horse, he found Walsingham sitting on his horse to the side, allowing the procession to pass until Edward caught up with him.

"Anything?" he said.

"Pardon?" asked Edward.

"Your search of the crowd. Anything of note? I saw you return to your horse."

"Nothing," said Edward. "Just happy revellers searching for a glimpse of their queen."

"Very well. Join Marcus at the front, if you would. We are about to meet the open road and I could do with your eyes." He smiled and Edward nodded, kicking in his heels and trotting forward to his oldest living friend.

Chapter Thirty Six

December 1584

Walsingham stood in the dawn light on the steps of the House of Commons looking out over the frosty street, not yet to be blessed by the pale brightness of the wintery day. A man stepped up to him and Edward saw him order the man away on what appeared to be errand as he himself appeared from the gloom and approached.

"Rothwell," said Walsingham.

"You called, Francis?"

"I did," Walsingham replied with what had become his signature frown. "Do you know why I called for you?"

Edward shook his head.

"Good, then it will be a surprise. I have something for you."

He led Edward in silence through the entry halls of parliament and down into the holding cells reserved for prisoners awaiting trial or representation before the Privy Council. He looked over his shoulder and nodded at Edward as he opened the door to a cell and stepped inside.

"Francis!" called a William Parry as Walsingham entered with Edward in tow. "Edward! Tell me you're going to help me?"

"That's unlikely, William," said Walsingham. "You

are being held on a charge of treason and we all know it was only a matter of time."

"Treason? For what? The shadows told me nothing when they brought me in. I haven't even been here, Francis. I have met with no one."

"Indeed you have not. No, you went to ground for what, eight, ten weeks? Until you were spotted near Whitehall leaving an inn."

Parry glanced at Edward who remained passive.

"Tell me what I am meant to have done. Please?" Parry said, finding nothing in Edward's eyes.

"I still struggle to believe it myself. Conspiring to remove our queen, I expected, but to turn up with a pistol to shoot her in the street? In the street!" Walsingham roared. "Yes, I saw you. And I saw you too, Rothwell. If you hadn't saved her, I would've had you stretched yourself, but why you protect this treacherous fiend, I do not know."

"It wasn't like that, Francis!" Parry exclaimed, his eyes once again filling with moisture. "It wasn't, I swear it. Please."

"Then how was it, William?" Walsingham shouted back. "How was it?"

Parry looked to Edward and though he found his confidant's gaze to be cold, his eyes were on fire with both warning and plea."

Parry twisted his jaw and nodded.

"I was trying to stop the assassination."

"It certainly didn't look like it. Who?"

"Neville. Edward Neville."

"Ed Neville? Cecil's agent?"

"Oh his loyalty is not to Cecil, of all people."

"I know of his quarrel with Cecil's son."

"He thinks you distrust him. He is downtrodden, disgruntled. He was desperate, Francis, and wanted to punish you. He came to me to help him after he heard of my communications with the conspirators in France. I kept him talking to gather evidence, and then the day came and he wanted to act. I…I wanted to catch him myself. Show you my worth. I pulled my pistol to spur him on and was planning to turn and shoot him as he moved to stab the queen in her carriage. Then when Edward saw me and stopped me, Neville panicked and ran. I am sorry."

Walsingham narrowed his eyes.

"And what did Rothwell say to you?" he asked without looking at Edward.

Parry looked at Edward then back to Walsingham.

"He said he knew I meant no harm but I would have to answer to you for my actions. He told me to leave so as not to cause panic and that you would come for me later that week. I went to ground."

Walsingham nodded.

"I don't trust you, Parry, and I believe you to be a traitor. You will be held while I investigate this claim against Neville. Edward, with me."

Walsingham stood and left the room.

Edward met Parry's eyes with thanks and followed behind. They walked in silence again until they met the icy air and the bright glare of the low sun once more.

"Does he lie?" asked Walsingham.

"I don't know, Francis. I guess we will find out when

we speak to Neville."

"How could you not have seen these conversations with Neville? You followed Parry for months."

"I don't know. I saw them speak once but it was of no importance."

"Well clearly it was!" whispered Walsingham through gritted teeth.

"I thought nothing of it. I am sorry."

"You told me he had met no one. Innkeepers and whores. Regardless, you told him we would come for him?" said Walsingham. "When you stopped him and let him go?"

"Yes."

"But you told me you saw no one."

"It was not the time."

"And yet with all of this time you still have not told me!"

"I looked for him but he went to ground. I had then let a possible assassin go and lost him. I could not tell you until I found him. But you did."

"And do you know how we did?"

"You caught him near Whitehall, yes?"

"Yes, after he met you."

"You had me followed?" frowned Edward.

"It is a good job we did, is it not?" Walsingham asked.

Edward shook his head.

"Whatever is happening here," Walsingham continued, "He is in chains and you know my eye is on you. Though whether you stopped an attack or it was a stunt, I do not know. Just carry on with your work but be available. No doubt Neville has gone missing as well. When we find him I will call for you."

Chapter Thirty Seven

February 1585

"Thank you for coming," said Edward as Cecil came into view in the corridor of the more comfortable upstairs cells of the Tower of London where Parry had spent the months since his arrest.

"What do you need from me, Edward?"

"I'd like your opinion. On Parry. I still have faith in him but Francis is so convinced of his guilt, I fear I may be blind. If you speak to him and feel him to be true, then we will make a final representation to the queen. The choice will then be hers, but with at least an unbiased opinion."

Cecil nodded.

"I have always trusted your judgement, Edward. And that of my own. Something of William Parry has always seemed somewhat genuine, despite his blunders. What does Francis say of this?"

"He doesn't know. He is already convinced, as I said, though I fear his paranoia is stronger than his judgement at this point. He is here though, at the Tower."

"He was. I saw him rush out with two soldiers who were not in uniform. Very well, let us speak with the man and see how I feel."

"Thank you, though may I speak with him first? Tell

him to be true. He trusts me and I want him to be comfortable. Dampen that desperate bravado."

"Ok, I shall wait here."

Edward nodded and entered the room, closing the door behind him.

"Edward," said Parry, rushing to his desk and offering Edward a seat. "What's happening? Did they find Neville? Has Francis spoken of me?"

"Cecil is outside. I have asked him to speak with you. We haven't found Neville yet and I think he still has faith in you. If we can convince him that you acted not in malice to the queen but in some misguided…"

"Why?" asked Parry. "You said you wouldn't defend me in this and, well, you were right."

"It is madness, I know, William. But oddly enough, you are the only other person on this…*mission*…that commands my life."

"It is too late for me, Edward."

"It is not."

"It is, my friend. Though you must carry on."

"But carry on with what? We have nothing."

"We do, Edward. Wellesley."

Edward squinted, his head tilting.

"Wellesley does not know of the Axe."

"Wellesley *is* the Axe. He must be! I did not know him at the time but he is the white haired man who questioned my master, Herbert. Then when I was arrested for the robbery of Hare, it was *him* that turned up and twisted it. I…I still could not see it, until you said he and Stafford are friends. Something is not right about Stafford. He is so keen to cut out Walsingham and someone, Edward, someone intercepted my letter to Rome."

"Stafford is a problem, though he is not in any way sharp enough to think at such levels."

"Wellesley is."

"But the fact that Stafford intercepted your letter and he just happens to be friends with Wellesley does not mean Wellesley is the Black Axe. Or either of them for that matter. I have looked far and wide and Wellesley passes every test every time. I am afraid it is just not possible."

"It's the reason no one intercepted my attack. Stafford knows me too well. Wellesley knows I am not a threat."

"I don't believe it, William, I am sorry."

"But Herbert. And Hare!"

"I am sorry."

A knock at the door told them Cecil had grown impatient.

"It is your turn now, Edward," said Parry. "Look into it. Look into Wellesley. Do it."

The door opened and Cecil walked in.

"William," said Cecil. "May we speak?"

Parry opened his hands confidently and offered another chair. Cecil sat down.

"What is going on?" asked Cecil.

"I have had enough, Lord Burghley," said Parry. "Enough. And I reacted poorly. I hold my hands up. I went to the procession to shoot the queen. I pulled my gun and only failed because Edward here intervened and put a stop to it. He is a hero. I am a traitor."

Edward's mouth dropped open. Cecil glanced at him, his eyebrows raised.

"And you will sign this confession?" he asked.

"I will," said Parry.

"Very well," said Cecil. "Edward, we have our answer."

Edward met Parry's eyes and found nothing but fire looking back at him.

"You have your answer," said Parry.

"You are surprised?" asked Cecil as he and Edward climbed the stairs towards the Queen's chamber.

"I am in shock," said Edward. "Your thoughts?"

Cecil shrugged.

"A confession is a confession," he said. "Though I am somewhat saddened by it. I trusted him too."

The guard nodded as they approached, opening the door and taking a breath.

"Lord William Cecil and Edward Rothwell, Your Majesty," he said.

"And Sir Francis Walsingham," said a voice behind them.

Walsingham stepped up to the top of the staircase, his face triumphant.

"Gentlemen," he said, stepping past them into the room. "Your Majesty," he said as the three of them entered and took a knee.

"Something looks serious," Elizabeth replied, wearing a simple, golden dress that brushed her bare feet as she walked to her window and indicated for them to sit down.

"It is," said Walsingham. "I am afraid young Rothwell is mistaken about William Parry."

"I am?" asked Edward.

"You are. Neville has recently been accosted."

"When?"

"It matters not. I spoke with him this morning and he has told me everything. I take no pleasure in this, Edward, but your trust of Parry is misguided. Parry approached Neville and presented to him the opportunity to assassinate the queen. Neville quite stupidly believed that Parry had good reason and thus conspired to carry out the act. They are, I am afraid, traitors."

"They are," said Edward.

"You agree?"

"Parry confessed this morning, Francis," added Cecil. "To Edward and I directly. We have a written confession and are here to discuss the queen's intentions for him."

"How can they be anything but of the most grave consequence?"

"I still do not believe him a traitor," said Edward.

Walsingham opened his mouth to speak but was silenced by the hand of Cecil.

"Based on the good work he has delivered for our monarch, I feel it must be discussed with an open mind. His service to the crown cannot be overlooked."

"And the intended peril of the crown must be dealt with absolutely, without bias!" said Walsingham.

"What of Neville?" asked Elizabeth.

"He too must be executed," said Walsingham.

"Agreed," said Cecil.

"Yet you would spare Parry?" asked Elizabeth. "Why, Edward?"

Edward firmed his mouth, knowing his queen's open mind but unable to reveal Parry's intentions in front of the other men.

"Just a feeling, Your Majesty."

Elizabeth nodded, seeing the truth in Edward's eyes.

"Francis? I am inclined to trust Edward's judgement, it has never failed us before."

"No, my queen.," Walsingham said. "No."

"No?" she replied.

"No. He went too far, and so did Edward's judgement in letting him go and keeping it from us. You are quite possibly only alive due to Edward's actions but it could have ended differently and Edward's secrets are once again simply too deep to overlook."

"Secrets to you," she said. "I am the queen, Francis. Do not think I cannot know things you do not."

Walsingham frowned at Edward.

"Nevertheless," he said. "Parry's actions were clear and Edward did nothing to apprehend a traitor. He let him go we very nearly lost two incredibly dangerous men who may have gone on to conspire further."

"My loyalty is…"

"Your loyalty is not in question, Edward. Only your judgement is under scrutiny," said Walsingham, interrupting Edward's objection. "You saved your queen and we are thankful. But Parry's intentions were clear and he masterminded the attack. As such, he must be publicly executed. His actions in this are known across the city and cannot go unpunished or else give rise to other hopeful assassins or lead to an uprising like those we have witnessed. Do not forget the scenes in Paris, Edward."

"I cannot," said Edward.

"I am inclined to agree with Francis," said Cecil. "He is correct. This *is* known and cannot go unpunished. Nor is it his first offence."

Elizabeth looked at the men and saw the defeat in Edward's eyes.

"I agree," she said. "An act such as this speaks volumes to those who target this crown. Parry is to be tried with only one possible outcome, then publicly put to death."

Edward nodded.

"Then it is done," said Walsingham.

Chapter Thirty Eight

<u>2nd March 1585</u>

    Once again, Edward found himself alone beside his queen watching the Tower Hill from the open windows of the White Tower. Together they had watched in silence as William Parry had been hauled across the cobbles under the unrestrained physical and verbal abuse of the crowd and had both his charges and his last rites read aloud to him. He had been hung from the neck until nearly dead and was now tied to a table as men armed with knives set about his body.

    Elizabeth closed her eyes as the first blade was drawn down the centre of Parry's chest and his exhausted cries could be heard over the cheers and cries for mercy emitting from the contrasted crowd. Edward grit his teeth as the man's genitals were removed and his organs pulled from his body. His head lulled lifeless to the side as large blades were brought forward to remove his limbs and then, finally, his head.

    "It is done," she said. "May his remains be posted around the four corners of this city as a warning to all who oppose this crown."

    Edward looked at her as her quiet words were repeated by the clerk who had conducted the execution.

    "It's not over, you know," he said.

"I know."

"He wasn't after you."

"I know."

She turned to look at him.

"What are you going to do?"

"Parry's plan," he began, taking a breath, "Was to pretend to attempt an assassination without being stopped by Walsingham so that the Black Axe would reveal himself in order to protect you. But it didn't work. I stopped him."

"Were you curious?"

"I didn't know it was happening. I saw them and intervened. He'd mentioned the notion but I had no idea he was capable of trying."

"And why didn't it work?" she asked.

Edward took another breath.

"He believed the Black Axe was inside our service and so he knew Parry was not a threat." He saw her question before she spoke it. "Wellesley," he said. "He thought the Black Axe was Wellesley."

"That's madness, Edward."

"It is, I know."

"Then why do you look conflicted? Edward?"

"He said it was Wellesley who questioned Herbert, and Wellesley again who twisted the story when he was arrested for robbing Hare. Coincidence, I know. Yet Baxter and Scammell were with the Black Axe. Baxter put me in that house when I clashed with the shadows. I fought them and yet Wellesley recruited me? He questioned me multiple times, such as in his test when promoting me to wolf. He gave Scammell a job. Someone questioned me in Marshalsea after

Scammell crossed me and he had a service coin."

"It is too far fetched. Wellesley is heavily vetted, he has served me for decades. He is famous for his unorthodox and zealous recruitment, and Scammell gave that interrogator the coin. Wellesley fights hard for this country."

"Which is what we believe the Black Axe does, is it not? Parry, Cobham. Maybe they were right. Maybe there is only one way."

"Absolutely not. I will not and cannot betray William and Francis. If it is as you say, the Black Axe does not threaten this crown. If you try the same, to lure them? I cannot protect you. I won't protect you. You will be at Francis' mercy. There will be nothing I can do."

"I know."

"Don't do it, Edward. You mean too much to me, to this country."

"I know. I won't, my queen."

She took hold of his shoulders.

"It is madness, Edward. Promise me."

Edward nodded.

"I promise."

Chapter Thirty Nine

"Talk to me, Albert," Edward whispered, sitting alone in the Shadows' office, swirling a mug of weak ale. "Tell me where to look." He looked through the window at the small office across the courtyard that had been set up for the operations of Walsingham's agents but the door had not been unlocked in days. A murmur of voices out of view by the courtyard gate caught his attention and he waited until Walsingham moved into view, followed by two of his agents. Walsingham saw Edward in the window and nodded once before moving out of sight and entering through the door moments later.

"Morning, Edward," he said as he entered. "Have you met my companions here? Thomas Phelippes and Robert Poley."

Edward shook his head.

"Robert, here," said Walsingham, "Is one of the best infiltrators you will ever meet and Phelippes is our best cryptanalyst. Gentlemen, Edward is perhaps the most intelligent and physically dangerous Wolf in my service and has a talent for artifice that could rival even you, Robert."

Edward greeted both with a handshake and sat back down as Walsingham nodded to each of them then left through the corridor towards Wellesley's office.

"What brings you here?" asked Edward.

"Francis needed to see Wellesley," replied Poley. "Where is everyone? The old man said this office is usually full of life."

"There are a number of raids ongoing this morning. Illegal imports and contraband, following a tip off from one of my informants. In fact one I picked up after my very first cypher-break back in seventy or seventy one," he added, nodding to Phelippes. "I used to love it but the nonsense codes used by the Bishop of Ross and Ridolfi almost broke me and now I leave such mind-stewing work to you. What's happening on your end?"

"With Parry executed, Francis had hoped for some quiet," said Poley, "But we have some activity that we need to monitor."

"Oh?"

"John Ballard, a Jesuit Priest, has been sent back to England by powers in France to convince northern rebels to join them. He's in London at present, staying in Cripplegate near the borders of the Cheap and Bread Street wards. And then we have multiple others lifting their heads above the parapet. William Gifford, cousin of Gilbert Gifford; a young lad named Babington; and an ex soldier, John Savage. Savage in particular is being watched. He has been paying attention to the rest of the group."

"Do they know each other? Does Ballard know Savage?"

"Not as far as we know. Savage has been watching the Giffords. We think he is biding his time before making an approach to build a catholic alliance in the city."

"What is your plan?"

"Right now? Pay attention to Savage and the Giffords. When Ballard leaves London, we will send someone to tail him up north."

"Good idea," said Edward. "Keep me posted?"

"Sure."

Edward nodded and stood.

"Thank you, gentlemen. One more question…"

Edward smiled as the doorway to the narrow apartment block where Ballard was believed to be staying opened and a man matching his description stepped out. Edward pulled his hat down across his face and his light coat higher on his shoulders as he walked across the busy street towards the man.

"John Ballard," he said, quietly.

"Who is asking?" said the priest.

"John Savage," said Edward, holding out his hand.

"Ah," said Ballard. "Your reputation precedes you. What can I do for you?"

"May we go inside?" He showed Ballard the seal of Morgan that he had still had with him, making him smile. "I have a…suggestion."

"Please," said Ballard, opening the door. "After you."

Chapter Forty

Deacon Gilbert Gifford stretched his back as he stepped off the fishing boat in Rye Harbour, Sussex. He thanked the captain with a wave and looked for the stables. In all of his twenty five years, he had waited for a chance to prove himself to his church and reinstate free catholic worship in England; though like his best friend, Christopher, he felt the violent ideals of the Jesuits were a step too far. When his cousin had sent both him and Christopher to a meeting with ex-soldier, John Savage, to hear a proposal that they assassinate Elizabeth and put Mary on the throne, his friend had declined but he had jumped at the chance to assist in the liberation of his faith without mass bloodshed.

He entered the stables and nodded to the boy who scrambled out of sight. Gifford frowned but waited patiently until the stable door was closed behind him and he was plunged into darkness. He turned in reaction and looked around in panic for a moment until his sight adjusted to the dim light and he found himself looking into a pair of eyes.

"Robert Poley," said the man before him. "Have you heard my name?"

"No," said Gifford, nervously. "Who are you?"

"Robert Poley. I just said so. And this is Phelippes," he said, indicating a man to the side who nodded back at

Gifford. "You may recognise the man behind you."

Gifford turned and found himself looking into the stern face of Sir Francis Walsingham.

"Oh God," he said.

"Oh God indeed," said Walsingham. "Pleasant travels?"

Gifford nodded.

"And how is our friend Thomas Morgan?" continued Walsingham.

"I don't know what you mean."

"Of course. The letter please," said Walsingham, holding out his hand. "The letter, Gilbert."

Gifford put his hand into his satchel and pulled out a scroll. Taking a breath, he handed it to Walsingham who opened it and read it swiftly.

"An introduction to the rightful Queen Mary from Thomas Morgan," the spymaster said. "Been elevating your status, Gilbert. Tell me who is involved."

"Involved in what?"

"Gilbert."

"Honestly, Sir Walsingham. I don't know. Involved in what?"

"In the plot to assassinate the queen. We know everything."

Gilbert took a breath.

"How did you know?" he said.

"We always know when there is a threat to the innocent English population."

"But there isn't. I would never incite or facilitate bloodshed. Just the freedom of my religion."

"Is that way you call it?"

"Of course."

"The activity you are involved with, Gilbert, is not only the death of the queen but the Spanish invasion of England in order to facilitate her murder. Hundreds if not thousands will die. First the soldiers, then protestant civilians across the country as the catholic extremists finally get a chance to eradicate the world of a faith they believe to be heresy."

"But, that is not my intention. It, it could never be," Gifford stammered.

"And you know what? I believe you. Nevertheless, treason it is and death by quartering while alive is what awaits you."

"Please."

"Unless you take another route, young Gilbert. Betray your accomplices, you would not, I know. But you have been fooled by those who have used you. Used you to enable an act you wouldn't dream of. They desire violence, Gilbert, and you can stop them. You can do what your *faith* requires of you. To protect life in the name of God."

"What do you want to know?"

"I do not want your words, Gilbert. I need your actions. Maintain a facade on our behalf and help us stop this madness. The queen was never opposed to the peaceful worship of the catholic faith, she simply desires peace and the protection of the subjects who follow *her* church. Work with us and you can not only save thousands but you can worship your god in peace."

"Yes. Anything. What do you need?"

"Let's start with names. Who is involved?"

"I do not yet know every body. My cousin arranged it, though he wasn't there."

"William?"

"Yes," said Gifford. "And another man, I forget his name. He has a scar on his throat. John Savage."

"Very good."

"Wait, Savage doesn't have a scar on his throat," said Poley. "Not when I last saw him. And I don't recall news of him being attacked or cut."

"Maybe as a soldier?" asked Walsingham.

"No, I have seen him since then, albeit not for some time. Maybe a year or so."

"And have you ever looked closely at his throat?"

"I guess not."

Walsingham nodded, content.

"Continue," he said. "Anyone else?"

"No," said Gifford.

"What about Christopher?"

"No. I mean, he was there, but he declined."

"Good," said Walsingham. "We know, of course, but it is always best to confirm. Any mention of other names? Ballard, for example?"

"He was mentioned but he wasn't there either. The same with a younger man, Babington. Oh and the French Ambassador, though his name is long. I do not remember it."

Walsingham smiled.

"Very well," he said, "Then this is what we shall do. Gilbert, you will get word to the French Ambassador that you and the northern rebels are ready. He will tell Paget and Morgan in France, I am sure, and then you will remain in this organisation and feed us the information we need."

"Surely you can arrest the men, with my word as evidence."

"No, we need Mary. This has gone far enough. We must have Mary."

"Word of her assent is not sufficient, Francis," said Phelippes.

"You are right, and the Bishop of Ross made sure she was protected before by communicating on her behalf. No we need her hand in writing. Her approval of the conspiracy. Then Elizabeth will have no choice but to execute her."

"But she is held incommunicado," said Phelippes again. "The decree of eighty four made it so."

"Thank you, Thomas, I am aware," said Walsingham. "We must go further." He paused to think. "Yes. Gilbert, you and Thomas will need to take place in Chartley Castle with Mary. Join her staff. Ballard will be able to make it so. You will join openly and Thomas here covertly, to decipher anything passed in and out. Using a cipher that we will provide ourselves. Letters will be monitored and she knows it, so she will not be trusting of any open communication. We must convince her that you have a method of getting her word out, and that the act will not take place without her consent. But how?"

"I heard of a ruse used in the French Wars," said Phelippes. "Letters smuggled via a water tight seal in the cork of a beer barrel."

"Excellent. Then that is what we will do. As if by sorcery, we just happen to have a Staffordshire brewer local to Chartley Castle within our service. Funny, that. Robert, make the arrangements. Gilbert, when you speak to the Ambassador, let him know how to pass the messages to you, using our man of ale. Inspire him to write to Mary requesting her approval for the assassination of Elizabeth, get her response, and then we bring them in. All of them."

"How will you protect me?" asked Gifford. "Your own side may not be water tight, you know. If my name is seen or heard, they will find out and I will be slaughtered."

"We will simply use an alias, Gilbert. You will be known as Number Four. Your true identity will not be spoken, nor written down. Not now, not ever."

Gifford nodded.

"Then I am at your service," he said.

Chapter Forty One

<u>3rd August 1586</u>

Ballard sat patiently, his elbows resting on the table and the glow from the single candle lighting his chin from underneath so that his eyes sat in complete darkness. Edward sat opposite him beside Anthony Babington and another five or six men as they waited. After a short moment of silence, the door opened, allowing daylight to fill the room, and Gilbert Gifford walked in, closing it behind him.

"Here he is, the man of the hour," said Ballard.

Gifford smiled.

"Why so dark, John?"

"Because I need to ensure we are not overheard and this is the best I can do.

"Right, gentlemen," he continued. "It is done. Thanks to Gilbert here, taking position in Mary's manor and working with her secretaries, she has approved our plan of action and awaits her liberty. Anthony?"

"I am assured that we have the support of the Catholic League in France," said Babington, "And the full approval of the Pope himself, giving us sixty thousand men even without the Spanish, though I am sure Phillip will not miss this chance. My concern remains with their ability to succeed while Elizabeth lives."

"Our very own John Savage will see to that, Anthony."

Edward nodded.

"You have a plan?" asked Babington.

"I do," said Edward. "We will discuss it in due course but will need the full contingent here when we do. All fourteen of us. But we *will* succeed. With Mary's assent, we are underway. The Duke of Norfolk, the Spanish Ambassador, the King of Spain; none of them have managed to achieve what we have. We are one step away. As soon as the first part of the army is in place, I will bring you into the plan. Then once Elizabeth is despatched, we can send the communications for the invasion to begin."

He stood and wiped his brow with his sleeve, looking at Ballard.

"John, with your permission, I would like to attend some business. Thank you for calling us together for this update."

Ballard nodded and stood to shake his hand.

"Good luck, John. And thank you."

Edward looked out from the mouth of the alleyway opposite the Shadows' office before turning back to Jacque.

"Is there much going on in there?" he asked.

"Not at the moment," said Jacque. "Walsingham's men are working but the Shadows are calm. Where have you been, Edward?"

"I have been following a lead. Listen, I have something to ask of you?"

"Something else?"

"Yes, I am sorry. I just need you to keep your ear to the ground in the French Embassy. If the Ambassador sends any word across the channel, you must intercept it."

"What will it say?"

Edward paused for a moment.

"It will give the order for catholic forces to cross the channel and invade England," he said, finally.

Jacque's mouth dropped open.

"Where has that come from? How can you know that? We must tell Francis."

"I cannot tell you, I am sorry. And you must not tell Francis."

"You can't tell me? Edward, this is me. You cannot ask me to go outside of Walsingham's directions and operate without his knowledge when *he* is running this investigation."

"It is sanctioned."

"It clearly isn't or else he would know. None of this has been said by Number Four."

"Number Four?" asked Edward.

"Number Four. It's Gifford's alias. I assumed you knew of Walsingham's infiltration operation after you said you were involved but simply couldn't attend the meetings due to the nature of your engagement."

"Of course," Edward lied, feeling his heart race. "I just didn't think anyone else knew of the alias?"

"No, Number Four's identity is not discussed outside of Francis, Robert, Thomas and I. Though Wellesley did discuss Gifford when I spoke to him."

Edward smiled, forcing himself to remain calm

despite the hot rush of blood closing in around his face like the warm towel of a city barber.

"You spoke to him, as I asked?" he said.

"I did this morning," replied Jacque. "Though why you needed me to, I am becoming unsure."

"And?"

"And, when I said activity was quiet in the embassy, he asked if Gifford had ever made it back from France. He'd known he was there and would be coming back through Rye, where Francis picked him up. Why was that, Edward? No one else knows of this investigation. I need to tell Francis there is a leak."

"You cannot."

"It is my job, Edward!"

"Please, Jacque. Give me one day."

"You need to tell me."

"Trust me, please. One day. Meet me here tomorrow morning at the same time. Nine o'clock. Please?"

Jacque worked his jaw in thought before nodding.

"One day," he said.

"Thank you," said Edward, looking back around the corner and seeing Wellesley leave the yard alone. He smiled.

"Come into the office," said Jacque.

"I am afraid I have some business to attend to," Edward replied, watching Wellesley disappear around a corner in the distance without being seen by Jacque. "I will see you tomorrow," he added, walking in the same direction. "One more day!"

Walsingham stood, sipping a warm cup of wine beside a street vendor and watching the bustle of London's upper class going about their morning routines.

"I still can't believe you can drink something hot in this weather," said Poley.

"It cools me down, Robert, I can't explain it. Maybe you should try?"

"No, thank you. I'll stick to cool ale from the cellar. What time is he arriving?"

"Any time now. What's the news?"

"Well, we were right. I managed to get close myself and Savage does not have a scar on his throat."

Walsingham looked around in surprise.

"He doesn't? Well that is a turn up for the books. Who *has* Number Four been talking to?"

"We can ask him," said Poley, seeing Gifford approach from across the street.

Walsingham looked round, welcoming him with a nod.

"Gilbert," he said. "Once again, what's the news?"

"It's happening," he said. "Ballard gave the word this morning that we are set up and direction has been sent for the forces to assemble overseas."

"Then we need to move, though I am still intrigued as to how they think an army can simply land on our shores and march into this country without resistance."

"Funny you should say that, Babington expressed that exact concern this morning."

"And?"

"And Ballard said Savage will assassinate the queen

first, though here's the catch, I don't believe the man going by the name Savage is John Savage at all."

Francis looked sideways at Poley who raised his eyebrows.

"My cousin brought the real John Savage to me last night and he himself has sworn to assassinate Elizabeth. He was a completely different man yet he knew of the plot and was deeply involved."

"Does Ballard know?"

"It appears not. It seems communications have been passed through my cousin William and John Savage has never been to any direct meetings with Ballard, though I am not sure why. And all the while, this man posing to be him has been Ballard's closest connection and sat there this morning in that very room, confirming he had a plan that would enable him to assassinate the queen. Sir Walsingham, I know your methods are complex but you must tell me if you have another man infiltrating this operation."

"I assure you I do not, Gilbert. Robert," Walsingham added, addressing Poley. "We must act now, before word can meet the coast and orders can be sent. Assemble the Shadows for action and I will meet you at the office shortly."

Poley nodded and left them to their conversation.

"Gilbert, tell me more," said Walsingham.

Edward kept his distance as he followed Wellesley through the streets of London, pausing at various intervals, both to keep out of sight and to ensure he himself wasn't being followed. As Wellesley approached a busy area, he moved closer and noticed he too would stop on occasion to take shelter or feign interest in the stalls of market traders before looking ahead and moving on. After observing the crowd ahead through a number of further pauses, Edward was able to make out the man Wellesley tailed, though it wasn't until the target turned to look over his shoulder that Edward realised it was indeed Gilbert Gifford. He smiled as his suspicions began to come together and watched as Wellesley moved on.

Wellesley moved into a trot as Gifford moved around a corner out of sight and Edward picked up his pace in order to follow. He rounded the same corner and found himself only a short distance from Wellesley who had stopped still and hid behind the column of shop front veranda. Frustratingly, Edward could only keep sight of Wellesley's hiding place by standing in the open air of the market himself but with the use of a well-placed stall, he was sure Wellesley could not see him. He briefly looked around the crowd and then brushed away a beggar, settling in to watch.

"And there is nothing else?" said Walsingham, draining the last of his wine.

"Not that I can think of," said Gifford. "This place is so busy, Francis. What made you choose here?"

"If you were to be tailed through quiet streets, young man, and you arrived to meet me, it would be obvious that you are there to feed me information and our targets may go into hiding or be spurred into acting rashly. Of course, it would be better for me to guide you through an observed path of gradually quieter areas in order to ensure you are not being watched but, alas, we do not have such time and therefore it is safer for us to bump into each other in a busy street as if by coincidence. Anyone watching will wonder what we discuss but would not have evidence of a coordinated meeting. Nor can we be overheard in the midst of such a racket. Gilbert," said Walsingham, frowning. "Do not get sidetracked now, what are you looking at?"

"I think I saw someone familiar."

"Who?" said Walsingham, looking in the same direction.

"I am not sure, it was just a moment. Behind that crowd around the man on stilts. Hang on, they are moving."

Both men watched a small throng of people before them, laughing at a grotesquely tall man, staggering through the crowd. As they finally moved to the side, Gifford's eyes opened wide.

"That's him," he said. "That's the man posing as John Savage. With the scar on his throat."

Walsingham followed his gaze until he saw it. Edward Rothwell stood, hiding behind a market stall, and watching something out of sight. Walsingham felt the rage build in his chest at his own stupidity as the suspicions he had ignored for a year were brought to life.

"Get out of London for a few days and keep low, Gilbert. You have served me well but now we will act. I don't want you caught in the melee to come."

"Who is he, Francis?"

"Go, Gilbert," said Walsingham, not allowing his

eyes to leave his new target. "Go, now."

Edward leaned against the wall in the alleyway opposite the Shadows' office once more. The sun had reached its highest point and the cool stone brought relief as the heat left his back. Wellesley had left his makeshift observation point and returned suddenly to the office without diversion, and now Edward waited, trying desperately to form a plan in his mind.

"Are you up to something or just taking a break?" said the voice of Poley behind him.

"Robert," said Edward, turning to face the man emerging from the maze of alleyways behind him. "Taking a break, you?"

"Had an errand to run. I hate the crowds so I always come through this way despite the flea-ridden vagrants grabbing my ankles from the floor."

"Any progress? How are things? I haven't caught up with Francis."

"We are moving today. We have word that Ballard and Babington's plot is in action so I have been ordered to assemble all Shadows and Wolves in the city for action. We better get inside."

"Wow, that's good news. What's the plan? Arrests? When?"

"When, I don't know, but they're all coming in. The lot of them, and both Savages if we ever find out who the other is."

"The other Savage?"

"Yes, it turns out John Savage is involved but not the man Ballard thinks he is. Some of the conspirators have made the connection that another man is posing as Savage to Ballard. If he finds out, he may get suspicious and call off the invasion."

"Good God," said Edward. "That *is* unexpected."

"Indeed. I've been out all morning so haven't been updated since Francis sent me to round up forces. Let's get in there and find out when Walsingham wants to strike. Every one of them is now under surveillance but my guess is somehow *someone* will get word to Ballard."

"Yes," said Edward, "Though I have a meeting with a Shadow informant that I must make first."

"Very well but don't be long. I don't think Francis will want to wait."

Edward nodded as Poley walked out into the square and towards the office. He looked around as his heart beat to a new rhythm and tried to think on his feet. If Ballard got wind of a stranger in their midst, he would suspect infiltration, call off the plot and go to ground, then all of Edward's risk would be for nothing. If he wasn't made aware and they were all arrested, Edward would be tasked with the interrogation of men who knew him as John Savage and he would be exposed. His queen was right, it was a step too far. He grit his teeth and turned away into the alley.

Chapter Forty Two

<u>4th August 1586</u>

Edward crept through the winding alleys behind Bread Street towards the rear of Ballard's lodgings. He had approached the building from the front but the early summer sun had disrupted his attempt at a stealth approach and he had spotted soldiers in plain clothes keeping watch on the premises from a carriage only a short distance away. Instead of hiding in the plain sight of a crowd as he usually would in a daylight setting, his intention to maximise the early hours of the morning would only betray his position in the empty streets. He cursed as the day met its fifth hour and he lost time moving far and wide in order to approach the building from the back. He finally met the rear wall of the small apartment building and took a breath. His only plan was to inform Ballard of an informer in their team before the real identity of John Savage was revealed to him. If he could move him to a safe house, he would be able to continue the plan up until the point the Black Axe showed himself and then reveal Ballard's location to Walsingham.

He looked up and down the alleyway, seeing nothing but the lifeless legs of a beggar emerging from a pile of rags, and then scaled the wall, dropping down into the small yard on the other side. He peered through the window, seeing only an empty room, and then slipped open the rear door, stepping inside. He crept slowly and silently through the empty ground floor but as he moved towards the staircase, his foot pressed on a loose board and the creak echoed around the house.

"Who is there?" whispered a voice from upstairs.

"Ballard, it is me, Savage," Edward said.

Ballard's face appeared in the gloom at the top of the stairs and he opened his mouth to speak before a rustling sound distracted them both from outside the front door. The sound of a whisper could be heard on the other side of the oak before it flew open with a splintering of wood and Edward found himself looking into the face of a soldier he recognised.

The soldier's eyes opened wide before he opened his mouth and took a breath.

"Rothwell is here!" he shouted.

"Seize them both," said a voice behind him in the street as Edward took his moment and threw a punch into the face of the soldier with all the force he could muster.

He turned on his heels and scrambled back through the hallway, hitting the door with his shoulder and bursting into the yard to leap at the wall.

The noise behind him erupted as men piled into the house and Edward dropped down into the alleyway only to be grabbed from behind by a rough pair of hands. He recognised the feet of the man who held him and saw that the pile of rags had been thrown aside as its occupant had given up his disguise in order to effect the arrest.

"Don't resist, we have you," said the man into

Edward's ear.

Edward stamped on the foot and reached behind him, grasping the testicles of his accoster, and twisting them until the man let go. He turned as he was released and headbutted the soldier, knocking him to the floor and then headbutting him again as they hit the ground together.

With the head below him lulling in shock, Edward clambered back to his feet and sprinted into the alleyway.

"Where is he?" he heard a voice call as voices reached the rear of the house and Edward disappeared into the dark shelter of a break between the terraced buildings.

His heart raced as he wound his way through the rotten mass of vegetables and excrement and slipped out into an open street where he blended in with the now thickening market crowds.

"Edward, what the fuck are you doing?" said Jacque as he stepped out of sight into the place they had agreed to meet.

"Thank you for coming, my friend."

"You are wanted, Edward. Number Four identified you as the man posing as John Savage, the very man who masterminded this assassination."

"You know that is not what is really happening. You know me better than anyone. The assassination was never going to happen. That's why I left that part of the job with me."

"Well whatever you were doing, it is over. Every man in the conspiracy is being arrested this morning for torture and Mary won't be far behind. I don't see how you will get out of this one."

"Then we have Mary, my artifice has been effective."

"No, Edward. Francis' plan was effective and has identified you as a conspirator. It is over."

"Shit," said Edward, almost to himself. "Then there is no more time and I cannot gather any more evidence."

"What evidence do you need? It is done."

"*My* evidence, my friend. Jacque, my life is now in jeopardy, I am at a dead end and have no other choice but to force it. I must take the ultimate risk. I need your help, one more time."

Jacque looked at Edward, open-mouthed, as his head began to shake.

"Edward, I…"

"Jacque," Edward interrupted. "You *know* me. You know I am not a traitor. And you know I did not plot to kill our queen. No one knows you have seen me, I am still in hiding. Please. If this goes wrong, you will have been the one who found and arrested me. There is no risk other than to let me walk away right now. Jacque…"

Edward waited as Jacque looked at him and then out into the courtyard. His jaw moved left and right in thought as it always did and then he turned back.

"One more time. What is it?"

Edward smiled in relief.

"Thank God," he said.

Chapter Forty Three

"Are you sure about this?" said Marcus, holding the chains binding Edward's wrists as they crossed the bridge into the Tower of London.

Edward recognised the glare of the guard who let them past, just as he had on the occasions he himself had walked suspected traitors into the Tower.

"I have no idea," he said, once they were clear. "I can only try. Thank you for doing this for me."

"It is of no risk to me, my friend. I just wish I didn't have to throw you into the fire. I wish I knew what you were planning."

They approached the inner gate and Edward waited until they were past and approaching the White Tower.

"It is safer if you don't," he said. "If Jacque gets the timing right, you will only need to stick to the instructions I gave you and I will do the rest. If it is possible at all."

"Marcus!" called a voice behind them, causing them to turn. "Are you not taking him down?" said the guard from the inner gate.

"No, the queen wants to see this one herself."

"I bet she does," said the guard, fixing Edward a stare. "Make sure you leave guards with her."

Marcus frowned.

"Really, Roy?"

The guard submitted and turned away, looking at Edward once more as he did.

"Here we go," Marcus said as the door to the White Tower opened and they stepped through. Together, they climbed the stairs to the queen's chamber and approached the hesitant guard at the queen's door.

"Let us in," said Marcus.

"Marcus, I saw you approach but you know my brief. No threat may enter the queen's chamber regardless of circumstances."

"I do, but on this occasion you must."

"Marcus…"

"I am the queen's bloody bodyguard, boy! It's my job to be the last word in her protection."

"I'm sorry, I…"

The young guard was cut off as Marcus stepped forward and headbutted him in the cheek. He fell to the floor with a thud as Marcus turned back to Edward and shrugged.

"You better pull this off," he said.

Edward nodded.

They turned and pushed open the door.

"Your Majesty?" said Marcus, drawing Elizabeth from a side room. Her face twisted in conflict when she saw Edward.

"Don't worry, Your Majesty," Edward said. "I need you to trust me, it is all coming to an end. The Black Axe is here." He pulled his dagger from its sheath and approached her.

"Edward?" she said, stepping back as her face

showed fear. She opened her mouth to speak but was silenced as Edward held up a finger and the sound of footsteps approached on the stairs.

"Hide, now," he said.

Elizabeth tilted her head, frowning for a moment before nodding and darting behind her dressing screen as the door was kicked open.

"Stop where you are!" shouted Wellesley as he burst into the room followed by Jacque.

"I'll stop them, Edward!" roared Marcus, diving at Jacque and wrestling him out of the door. He threw him to the ground and turned back to close the door, looking around and seeing an empty floor. "Where is the guard?" he said.

"You're lucky, she's not here," said Edward, throwing down his blade. "What are you doing? Why are you stopping me?"

"What are you talking about?" asked Wellesley, incredulously.

"You want her dead!" said Edward. "You plot to kill her, do you not?"

Wellesley frowned.

"Of course not," he said.

"I know you do. I've watched you, followed you. You, Baxter, Scammell. Traitors."

"How dare you!"

"Traitors! And I will make sure everyone knows it."

"I have protected her for decades, you fool."

"Only Francis Walsingham can protect her. You are nothing."

"Walsingham?" cried Wellesley, with a laugh. "I have picked up the pieces every time he failed. Who do you think gave him Gifford?"

"Bollocks. The Black Axe is a traitor!"

Wellesley tilted his head.

"I know about the Black Axe, Richard," continued Edward. "Pathetic traitors."

"I have no idea what you are talking about."

"Come on, there is no one here. Admit it, admit it for once. You are armed, I am not. Come on!"

Wellesley sneered as he looked at Edward.

"You have no idea what the Black Axe is capable of."

"Well he hasn't done a good job of killing me *or* the queen."

"You could have been killed any time. And the Black Axe protects the queen!"

"*Protects* the queen?" asked Edward, slowing down.

Wellesley roared with laughter.

"Of course he does!" he said. "You stupid boy. You thought you knew about him all along."

"I killed the Black Axe the day Baxter burned to death."

"You did nothing but burn my friend. That was not the Black Axe. He would never be so stupid."

"But the man? The man who ordered Maggie's death. He was the Black Axe. I killed him!"

"Of course he wasn't the Black Axe. You were meant to be intelligent, Edward."

"That wasn't the Black Axe?" said Edward, in thought. "And the Black Axe protects the queen. How did I not see this?" He focused his eyes on Wellesley. "Then only one man possessed the skill and resolve to be him and I have known him all along. It is Walsingham."

Wellesley's eyes opened wide.

"Walsingham? He is not!" he said.

"He must be."

"No."

"Yes, only he has the queen's ear. He and Cecil but Cecil does not have the ability."

"He is not, you idiot."

"He must be. Only he has the power and position. Other than you, but you could never…"

"I could never what?"

"Never have the strength and power."

Wellesley opened his mouth.

"How dare you," he said.

"I am sorry but…"

"I *am* the Black Axe, Rothwell. Me! There, I said it."

Edward laughed, almost uncontrollably.

"How dare you laugh at me, boy. I have more power than Walsingham could ever imagine. More than the queen herself. It is I who has moved the powers in Europe. It is I who determines who and where and how."

Edward stopped laughing and stood straight.

"I don't believe you."

"Then you are even slower than I thought. Who do you think got you your position? Got *Scammell* his position? Caught John Felton for posting the Papal Bull? Put Baillie at

Dover? Convinced you to leave Spain?"

"That was the King's Secretary."

"Indeed. Friendly man, don't you think? And who convinced the King of France to marry his catholic sister to a protestant leader? And what a plan that was until Coligny put his nose in the way. I hadn't known taking him out would lead to such a massacre of *our* people."

"You assassinated Coligny?"

"Of course, the meddling fool, though we learnt our lesson and we were much more subtle with the French king. Tuberculosis, I believe it was recorded as," he said, with a smile.

Edward opened his mouth in shock.

"Oh, I am everywhere, Edward," Wellesley continued. "Everywhere. The lives that have been given, taken, for me! How dare you suggest Walsingham has power. Even that filth, the Pope, has nothing; nothing of my reach."

"Then why haven't you killed me, Richard?"

"Lucky does not do your pathetic existence justice, Rothwell. We set you up with your street whore but she failed. We put you in the merchant's house but you kept that mouth shut. So I brought you in and still, you did not talk. We drip fed you Westminster Abbey, held a knife to your throat in Spain. And then others began to chase our tail. That pest, Cobham, and then Parry who would not let the death of his master go. Eventually he too fell to the blade at the end of my reach. As will you, finally, this day. Your girl didn't expose you. Your old friend in that shithole didn't give you up. Your friends didn't betray you. But you did. When you chased Eoin one step too far. Only by then the Queen was too keen on your pathetic charm and you were watched everywhere you went. But here we are, there is no one left. No one knows. Just you, and me. And it ends here."

"But why? Why me?" Edward asked, honestly.

"Because you are the embodiment of all that we fight against. The root of catholic poison that destroys this continent with its archaic tradition and corruption. People must be free to worship their way, Edward."

"I am not catholic."

"Oh but you are, Edward. You see, the Earl of Shrewsbury, George, was one of the greatest warriors of our time. For the queen's grandfather *and* her father. But he lost faith in the catholic church after the atrocities he witnessed in his many battles. When Catherine, the queen's stepmother came to England from Aragon to marry Arthur, King Henry's brother and heir to the throne, George knew how close she was to Rome and vowed to stop the wedding. Such proximity to the arrogance of Rome on the throne of *our* country could only cause more death and destruction for our people. Sadly, his attempts to poison her led only to the death of the prince, but though heartbroken, he had achieved his aim, until she was betrothed to his brother Henry, the new heir. Do you know she could not produce a son? Why do you think that is, Edward? Even those that made it to this world were stillborn, thanks to George, and he didn't stop there. Opening the path of the Boleyn family to the foot of the throne planted the very seed he desired in the king's mind and through his cunning and guile, he managed to convince Henry to divorce Catherine and create the Supreme Church of England as we know it today."

"This cannot be true."

"Thankfully, Edward, it is. Though it didn't stop there. The strength of catholic resistance led George to create the organisation we know today, and when Mary took the throne, the effort intensified. She too suffered two phantom pregnancies and became unwell, thanks to our power, leading to an early death. Finally, her sister could take the throne and the faith of this country was in safe hands. Until Herbert, Parry's master, married Anne Talbot and discovered who his father in law, our founder George, had been. Herbert had been a fierce warrior for Mary and his proximity to Elizabeth was not safe. So once again, we intervened and he was implicated in the plot to marry Mary of Scotland to the Duke of Norfolk. You see, Edward, the shape of the Tudor Monarchy, of this country, is because of us."

"You designed it all."

"Of course. And now you know our power."

"Yet you have not managed to kill me."

"Until now."

"Then tell me why?"

"You would never understand."

"Try me."

Wellesley's eyes worked in thought before his sneer returned.

"You want to know who you are, Rothwell?"

"I want to know."

"You want to know why you are the poison of this land?"

"Tell me, Wellesley!"

Wellesley laughed.

"Very well," he said. "All of Queen Catherine's sons were stillborn."

"You said."

"*Or* so we thought. All but one."

"One?" Edward asked, feeling his heart race and the ears of his queen only an arm's length away.

"One. Though she knew it would break her husband and lead to her downfall, Catherine suspected foul play and her one living son was taken away to be protected. That young boy grew up and had a son of his own. We found him eventually and he was removed, but it was to be years before we found the location of Henry's grandson. We followed the trail to France, where your family of protectors killed themselves to allow your escape. And so became the second endeavour of our life's work, the hunt. Our trail dried up until one young, reckless Edward Rothwell arrived in Southwark, right under the nose of one of my most trusted men. We called him Blue. You knew him as Robert Baxter."

"And so now you must kill me."

"You are the grandson of King Henry the Eighth, Edward *Tudor*. The true heir to the throne from this country's catholic union to Aragon. You threaten the very essence of what we fight to protect. You put the country and the protestant crown in peril."

"But I am not catholic."

"It matters not," said Wellesley, finally raising his sword.

Edward reacted and rushed towards the older man, only to have a gloved hand thrust into his face, knocking him to the ground. He scrambled backwards as his former employer stepped over him and trod on his ankle, making him wince.

A shout of, "Protect the queen!" echoed in the hall outside the door as Wellesley smiled and raised his sword. His eyes didn't leave Edward until the door flew open and Walsingham stepped in, red faced with panic.

"Where is the queen?" he roared, causing Wellesley to look around and allowing Edward a moment to pull his second dagger from his coat and drive it into the groin of the man above him.

Wellesley turned to look down as blood rushed over Edward's arm and grit his teeth, aiming his sword with a roar until his eyes began to fade and he fell to his knees. He dropped his sword as he focused on Edward one last time. The moment stretched as all present watched without a sound, and then finally, as his eyes regained their intensity, Wellesley mouthed something silently and crumpled lifelessly onto his side.

"Seize Rothwell!" shouted Walsingham, sending his men forward.

"No!" replied Elizabeth, firmly, stepping out from behind the screen and looking down at Wellesley for a moment. "I am here and I witnessed everything," she said, turning back to Walsingham and stepping in front of Edward with her chin held high. "*Wellesley* was the traitor and only Edward was able to draw him out. He has been working for me to flush out what we knew was an inside threat and," she looked at Edward, "He saved my life."

Walsingham lowered his blade.

"Wellesley?" he asked. "How?"

"I didn't believe it either but Edward extracted a confession."

"But, Rothwell," said Walsingham. "He, he…"

"Saved my life," Elizabeth repeated. "Believe it, Francis, it is over. And other threats?"

"Neutralised, Your Majesty. With Mary's hand in writing, authorising and compelling your assassination. I am sorry, Your Majesty, she ordered your death."

"And then she must face the consequences, as must her accomplices."

Walsingham nodded.

"Your Majesty, I…"

"Leave Edward and I to speak, please, Francis."

Walsingham nodded again and bowed as he backed from the room.

Edward caught the eyes of Marcus and Jacque and nodded subtly to each, in turn. They both responded with a smile as the door was closed and they disappeared from view.

"You have good friends, Edward."

"I do, Your Majesty." He paused. "What do we do now?"

"Well, that may be up to you, nephew," she said, grimacing with embarrassment. "Are you the true heir to my throne, Edward?"

"I am not."

"Yet this traitor's story says you are. You understand why that presents a problem?"

"I do not consider what he said to be a factor in my life or position, my queen. I am no threat to you. I will defend your crown until my dying day. And more importantly, I will defend you. My friend, my idol, my queen."

She smiled.

"I know you will," she said. "Oh, Edward. My father's grandson? And to think of how I looked at you once." She reached forward and held his cheek. "You truly are my friend, and what a man you are. Your wife, she is well?"

"The last time I saw her, she was."

"And how long has it been?"

"I have been in London for many weeks, Your Majesty."

Her eyes looked pained as she made a decision.

"Then once again I must send you to her. Your position is one of some importance, when it becomes known…"

"It will not, my queen. Not even to Amelie. She is my wife but you, I have love for you I will never understand."

Elizabeth smiled.

"I guess we can understand it now. I can make your life comfortable, you deserve it. If you plan to retire?"

Edward almost barked a laugh.

"Retire? Your Majesty, I am your Wolf, and always will be."

She looked at Wellesley.

"To think we may have never met if not for this excuse of a man beside us." Returning her gaze to Edward she leaned in and kissed him once, her eyes closed, and then gave way to instinct and squeezed him tightly. "Go," she said, stepping back with a shine in her eyes. "You have worked quite enough for one day. Go and be with your wife and I will see you again."

"Are you ok?" he asked.

"I am," she said. "I am."

Chapter Forty Four

<u>10th February 1587</u>

Edward sat in the queen's chamber at Greenwich Palace and looked at the men around him. He chuckled silently as Marcus stopped chewing his nails and looked at them as though crafting the finest instrument, and then looked at Jacque who watched the gardens in thought.

"It reminds me of the chateau at Chambord," he said. "The gardens, the water. You should see it, Edward."

"Why?" said Edward. "If this reminds you of it, why is this not enough for my eyes?"

Jacque opened his mouth to answer him when he saw Sir Francis Walsingham watching them both curiously.

"Francis?" he said, turning Edward's gaze to the older man.

"You two," Francis said. "Not many people surprise me, and you two? Well. I have not had a chance to see you together since you returned to your homes. Time was short before and I wanted to say…well…we wouldn't be here now without you."

"Wellesley surprised you," said Edward with a grin.

"Edward, please, that is not tasteful."

The last three men Francis expected to find himself sitting alongside in the queen's chamber chuckled at his response and then only laughed harder when they saw his expression of hurt. The old man allowed himself to smile and held up his hands.

"I am sorry," he said. "Sorry I doubted you. Your personal mission confused me, Edward, but your intuition was correct. The queen owes you her life, we all do. And I am glad you got closure."

Edward nodded.

"Are you at peace?" Francis added.

"I am."

"Then, Rothwell, I hope you continue to serve your queen for years to come. I, myself, need you all, and I do not say that lightly. She wants to honour you, you know?"

"You lead her protection, Francis. Your name will certainly go down in history, whether you like it or not. For me, I am content in the shadows."

"As am I," said Jacque.

Francis nodded and they all looked at Marcus who finally glanced up from his hand.

"Don't look at me, I want a medal and a large house like you fine gentlemen."

The men laughed.

"I am sure that can be arranged," said Francis. "One thing *will* be written, without doubt. The success of my network and the safety of our queen was not possible without the brave men that served us both."

Edward raised his small glass.

"To Sir Francis, the Spymaster," he said.

"The Spymaster," Jacque and Marcus repeated together.

I pray you do not toast our mournful news," said Elizabeth, entering the room.

"Only your safety, Your Majesty" said Francis as they all stood and bowed their heads.

"Sit down, gentlemen. I am certain you have earned it." She looked at each of them and smiled. "Thank you for coming to see me. I assume we all know the news?"

"The traitor has been executed, Ma'am."

"Indeed, Francis. And I take it you each know the circumstances?"

Francis nodded.

"Your Majesty, when parliament petitioned you to execute Mary, Cecil saw how the decision pained you significantly. I hear he felt that to execute her without your word would remove you of such burden and ensure both the safety of this country as well as the peace in which you sleep."

"Did he? And where is William?"

"Well, with Davison, whom you asked to arrange Mary's private death, now locked in the Tower for allowing her public execution, Cecil felt it wise to leave the city for a while."

Elizabeth smirked.

"And so he should," she said. "I will deal with him when he returns, and for now, I will have to deal with my guilt."

"My queen, Mary attended her trial dressed in black and denied her involvement even when the overwhelming evidence was put to her."

"I know what happened, Francis."

"And she would have risen again, Your Majesty. The

Bond of Association Cecil and I drew up in fifteen eighty-four permitted the private death of suspected assassins but would only have made her a martyr. The public death of such a threat was the only way to protect you from further uprising."

"And yet now I am guilty of regicide and the powers in Europe will want my blood."

"Not exactly, Your Majesty," said Edward. "If I may?"

She nodded.

"Your unwavering compassion for Mary is known across the continent. With her killed under the Bond of Association, yes you would remove yourself from blame. But with Cecil secretly sealing the warrant and sending it to Fotheringhay behind your back, you are the victim of court-conspiracy. I was at Mary's trial, Your Majesty. Through tears, she said, 'I would never make shipwreck of my soul by conspiring the destruction of my dearest sister.' And then her secretaries' confessions were put to the court and in defiance she proclaimed that even an act of war would be legitimate if it freed a queen. She played any hand she could and desired your death for her own reign. You are the *rightful* queen and have done nothing but lead with integrity. You are safe now, *Elizabeth*, and always will be."

Elizabeth smiled, looking around at the nervous men and then back at Edward.

"I know I will be, thanks to you, *Edward Rothwell*. Thanks to each of you. Let us continue on," she said, standing. "I hear our supposedly sanctioned pirates have driven Phillip of Spain to the edge of his somewhat delicate tether and we will need to prepare. Get to work, Gentlemen, but Francis, let Cecil sweat for a while, yes?"

"It'll be my pleasure, Your Majesty."

She looked at each of them proudly then back at Edward with a warm smile. She curtsied with a shy smile and left the room.

They shared a moment's silence before Walsingham took a breath.

"Well? What are we waiting for?" he said.

Printed in Great Britain
by Amazon